CONFRONTATION IN SPACE

Gerswin pursed his lips. The four alien space ships were still approaching. If they were xenophobic, they would have already tried to destroy the *Fleurdilis*. That they hadn't meant that either they couldn't, or didn't want to.

"Permission to destroy attackers, Captain!" demanded Strackna.

"Permission denied," snapped Gerswin. "Retreat our screens. That's a boarding party, Major. They're not about to fry their own."

"Batteries on full—stand by to fire!" ordered Strackna.

Gerswin stabbed his overrides. "Negative the last. All batteries stand down." He dove off the command couch like a hawk. Gerswin's shoulder knocked the Major away from her console. His hands flashed twice.

"Major Strackna is relieved of duty," Gerswin said, checking the unconscious figure lying on the deck. "Get my suit ready. If I'm wrong and the aliens blast me, you can release Major Strackna with my posthumous apologies."

Look for these Tor Books by L. E. Modesitt, Jr.

L.E. MODESITT, JR.

THE SILENT WARRIOR

A TOM DOHERTY ASSOCIATES BOOK

THE SILENT WARRIOR

Copyright © 1987 by L. E. Modesitt

First printing: December 1987

A TOR Book

Published by Tom Doherty Associates, Inc.
49 West 24th Street
New York, NY 10010

ISBN: 0-812-54588-5
Can. No.: 0-812-54589-3

Printed in the United States of America

0 9 8 7 6 5 4 3 2 1

For Catherine, and may her songs brighten her life and the lives of others through the 'miles to go.'

I

TECHNICALLY, THE ROOM was not supposed to exist, for it appeared neither on the official floor plans of the Admiralty, nor in any of the references, nor even in the classified briefing materials provided to the Admiral of the Fleets.

The Admiral of the Fleets knew of the room with its unique equipment, as did the man called Eye. That they did was obvious from their presence within.

The interior walls were not walls, but an arrangement of polygons upon which other equipment remained focused. The soft flooring was designed as well to resist echoes and any duplication or recording of the proceedings.

The Admiral wore dress blacks, as he often did. The three others around the table were garbed in black full-fade cloaks with privacy hoods. The man called Eye was distinguished only by the seat he had taken at the head of the five-sided table.

"You called the meeting, Admiral." The scratchy tone of the voice indicated that Eye employed a voice distorter.

"I did. I have a commission. The file is there." He pointed to the blank cover of the folder on the table in front of Eye.

No one said a word as the Intelligence chief read the material, then passed it to the figure on the right, who in turn scanned the contents before passing it back to the last intelligence controller.

"We have some questions," began Eye. The hooded

heads of the other two nodded in agreement.

"Questions yet?"

Eye said nothing, and with the face lost in the shadows of the hooded cloak, the Admiral wondered if he had pushed too far.

Finally, Eye cleared his throat, and his distorted voice, low and even, responded.

"We probably know more about the subject than you do. We considered him as a candidate for Corpus. We chose not to pursue the matter, and based on your material, I would agree that choice was probably wise.

"For many of the same reasons, we are concerned about reopening any possible involvement here, and question the advantage to the Service of doing so."

"Would you feel free to explain?" the Admiral asked, not pleading, but with his tone making the other aware that he was asking so far, not demanding.

"His personality is stable, except under extreme stress. Under such stress, he will lose all sense of restraint, common morality, and go for the jugular. His level of stress is higher than anyone ever tested, however, which offers us all protection. His reflexes are naturally better than any single agent, possibly by a factor of two or three, and he has spent at least the last fifty stans teaching himself virtually every single personal weapon known.

"He is adept at circuit design, is probably a good journeyman systems breaker, and is one of the best pilots in Service history. We checked the drives of the *Sanducar* after she was returned. Although they tested normally, indications were that the grav governors had been reset to a higher tolerance, then returned to normal. Given any amount of time, he could do the same to any ship. We do not know what level of acceleration he could tolerate and still function at peak efficiency, but it is high enough to give him an insurmountable edge over any ship fast enough to pursue . . ."

The Admiral nodded, not quite impatiently.

". . . also has contacts within the Court able to gain

him an open portal to any installation. With his skills, only access would be necessary."

"But the man sleeps, doesn't he?"

"He may. Remember there are at least eight other so-called devilkids fully trained, most of whom have similar skills, who remain within Recorps. All are fanatically loyal to him, and he has charged them with carrying out the reclamation effort on Old Earth. That means that they are effectively neutralized at this time."

Eye's hood lifted, and although the Admiral could not see the man's eyes, he felt a chill in spite of himself.

"Don't you see, Admiral," asked the Intelligence head, "where this all leads? Do you understand why I am reluctant to take on a commission that could lead to eight totally unrestrained fanatics declaring war on us? It could take a full battle group to catch and subdue each. And for what? Because your subject made you look silly? His actions are centered on one planet. Those actions are considered idealistic by the majority of the Imperial citizenry, by the majority of the Court, and probably by the majority of the I.S.S. officer corps. Further, he has removed himself from the scene in order to prevent any reprisals at him from affecting the reclamation effort. With all that, you ask that we stir up the mess by trying to remove him?"

"Yes. No individual should be bigger than the Empire. No individual should be able to manipulate public sentiment to break Imperial laws with impunity."

"He didn't, Admiral," added Eye, his voice even softer. "He renounced any claim to return to his planet, even in death. For someone that dedicated, that is punishment. Perhaps not what you wish, but punishment nonetheless. More important, it is regarded as punishment by the majority of the older devilkids. Some of the more recently commissioned officers, as you know, still opted for the Service, and I seriously hope you rereview their records and expunge the Board of Inquiry findings."

The last sentence was nearly a command, and the

Admiral stiffened. "Are you telling me what to do?"

Eye shook his hooded head. "No. Just hoping you would understand all the factors Intelligence must consider. The man wants to restore his planet. He used force only when necessary and went to elaborate lengths to avoid injury to Imperial personnel. He willingly gave all the credit to the Emperor, and I might add that such news was worth a plus ten week rate for nearly a month. The Emperor knows that and appreciates it."

"But he stood the Service on end."

"That I doubt. He did upset the High Command. The Service is alive and well." Eye cleared his throat. "Do you want us to deal with the problem?"

"Yes."

Eye turned to the figure on his left.

"Clause five," suggested the cloaked figure, and even with the voice distorter, the softness of tone suggested that the speaker was a woman.

Eye returned his attention to the Admiral, whose fingers drummed on the table with scarcely concealed impatience.

"We will solve the problem in our own way, subject to clause five of our charter."

"That means . . . ?"

"We undertake to solve the problem, either within or without the solution suggested, subject to the Emperor's personal review."

"Which means?" asked the Admiral again.

"It means, Admiral, that I will not undertake an ill-advised removal action surely geared to cause severe casualties to both Eye section and the Service, as well as public relations and public opinion reversals of the first order, just to soothe the wounded pride of the High Command. Because you feel so strongly, however, I will take action to insure that the Emperor is protected. If my decision is incorrect, I will be removed. Removed, not replaced."

Eye nodded to the figures who flanked him.

The Admiral's eyes widened, trying to focus on all

three figures simultaneously, on the way the two at Eye's sides lifted their robed hands, with the strange devices.

"No—"

The Admiral could feel the sudden constriction in his chest, feel the alternative waves of red and black washing up over him.

"Get him back to his office, and call a medical tech. I believe the Admiral is suffering a massive heart seizure, poor man."

Clause five. That was the Admiral's last thought. *Clause five.*

II

There was in those times a prophet, and when the people asked his name, he answered not, saying instead, what I do should be remembered, for in deeds there is truth, and that truth should be remembered and live, even as men die.

A man from Denv asked the prophet this question.

If a mountain is called a mountain, men call that a fact, for the mountain is, and they can see it is. Likewise a wilderness. Likewise the stars. But when a man calls his deeds truth, are they?

When he calls a mountain the ocean, all can tell he is mistaken. But when he calls himself a prophet, or allows others to call him a prophet, no man can prove or disprove his naming.

Should the prophet walk on water and heal the sick and raise the dead, no one can say whether he is prophet or no, whether he is sent by the angels or the devils, or whether he is master or slave.

Goodness may be done by the evil to ensnare the unwary, and evil by the good to test the worthiness of the people. So by what measure can any person weigh the truth of another's deeds?

The Book of Deeds
Authorized Version (First Revision)
Old Earth, 3788 N.E.C.

III

GRIM—THAT WAS the appearance of the gardens in the central courtyard of the senior officers quarters, reflected Gerswin.

Heavy gray clouds poured out of the eastern hills and down over New Augusta, scudding across the sky so swiftly that their motion was apparent with even a single glance through the narrow windows of his room.

No rain dropped from the mass of gray, and the air beneath was preternaturally clear, as if the sky held its breath.

The senior Commander turned and glanced toward the vidscreen.

"Seems like you've done this before," he said quietly, but neither the screen nor the room answered him.

High Command had not expected him to choose the Service over the newly created Recorps, and now the Admirals didn't know what to do with him.

Gerswin could understand their dilemma. A desk job

in New Augusta might give him access to influence or to make more trouble. At the same time, his rank would guarantee him a job with access to people and resources at any out-Base. At the moment, there were no handy combat or high risk assignments for Commanders where he could be placed with the hope of his not returning.

Although Corpus Corps involvement in shortening his life span was a possibility, Gerswin hoped that no one in their right mind would seriously consider assassination or removal. The subsequent inquiry would prove too unsettling and would expose too many weaknesses in both the Empire and the Service, not to mention the possibility that the devilkids might feel compelled to take on the Empire because they would regard the Empire's commitments as worthless.

But ego was a touchy subject, and Gerswin would not trust rationality to prevail, not for a time at least. For that reason were the throwing knives concealed behind his artificially stiffened waistband, the sling leathers in place. He also was devoting increased attention to his surroundings, especially when he went out.

In the interim, while the Admirals decided, he reported to the detail section every morning, was updated on how no new assignments were yet available, and asked to check back the next morning. Three days earlier, he'd spent the day taking a battery of tests, and the first thing after he'd arrived had been a three-day physical.

The fact that they were still looking for somewhere to put him told him that he was disgustingly healthy, and as sane as anyone could test out.

He paced back from the portal toward the window and stopped, staring out at the grayness. Still holding back rain, the heavy clouds continued their race across the central city.

Buzz!

Making an effort not to charge the screen, he took three slow steps and acknowledged the call.

An unfamiliar face filled the screen—a tech of some indeterminate rank.

"Senior Commander Gerswin?"

"Yes?"

"This is Curvilis at the orderly's console. There is a messenger here for you."

"Yes?"

"Ser. This is very unusual. It is from the Duke of Triandna, and his person insists upon handing it directly to you."

Gerswin shook his head, then stopped as he realized that meant exactly the opposite of what the orderly expected.

"I'll be right down."

Was it Caroljoy or the Corpus Corps?

He tapped off the screen image before checking his knives. Then he palmed a miniature stunner and slipped it into the special pocket in his left sleeve.

As he departed he pulled the privacy cloak from the locker and swirled it around him. He didn't need the privacy, but the material was supposedly designed to block low energy projectiles and lasers. He let the hood fall back on his shoulders.

The corridor was empty, but rather than taking the passenger drop shaft, he turned left and headed for the freight shaft.

In quick and quiet steps from the back of the exit on the main floor, he slipped toward the main entry and the orderly's console. From the archway that separated the triangular entry hall from the back corridor where he stood in the shadows, Gerswin could see the "messenger" from the Duke, or most probably from the Duchess.

The messenger was none other than the retired I.S.S. pilot who had taken him to the Duke's estate the last time he had been in New Augusta.

No one else entered the area, nor was anyone else in evidence besides the pilot and the orderly.

"Commander?" Gerswin offered as he stepped out

boldly toward the lavender-clad pilot.

"Senior Commander Gerswin, a pleasure to see you again, ser." The older man bowed slightly from the waist and straightened, handing the I.S.S. officer a sealed package that weighed close to a kilo. "Those are the papers the Duchess wanted you to have."

Gerswin covered his confusion by bowing in return. What papers?

"My thanks, Commander," Gerswin responded. "Her Grace . . . ?"

"Perhaps you should read them before . . ."

The pilot did not meet Gerswin's eyes.

"Appreciate your bringing them."

"No problem at all."

With that, the Duke's pilot was gone, leaving Gerswin holding the sealed package.

This time Gerswin took the passenger lift to his third floor room. The corridors were deserted, unsurprisingly, since most of the senior officers billeted there were undergoing full-day briefings at the Octagon, or were stationed there.

Once inside his quarters, he used some makeshift extender tools to open the package, still unwilling to stand over it and unseal the tape.

His fears proved groundless, though he put a small slit in the cover of the loose-leaf book which had been enclosed within the wrappings. A small sealed envelope, with only the notation "Lieutenant Gerswin" on it, was tucked inside the black leather covers, just in front of the title page, which stated simply: "OER FOUNDATION."

He opened the letter, setting the book on the top of the console.

Dear Lieutenant (please pardon my remembering you this way),

I think it is fair to say that I understand you a little, and have helped you in the ways that Merrel and I can. The book represents, in its own way, my only lasting gift of a material nature. Jane, of course, is another gift, but it is rather unlikely you will cross paths.

You are trying to light a light in darkness, and may this help. Other than this note, which for my own selfish reasons I cannot resist, there is no connection between the Foundation and us, nor would His Grace wish it otherwise. The Foundation is yours, and you are the Foundation. While it is modest by Imperial standards, it need not remain so, and used properly may provide you the lever you need to reclaim your heritage, and Martin's.

You have a long future, or, as the ancients put it, "many miles to go before you sleep." My rest will come soon, sooner than I had thought.

To that I am reconciled, my lieutenant, and with you go my thoughts, my memories, and what we have shared, and might have shared.

Farewell.

CJ

The scent of the note, like the clean scent of her, burned through him with the words as he stood staring, his eyes looking through the narrow window at the courtyard garden he did not see, his left hand clutching the note, his right the envelope.

Sooner than she thought?

OER Foundation?

Miles to go before you sleep?

Reconciled to what?

The questions swirled through his thoughts like the fringes of a landspout, ripping at his composure, tearing at his guts, until the tightness in his stomach matched the stabbing behind his unfocused eyes.

Darkness, the darkness of youth, and the touch of lips under his, with the cool warmth of New Colora outside the louvered windows of a junior officer's room. Darkness, and the cooling silence of rest after fire. Darkness, after the first time he had ever whistled his song of Old Earth for anyone.

Darkness . . . darkness . . . always the darkness.

A flash of light across the rain-damped gloom of the courtyard outside finally broke through the ebbing flow of his memories, and he looked up from the chair he found himself sitting in.

1534. That was what the readout on the screen indicated. Three hours . . . more than three standard hours he had wrestled with the past, a past he had not even known meant so much until he found himself losing it, piece by piece.

He stood, squinting, shrugging his shoulders to loosen the stiffness, and trying to repress the shivers that threatened.

He looked down. The envelope was on the flat section of the wall console, but the note itself was still clutched in his left hand.

Caroljoy. I never knew . . .

"Didn't you?" he asked aloud. "Didn't you?"

There was no answer from the dark green walls, nor from the blank screen, or from its flashing red light that indicated messages stored in the system.

He ignored the messages and turned to the book —only because the pilot had suggested he read it before reacting. Carefully refolding the note, he placed it in the pocket inside the front cover, though he would remove it shortly, as she had implied he should.

"OER FOUNDATION"—that was stamped in silver letters on the spine of the book and on the otherwise blank front cover.

He leafed through the pages, skimming the contents, still standing before the console.

The shakiness in his knees reminded him that he had some physical limits, and, flicking the room's light level higher, he sat down in the single gray swivel.

After racing through the first ten pages, he shut the cover. The rest could wait until he could devote the right attitude to study and learn the contents.

Caroljoy had been right. He was the OER Foundation. Of course, she was right. She had designed it. While the Halsie-Vyr Group controlled the base assets, all income from the trust went to OER, to an account blind to Halsie-Vyr, and from which only one Senior Commander MacGregor Corson Gerswin could draw.

He shook his head. The details were overwhelming. In essence, the book was a personalized how-to manual for him . . . how to set up a double blind operation to protect himself . . . how to comply with the Imperial Tax Code—

"No!"

Caroljoy had been so thorough. She had personally picked out the offices—through an intermediary—and included a floor plan. So thorough, as if everything had to be done completely right the first time, as if there were no tomorrow. As if . . .

"Farewell?"

This time he could not stop the shivers. So he sat and trembled until they passed.

After a time he stood and went to the screen, tapping out the combination he had never used.

A woman's face appeared in the screen—hair snow-starred in the latest pattern, but slightly askew, composed, but with the smudged circles of tiredness under her eyes, eyes from which radiated the fine lines of a middle-aged woman under stress.

"Commander Gerswin, I believe."

"How did you know?" He could tell his voice was ragged.

"The Duchess left a solideo cube. She thought you would call. I think she hoped you would not accept a mere farewell note."

"Could . . . I'd like to talk to her. Come and see her if at all possible."

"It's not possible, Commander, though we all wish it were. She has some pride, and forbid it."

"I don't understand."

"She left for H'Liero yesterday, for the Mern'tang Health Center."

"Oh . . ." Another chill passed through him. The famous center accepted only cases diagnosed as terminal, and only patients who could afford the astronomical costs.

"Her mother and grandmother both died of Byclero's Syndrome. His Grace had hoped that continual treatment would lessen the chances . . ." The woman's voice died off.

Gerswin shook his head again, and again, his eyes unable to focus on the screen.

He reached out to break the connection.

"Commander." Her level tone reached him.

He stopped, blinked back the tears he did not know he had shed, wiped his eyes with the back of his sleeve, and cleared his throat.

"Yes."

"I wish she could have seen you, but you know the final stages of the disease break down most of the body's cartilage. She refused to have either you or His Grace accompany her. His Grace would have had you go in his place, even. He did not want her alone—" The woman's voice broke this time, and Gerswin waited, swallowing hard. "You know how strong-willed she was . . . she is.

"She insisted I wait for your call. She did not want to upset His Grace, but she *knew* her lieutenant would call, and someone had to tell you . . . she knew her lieutenant would call . . ."

The woman with the snow-starred hair looked down, saying nothing. Gerswin could see her fists clinched, feeling his own knotted at his sides.

"She knew you would call . . .," repeated the woman helplessly.

"She knew," repeated the senior Commander. "She knew so much." The silence fell on both screens. "What can I do?"

"You have done all that you can . . . more than . . . many . . ." The woman visibly pulled herself together. "I asked her what I could say to you—if, when, you called. She said you would know, but that if

I had to say anything, that she would see you at the end of time. That hers was the shorter journey, and the easier."

He said nothing, but nodded twice. Then he cleared his throat again. "Let me know. Let me know." He could say no more, and his hand lashed out at the screen controls. The image faded into gray.

Forcing himself to unclinch his fists, he took four steps to the narrow oblong window and peered at the smudged lights above the rain-damped garden.

"Hers was the shorter journey . . . Caroljoy . . . I never knew . . . never knew . . . But you did . . . You always did."

As he stood before the rain and storm, the darkness solidified within.

IV

THE FOREVER HERO

Call him hero after all heroes had died.
Call him champion when none else had tried.
Call him saviour of a land left burned.
Call him destroyer of shambles unlearned.

Call him a name, a title, a force.
Call him devil, or the land's source.
Call him soldier, pilot, or priest.
Call him the greatest, or term him beast.

But remember he stood, and stretched tall,
Where others crawled, or stood not at all.

Remember the Captain, and call him Lord.
Remember the sheath is not the sword.

> Anonymous
> Quoted in *Ballads of the Captain*
> Edwina de Vlerio
> New Augusta, 5133 N.E.C.

V

THE CAPTAIN OF the *Fleurdilis* frowned as he studied the hard copy of the schematic. He supposed he could have used the screen, rather than having gone to the trouble of having the pages printed, but he liked to be able to wander around the cabin with the diagrams, to be able to make notes at odd times without having to code up the file, to puzzle through the codes and routings.

He still didn't understand all the details represented in the diagrams, but he knew enough to understand that the ship whose command he had just assumed was not configured according to her own specifications, or that the ship's own databanks did not register the differences.

Admittedly, the majority of discrepancies were minor, where conduit blocs had been shifted less than a meter, in one case, to accommodate modifications to the forward launch tubes. But some were scarcely minor. The *Fleurdilis* no longer carried the installed equipment for its own emergency field recharging, nor did it carry the original energy capacitators, nor the original drive field equipment.

The newer equipment was not only smaller, but,

compared to the original specifications, far less powerful.

In short, he was saddled with command of a nominal cruiser, but one with less real power than an old-style corvette. The lower power capability reduced range, screen defenses, and survivability.

He touched the console, without looking at the image that formed on the screen.

"Yes, Commander?"

"Send up Senior Technician Relyea, if she's available."

"Yes, ser."

The senior Commander straightened his blacks, set down the schematics, and paced in a narrow circle in the small stateroom as he waited.

"Technician Relyea, Commander."

The woman was petite, scarcely even to his shoulder, with brown hair knotted into a neat bun, black eyes, and new senior tech insignia on her collars.

"Sit down." He pointed to the single guest chair.

She sat.

"Have you studied the basic schematics?" He pointed at the diagrams on the console.

She peered at them momentarily. "Not in detail. Those are really not much good."

"Figured that out. Why weren't they updated? Means that the information in the databanks isn't reliable."

The senior tech pursed her lips. "Not exactly, Commander. The data entries are not all they should be, but the correct information is there. Provided you know the keys . . ."

The Commander, still standing, turned and looked down at her.

"Go ahead."

"When the downsizing orders came through, as each ship went through refit, new specs were added to the databanks. The originals were left." She lifted her shoulders. "Just in case, I suppose."

"Downsizing orders?"

"The CommFleet Order . . . about five years ago . . . the one that was to reduce fleet energy consumption by thirty percent, except for the First and Fifth fleets, and, of course, the scouts."

"Did the rest of the galaxy downsize as well?" the Commander snapped. "Forget that," he added abruptly. "Planetside at the time." He paused before continuing. "Was there any official explanation?"

Relyea cocked her head to one side. "Then I was number two on the *Bolivar*, chief tech ops, not on admin, but I recall the official reason was that an analysis of the Fleet had shown that in ninety-eight percent of all operations no more than fifty percent of the available power levels was ever required. Don't hold me to the exact numbers, but that was the general idea."

"Too much peacetime." He frowned. "About the specifications?"

"Yes. The new ones are under 'Ship Specifications —downsized.' As you'd expect . . ."

"If one knew," added the Commander.

"If one knew."

The five-by-five cabin seemed to shrink, though it was more than twice the size of most cabins on the cruiser.

"If I might ask . . . Captain," ventured the technician.

"Ask."

"How did you end up with the *Fleurdilis*?"

The Commander smiled. The senior technician, for her more than thirty years of service, shrank from the expression.

"Because someone wants to file me away, preferably to make a mess of it as well, Relyea, and I don't intend to." The hawk-yellow eyes bored into her. "Now. What other technical changes and booby traps are buried in this obsolescent excuse for a fighting ship?"

"That would be hard to say, Captain."

"Don't care how hard or how long. You either know, or you don't. If you know, start telling me. If you don't, tell me, and go and find out. If I find out before you, we'll discuss your request for a transfer."

"You aren't serious . . ."

"Relyea, I am very serious. We have orders to break orbit for my first patrol in two standard weeks. I intend to know the personnel background on every crew member cold before we break. Same for technical specs. Same for the teamwork that exists or doesn't."

"Captain, I doubt that any line officer has requested or learned the technical details of his command."

"I did, and I will here. As for the others, I wouldn't be surprised. Precedent is irrelevant. By the way, can you install a power diverter from the screens and grav fields to the drives?"

"Could be done, I suppose."

"Good. Let me see your proposal by, say, 1800, tomorrow."

"What do you have in mind?"

"Without full screen power, at least ought to be able to get to hell and gone out of trouble."

Relyea nodded slowly.

"Anything else I should know?" asked the Captain.

The senior technician frowned, looked at the deck, then into the hawk-yellow eyes. She looked back at the deck. Finally she stared at the wall.

The Captain waited, knowing this time he could not afford to push.

The technician cleared her throat, once, twice.

The senior Commander slowly folded the older schematics until they were small enough to fit into the single drawer under the console.

"Personnel . . . have you studied any . . . ?"

"Taken a quick scan through the entire crew."

"Your initial reaction?" The brisk voice was now tentative.

"Take some work to shape up."

Relyea nodded once.

Again the Captain smiled the smile that flared like a predator's before he spoke.

"Noticed a few other things, Relyea. Not one senior rating with time in grade left. Not one outstanding performance score. Forty percent of the crew transferred in within the last three standard months. The scheduled refit postponed until *after* our first two patrols. Are those the sorts of things you're suggesting?"

The senior technician frowned, "Outside of the specs, you seem to have found out a great deal in the three days you've been aboard."

"One thing I haven't found out, Relyea. Most important of all."

"And that is, ser?"

"Who I can trust. Who is responsible."

The senior technician swallowed. Swallowed again. "Captain . . . you give us orders. We'll get them done."

The senior Commander nodded. "Understand." His voice was surprisingly soft. "I understand, Chief Technician. And I'll make it clear, quite clear, that *you* are the senior technician."

"Thank you, Captain." Relyea's voice picked up. "Do you want a quick rundown on what the other spec changes are and the difficulties? Now? Or later?"

"Can you run it into the system, under 'Captain's Specs,' for me to study later tonight?"

"Give me two or three hours."

The Captain nodded. "Tomorrow," he added, "right at 1400, Relyea, you'll take me on a tech walk-through. Want to meet every one of your techs. Every last one. Let them see me, see that line and tech work together."

He turned directly to the thin-faced and older-looking woman. "I will work through my senior tech, and the senior tech will work for the Captain and for the good of the ship."

Relyea shivered at the intensity in the yellow eyes.

"I understand, Captain."

His face smoothed out into a calmer expression,

somehow, although none of his features had changed. "Looking forward to seeing your analysis. Very much. Anything else?"

"No, ser. No, ser."

"Until 1400 tomorrow, then."

She stood, saluted, and left.

The Captain slowly shook his head. He hoped he could pull the *Fleurdilis* together . . . somehow.

VI

"Torp away, Captain."

"Stet."

Gerswin returned his full attention to the ranked screens before his control couch, but did not tighten the acceleration harness.

"Determined their frequencies, Comm?"

"That's affirmative, Captain. But they're using a nonscanned transmission. Burst-blast."

"Complete new image with each burst, rather than a continuous scan?"

"Stet."

"Can we convert?"

"Negative. Not within orbit time."

"Guns, do we have a better screen analysis?" Gerswin's eyes flickered over the third screen.

"Negative."

Take one outmoded cruiser, underpowered, out on the Imperial fringes, and order the Captain to investigate strange transmissions, without any backup. Then have the ship find a new alien space-going civilization, and leave the decisions in the hands of the Captain. That was what he faced.

No time to torp back for instructions, instructions that would probably amount to "Use your own judgement."

"Captain?"

Gerswin snapped his head up at the voice of the Executive Officer.

"Yes, Major Strackna?"

"Do you intend to continue toward orbit around the home planet?"

"Yes."

"Might I ask why?"

"Because our orders indicate that if initial survey indicates the culture is less advanced, we are to initiate contact."

"There are four large ships there, waiting, and the emissions beyond their screens indicate they are all carrying fusactors, or the local product." Strackna's thin lips pressed together tightly after she finished.

Gerswin nodded. "That would seem to indicate no jumpshift technology."

"Captain, Comm here. How soon before the next out-torp?"

"Hold on that until we have something new to report."

"Stet."

"That gives them more than eight times the power reserves we possess," persisted Strackna.

"Without anywhere near the screens we have, Major."

"This could be suicide."

"I'll do my best to avoid that, Major. Suggest you return to your station. May need all the screens and power I can get."

Gerswin refrained from shaking his head. Of the entire crew, the Executive Officer remained the biggest headache he had inherited. The only possible reason for her rank was her family connections. Once Gerswin had thought the I.S.S. above that. While he knew better, it didn't make solving the problem any easier.

The *Fleurdilis* was edging toward the alien's geocentric orbit station, right above the largest broadcast power source on the planet. Gerswin would have bet that the station was close to directly above the planetary capitol or what passed for it.

The ship shivered slightly as the antique antigravs failed to compensate evenly for the deceleration. Gerswin frowned as he scanned the screens, but he did not move to take over from Senior Lieutenant Harsna as the lieutenant continued the approach to the orbit station.

A tight smile played around the Captain's face.

He knew all too well the gambit the *Fleurdilis* represented. An obsolete ship, crewed by a group of misfits, would be no loss to the Empire. Since the Dismorph Conflict, and the years that had passed since without event, more and more systems had come to question the value of the Empire and the resource taxes necessary to support it. Another alien adventure would be just the thing to drum up enthusiasm.

The Imperial strategists couldn't lose. If the *Fleurdilis* succeeded, then the newshawks would be told how a single obsolete ship, which was all that could be spared, overcame incredible odds continually one step from disaster. And if the *Fleurdilis* failed . . . what could one expect without greater support from the allied systems?

Besides, if the failure led to another war, then the Empire could use the war as an excuse to rebuild and strengthen its holds on territory and resources and to discredit the peacemonger critics.

Gerswin glanced across the command bridge at Major Strackna, who scanned the power screens, all of them, not just the summaries represented on his console. Her jaw was tightly clinched, he could see.

He doubted she would ever understand just how expendable the Empire thought she was.

"Stationary in orbit, Captain."

"Thank you, Harsna."

"The four alien ships are spreading."

"Stet." Gerswin could see that himself. He stabbed a glowing stud. "Captain here. Any guesses on the magnitude of their screens?"

"Nothing definite, but from the background radiation, which seems to be residual secondary associated with fusactors, I'd have to say that their screens are not designed to block energy weapons or even high-speed torps."

Gerswin pursed his lips. If so . . . the aliens had one or two obvious options.

If they were xenophobic, they would have already tried to destroy the *Fleurdilis* before it settled in orbit. That they hadn't meant that either they didn't think they could or didn't want to.

If they couldn't—

"Multiple launchings."

"Permission to destroy attackers, Captain!" demanded Strackna.

"Permission denied," snapped Gerswin, touching another stud.

"Estimated ETA at *Fleurdilis*?"

"Twelve plus, Captain."

"Strackna, draw our screens back to hull plus one."

"Retreat screens, Captain? Hull plus one?"

"Screens at hull plus one. Screens at hull plus one."

"But—"

"That's a boarding party, Major. They're not about to fry their own, which means they either don't have penetrating lasers or particle beams or tacheads, or that they don't want to use them. Blast their boarding party and Istvenn knows what they'll do."

"Batteries on full. Stand by to fire!" ordered Strackna.

Gerswin could see Lieutenant Harsna's mouth drop open, and the look of disbelief in Relyea's face.

Gerswin stabbed his own overrides.

"This is the Captain. Negative the last. All batteries stand down. All batteries stand down."

No sooner had he finished the statement than he dove off the command couch like a hawk toward the Exec's station.

"Stand by! Stand by—!"

Thud!

Gerswin's shoulder knocked the Executive Officer away from her console. His hands flashed twice.

Then he stood up abruptly and touched the vacated console.

"All batteries stand down. I say again. All batteries stand down."

"Standing down. Standing down."

"Lieutenant Harsna!"

"Yes, ser."

"As of this instant, you are acting Exec. Have Major Strackna confined to quarters and a guard posted. She is relieved until further notice."

Gerswin ignored the collective sigh that crossed the bridge and checked the figure lying on the deck. Strackna, unconscious, was breathing evenly, and had no obvious injuries.

"Estimate plus eight for arrival of alien boarding party."

"Get my suit ready, Riid. My suit and a scooter."

"Captain . . . do you think that is wise?" That was Relyea, the senior tech.

"If I'm wrong, and if the aliens blast me, or if I don't return within a standard week, then you can release Major Strackna with my posthumous apologies. Until then, Lieutenant Harsna will be acting Captain."

"You're not leaving the ship?"

"You must have a reason, Captain," said Harsna slowly.

"I do, Harsna. I do. Too many people lost their lives unnecessarily in the last great Imperial adventure. Some were close to me. These aliens aren't a threat now, and they may never be one.

"If I'm right . . . well . . . you'll see. Guns! Have a spare tachead?"

"Not spare, Captain. But we have one."

"What's the closest point at which a detonation is safe for those aliens? Assume our metabolism and no suit shields."

"I wouldn't recommend any closer than a thousand kays, and that's probably too close."

"All right, set one for two to two point five straight out. Ninety from the orbit station. Launch when ready."

"Plus one from launch, Captain."

"Five plus for alien arrival."

Gerswin nodded.

"Suit ready, Riid?"

"Ready, Captain."

"As soon as we get a burst on the tachead, I'll be down. Have the scooter ready."

"Yes, ser."

"You think the tachead will awe them?" asked Harsna.

"No, but their techs will note torp speed and burst size. Shortly it might dawn on them that we possess the power to pulverize their system. That won't awe them at all, I suspect, but it should make them cautious."

"Tachead away! Tachead away!"

For the miniature jumpshift of the torp, two thousand kays amounted to an instantaneous burst.

For an instant, a second sun flared far behind the *Fleurdilis*.

Gerswin did not wait for the light to fade, but headed for the main lock, and the suit that waited for him.

"Plus three to alien arrival."

Now all he had to do was survive and return before an entire week passed.

"Confident, aren't you?" he muttered as he swung into the armorer's bay.

"Suit's here, Captain," Riid said quietly.

Gerswin repressed a smile.

Riid had ignored the letter of his order, instead had readied one of the five Imperial Marine Marauder suits, obviously previously tailored for Gerswin without his knowledge.

"Feedback circuits might be rough, Captain, but you're not going without the best I can do."

"Appreciate it, Riid. Appreciate it."

He reached across to the console. "Bridge, Captain here. Harsna, bulge the screens a little, and push them back gently for a couple of minutes. Soon as I'm clear of the lock, drop the screens and reform them right on the hull itself. Understand?"

"Stet. You need the time, and we'll reform behind you. Major Strackna's under restraint. No problem."

"Thanks."

Gerswin devoted his energies to getting installed inside the armor.

It could be a damned-fool idea, but he owed something to Martin, and to Faith, and to the poor, unsuspecting aliens. And this was the best he could come up with on short notice, the best possible with an obsolete cruiser that the Empire would have preferred as a martyr to Imperial expansion.

Not that any devilkid, even one who now wore the insignia of an Imperial senior Commander, intended to submit to martyrdom, inadvertent or otherwise.

He grinned behind the suit's face screen. All the years of practice in esoteric and often theoretically obsolete weapons just might prove useful in the official line of duty. Official line of duty—wonderful phrase.

Absently he wondered if Martin had felt the same inane relief at the thought of action and the ability to use long-sharpened skills. Had his son felt the same way on that day so many years earlier? He could feel the sweat beading on his forehead. Martin certainly hadn't wanted to be hero or martyr, any more than his father now did.

"Are you subconsciously out to avoid the duty Caroljoy laid on you?" The words were low, addressed only to himself.

"What's that, Captain?"

"Muttering to myself, Riid."

He wanted to wipe his damp forehead with the back of his hand. He settled for rubbing it against the suit's sweat pad.

Besides, Caroljoy hadn't forced him to do anything. Just made it possible to follow his own expressed dream.

Dream?

He pushed away the question, refocused his eyes on the suit's internal indicators, and steeled his thoughts on the encounter ahead.

VII

THE WAILING FROM the four-piece group reminded Gerswin of a landspout when it struck a fast-flowing river—screeches, gurgles, and dull thuds. Despite the strange assortment of sounds, behind the surface chaos was a clearly identifiable theme—harmony.

Only the silence of those listening around the arena kept Gerswin from snorting aloud, but he maintained his attentive and superficially reverent position while studying the guards around him, and beyond them the red stone arena. He had mentally dubbed the aliens Ursans, for want of a better term, and because they resembled bears more than any other of the animals he had run across.

One of the Ursan officers, or clan leaders, or whatever their class of leaders were called, stepped a pace closer, but did not look directly at the I.S.S. officer.

While Gerswin didn't understand the language, he

had a fair idea why he had been escorted to the arena near what he thought was the capitol. He hoped he was right.

Although he had misgivings about leaving the *Fleurdilis* in Lieutenant Harsna's hands, with Major Strackna unstable and under restraint, there hadn't been any real alternative. Strackna was not only Imperialistic, but xenophobic to boot. While she was a competent Service officer in peacetime or in all-out war, she was precisely the wrong person for any sort of alien contact. Strackna would have no compunctions about unleashing all of the *Fleurdilis*' tacheads at the Ursan capitol, without even understanding the implications.

Gerswin repressed a sigh as the strange musical wheezings continued. While the Empire might benefit from another repeat of the Dismorph Conflict, that was the last thing he needed, the last thing needed by the majority of the people of the Empire, and certainly the last thing needed by the Ursans, whether they understood or not.

Gerswin brought his mind and thoughts back to the present and the red stone arena. To forestall Strackna and the rest of the hawks, he would need every bit of skill he had developed over the last half century. He wondered if it had really been that long.

The Captain of the obsolete cruiser that orbited directly overhead, albeit nearly thirty-five thousand kays above his head, hoped he had guessed correctly about the aliens, and about their culture.

He shrugged to himself. If not, it was already too late, but the signs were there that he had not.

He took a deep breath and almost choked. The Ursans smelled like a cross between wet coydog and rancid fish.

They resembled the pictures of bears he had seen in the archives, but their pelts were red—eye-searing red. Their heads rose directly from broad shoulders, with no necks as such. Their respective heights varied only slightly, but most stood ten to fifteen centimeters shorter than Gerswin. Their squarish bodies massed more; how much would have been a guess.

Like bears, they had claws, but thinner claws and fully retractable. Their fingers were more like claw sheaths, and the lack of flexibility was offset by two opposing thumbs on each hand, which did not contain claws.

He studied the Ursan closest to him, watching the slight chest movements in an effort to analyze the breathing patterns. From what he could tell, both chest and back expanded. He speculated on whether the lungs were based more on a bellows concept and jointed cartilage separating two stiff rib plates.

The anthem, if that was what it had been, screeched to a close, and the honor guard shambled forward, their motion designed either to force Gerswin to come along, or to start a fight under the arched gate to the arena.

From the opposite gate he could see another guard group, although the individual being escorted was an Ursan of some rank.

That, again, was a guess, but the guards around Gerswin wore only plain purple leather harnesses, on which hung servicable long knives and short swords. The dignitary around whom the other guards clustered wore a silvered harness with clearly more refined weapons.

Gerswin carried no weapons, none except for the throwing knives concealed in his waistband.

Despite the lack of technology in their personal weaponry, the Ursans were not primitives. The four spacecraft that had met the *Fleurdilis* had been nuclear powered and carried defensive energy screens against meteors. They had to have chosen the boarding party technique for cultural reasons, not for lack of more sophisticated weapons.

Gerswin almost shook his head in retrospect. With a handful of devilkids, he could have disarmed the Ursan boarding parties on the spot.

With Lerwin and Lostwin and Kiedra, or Glynnis . . . but the devilkids were on Old Earth, busy trying to reclaim their poor poisoned planet, busy buying time for Gerswin, busy and secure in their belief that their efforts mattered.

They did, but not in the way the left-behind devilkids thought.

Still, a handful of trained devilkids could have prevented the situation in which he found himself. When the Ursans had launched four shuttles filled with warriors, Gerswin had faced the choice of incinerating the shuttles and possibly starting another system war, which meant the destruction or immediate subjection of the Ursans, or ignoring the shuttles, leaving the *Fleurdilis* safe behind unbreachable screens. The passive use of screens could only have encouraged the Ursans in the belief that the Imperials were personal cowards, and such a belief would lead to contempt . . . and to eventual rebellion and war.

That had left Gerswin with the need to outface the Ursans personally, meeting them alone outside the *Fleurdilis*, in the hope of instilling respect for the Empire without the cost of destroying the Ursan culture and society. Not that some Imperials wouldn't have relished that destruction.

Strackna had tried to blast them out of existence —until Gerswin had her locked up. And Harsna thought he was crazy. Maybe he was.

So . . . here he was, standing in the middle of an arena, basing his future on the possibility that he was facing a warlord-personal-honor-type mentality.

The guards backed away abruptly and left Gerswin in the center of a hollow square of Ursans. The silver-harnessed Ursan stood on the other side.

Gerswin saw the scars, the slight discoloration of the bright red pelt hairs, and spit on the hard-packed clay in the direction of the other.

A hiss ran around the arena. Gerswin couldn't tell what it meant for certain, but it was the first reaction of any sort, and he couldn't tell what the following grunts and clicks signified.

Two of the guards lifted their knives. Gerswin stepped toward the guards and motioned them back. They looked at each other and halted.

"Look. I didn't say I wouldn't fight. I said I wouldn't fight him or her, or whatever. No status."

He elaborately raised his hands and frowned, dropped his arms to his sides, half-turning from the Ursan champion.

A series of sounds, more screeches and gurgles, issued from the four Ursan instrumentalists, and the square of guards opened. From the far side of the arena a series of steps was extended, and another Ursan appeared sedately strolling down to the hard-packed clay.

Gerswin turned back to study his potential adversary. The second Ursan was not scarred, not obviously, though the reddish pelt could conceal most anything, and it moved with greater assurance than the first.

Gerswin repeated his charade.

This time the entire squad of guards reached for their knives.

"Only once?"

Gerswin motioned them back and turned to face full on the recent arrival, noting that the first "dignitary" had retired to the side of the arena.

His current opponent motioned to a guard, who stepped forward carrying a short sword or long knife, and a longer sword, apparently a match to what the Ursan wore strapped to his or her harness.

The Commander took the knife first, testing its balance and construction. It was designed as a thrusting instrument.

The sword was more of a heavy cutting blade. Both fit with what Gerswin suspected about the Ursan physiology. He hoped he could give the aliens a lesson in psychology as well.

Smiling wryly, he took the heavy blade, after thrusting the knife into his waistband.

Talk about ethnocentrism! The Ursans obviously believed that any culture would follow patterns similar to their own. Most I.S.S. Commanders would have blasted all four boarding parties and proceeded from there.

Gerswin was gambling, gambling that his reflexes and abilities would enable him to come out on top, gambling that his observations were accurate enough for him to do what he wanted.

Each of the score of Ursan guards stepped back several more paces and the square expanded again.

The Ursan champion faced the I.S.S. Commander and touched his sword to the clay before him.

Gerswin raised his sword, then touched it to the arena clay, whipping it up and dancing aside just in time to avoid the pounding rush of the Ursan.

No polite fencing here! Gerswin avoided three back to back cuts from the other's heavy blade with footwork, using his own more as a shield than as a weapon.

The alien's slashes, seemingly awkward, whistled by Gerswin's legs or arms.

Gerswin leaned in, back, forward, occasionally deflecting the other's slashes, but carefully avoided taking the full brunt of the other's attack.

Almost as suddenly as the rushes had begun, the Ursan circled backward and began a circling stalk, as if to get behind Gerswin.

The Ursan's breathing deepened into an odd wheezing sound.

Gerswin moved toward the Ursan, bringing the heavy blade around.

The Ursan countered, trying to catch Gerswin's blade edge on. Gerswin twisted the borrowed blade, letting it slide off, and ducking inside the other's sweep, tapped the alien on the chest with the dullish point. There was no penetration of the solid bone plate under the reddish fur and muscles.

"Wheeze!"

Rolling hard left, Gerswin could feel the other's sword crossing where he had just been.

Once more, the Ursan began a furious attack of crisscrossing sword sweeps that would have been awkward were it not for the speed of the blade.

"All right, friend. Play for keeps."

Again, after the mad and sustained fury of the attack, the Ursan backed off and wheezed; almost as if pumping up his system with oxygen.

The Ursan tactics were becoming painfully obvious. Whichever fighter could last longer in the high effort attacks, whichever fighter needed less of a recharge would inexorably force the other into an ever-increasing oxygen debt—unless the less conditioned fighter was far better with the pair of blades.

Already Gerswin's arms were feeling the strain, and he'd been careful not to take any blows directly. So much for conditioning.

Thud! Thud! Hiss! Hiss!

The Ursan was back at it, throwing quick stroke after quick stroke at the I.S.S. Commander.

Gerswin continued to duck or deflect the other's blows, watching the pattern of cuts.

This time the Ursan kept at it nearly twice as long, as if he sensed the human's tiredness, before retreating to the circling and defensive stalk.

As soon as the Ursan dropped beyond quick thrust range, Gerswin switched the long blade into his right hand and the short thrusting blade into his left hand.

With a flowing motion, he threw the thrusting blade, rifling it straight at the right-side junction between the Ursan's shoulder and head.

The sharp-edged blade went half its length into the heavy muscles and stopped with a clunk. Maroon fountained darkly down the Ursan's chest for an instant before the alien dropped both knife and long sword and collapsed in a heap, still clawing at the embedded weapon.

"Hsssssssss!"

The disapproval of the crowd was deafening, but Gerswin marched forward and extracted the short knife, picked up the deceased dignitary's weapons, and marched through the square of Ursans toward the black-rimmed box from where he hoped the powers-that-be had watched.

He located an Ursan wearing a black-rimmed silver harness, bowed, and placed all four weapons on the clay between him and the senior Ursan.

"All right, fellows or ladies, I'd like to go home."

The Ursan looked undecided. At least, he did nothing.

Gerswin took a deep breath and pulled one of the throwing knives from his belt, displayed it, then let it rest on his palm. He studied the crowd, looking for a suitable target. The arena was plain, with a straight metal railing and no statues. Gerswin shrugged.

Finally, he took his foot and scratched an *X* in the clay, then turned and walked five, six, seven, eight paces, then whirled, throwing the knife as he turned.

The heavy blade buried itself to the hilt at the crossed lines of the *X*.

Another "*Hssssss*" roared from the crowd.

Gerswin continued his steps and stooped, pulled the knife from the clay, wiped it clean on his tunic, and replaced it in his belt.

Then he walked the last steps to the laid-out weapons, picked up the Ursan knife he had used, raised it as a salute, and plunged it into the clay so it stood like a cross between him and the Ursan leader.

The Ursan stood, and in turn raised his arms, claws extended, then lowered them, retracting the claws and turning his hands upward, so that they remained empty and weaponless.

Gerswin repeated the gesture, minus claws, since he had none.

"*Ummmmmmhhhhh.*"

Gerswin could sympathize with the disappointment of having to acknowledge the loss of the local hero, but when they learned the real score, he suspected the Ursans would be much happier that the local hero had lost to the outlander who had cheated by, stars forbid, throwing a short sword.

Already the guards who had escorted him were reforming, but this time he noticed with a scarcely concealed grin, the leader was offering, by gesture, the place of honor.

He followed the guards back to one of the Ursan shuttles for the ride up to the *Fleurdilis* and a sure-to-be-disappointed Major Strackna.

VIII

FOR THE FOURTH time the Commodore frowned at the senior Commander across the wardroom table that had been covered temporarily with the red felt that signified a Board of Inquiry.

"Let me get this clear. You felt that accepting a single combat challenge would make life *easier* for the Empire? By setting a precedent where every time the Ursans feel like it, they could challenge an Imperial ship on a man-to-man basis?"

The senior Commander shook his head. "No, Commodore. The point was much simpler. They lost on their own terms, on their own territory, with their own weapons, to an outlander who had no experience in their rituals. The next step is to demonstrate that they are so outmatched in weapons and technology that they have to join the Empire on our terms."

"What about the risk? How did you know you could win?"

"I didn't. Good guess. Based on several factors. Had to be a unified planetary culture. Also had to be based on individual combat."

The Commodore waved vaguely at the sheet before him. "I know it's in the staff report, and the ethnologists have supplied sheet after sheet of ethnology equations that support your guesses. But how could you subject the Empire to that kind of risk through mere guesses?"

"Commodore, ser. Considerable risk for me. None for the Empire. Also considerable risk for the Ursans."

The Commodore motioned for the senior Commander to continue.

Gerswin cleared his throat. "If I had been defeated, then the Empire still could have blasted chunks out of Ursa IV, and with even greater justification. Done what most Commanders would have done in the first place. Ursans have no heavy screens, only for debris, and have avoided developing long range weapons. That's why they have to have developed a workable planetary culture."

"How does that follow?" The Commodore's puzzled expression indicated his lack of understanding.

"Nationalism always puts the culture above the individual. Culture based on individual prowess almost always loses to one based on nationalism. In the crunch, nationalist cultures use whatever they have to, no matter what the consequences. What nearly destroyed Old Earth the first time.

"In an individualist culture, some things you will not do. If you do, the culture will destroy you. So . . . Ursans couldn't have space travel, advanced technology, *and* individual prowess tests unless they had unified planetary culture."

The Commander was still shaking his head. He could not understand, and Gerswin understood why.

Finally the Commodore asked another question. "Why did you say there was considerable risk to the Ursans?"

"Simple. If I lost, the Empire would have blasted the planet, or at least the space-going ships. Would have claimed that the Ursans were barbarians who demanded that their leaders solve disputes through personal combat. Incompatible with civilization and decency."

"Barbarians indeed," confirmed the Commodore. "One last question, Commander. Why didn't you just ignore their boarding parties?"

"Thought about that. Problem was that it would take years to undo the image. If we didn't at least meet them face to face, then the Empire would be regarded as bullies and cowards rolled into one. Ursans might knuckle under to brute force, but would begin relation with the Empire from a basis of contempt. Leads to unrest, maybe revolution. So we'd be back on a conflict basis within a decade. This way, we bought some time."

"How much?"

"A good century, my guess, if you get a couple of good Corpus Corps types to act as champions every once in a while."

The Commodore nodded, then tapped the stud on the control box by his right hand.

"Now, Commander," growled the Commodore, "the question is what to do with you."

"Nothing," suggested Gerswin.

"Commander—"

"I'm not being flippant, Commodore, ser. Your experts have begun the real work with the Ursans. I made the entry easier. Take credit for the peaceful contact. If I had failed, you would have taken the blame."

The Commodore reflected, pursing his lips. "And what about Major Strackna? Your Executive Officer? She recommends your court-martial."

"That's because she wanted to blast the Ursans out of existence. Wouldn't let her. Her specialty was alien relations. She had an attack of acute xenophobia and tried to blow the Ursan boarding parties into dust, after I ordered her not to. Not for her distrust of my decision that I recommended her court-martial and dismissal. Because she disobeyed a direct order when the ship was not in danger."

"Wasn't your report rather harsh?"

"Don't think so, Commodore," answered Gerswin, ignoring the implied suggestion that he change his recommendation that Strackna be cashiered from the Service. "Major Strackna did not act to override me from a well reasoned difference of opinion or knowledge, nor to save the ship. Just because she hated aliens she hadn't seen. Aliens couldn't hurt the *Fleurdilis*.

"Preliminary evidence showed they had no projective weapons, no screens to stop our weapons. She kept trying to destroy them against evidence, against orders." Gerswin shook his head. "No Captain should ever have to tolerate that, and no subordinate should have his or her life risked by such an attitude."

"How should we handle you?" The Commodore's glance was direct.

"Don't. Ships survive because they act as a team. Think you should give the entire ship a letter of commendation, outlining the contribution the whole crew made."

"Commending them for what?"

"For handling a delicate situation with the care that reflects favorably upon the Service and the Empire. The Ursans are learning who's boss, and it only cost one tachead and not one casualty for us. Only cost them one casualty."

The Commodore worried his thin lips, darted a look at the closed portal before speaking again.

"Assuming your analysis is correct, and the experts seem to feel it is, *you* deserve the commendation, not the ship."

"Commodore, the crew deserves the commendation for not going off half-blasted and trying to pull their C.O. out of a mess. I blasted it. Nearly failed. Didn't because the Ursans have some common sense, and because their leader's sharp."

The Commodore sighed. "Everything is more complicated than it seems. Would you mind explaining, since I don't seem to understand the logic here?"

"Ursans don't fight to kill. Probably only have a few flesh wounds. We're not built like them. I had to kill him—her—because I couldn't figure out the rituals.

That's why the Ursan crowd was so upset. Don't like unnecessary killing."

A wintry smile crossed the Commodore's leathery face.

"The implications are obvious, and far-reaching, Commander." He looked down, then at the red felt covering the table, picked up the sheet before him, and looked up. "Your talents are underestimated, and I wish we could afford to promote you to the General Staff. In any case, I'm taking your recommendation, with a slight upgrading. The *Fleurdilis* will be recommended for a distinguished service medal for all crew, and you will receive a polite letter of personal commendation. Enough to make it clear that you did a good job and that the letter is *not* a formality."

"Thank you, Commodore. The crew will appreciate the honor, and they do deserve it." The senior Commander waited, eyes meeting the Commodore's.

"That will be all, Commander Gerswin."

Gerswin rose. "Yes, ser. By your leave, ser?"

The Commodore nodded. "I'll have the announcement made shortly." He gestured toward the portal.

Gerswin saluted, then turned and left.

IX

Wars are fought because someone can generate the impression of loss, or the impression of gain. Take away that impression, and you make it that much harder to generate support for war.

Wars can only be fought with popular support

or with centralized government control. Centralized and strong governments arise because of the perception of unmet needs. They maintain power because they generate new perceptions of needs which are unmet or by fueling the impressions which lead to war—or both.

Take away the perception of unmet needs, and strong governments find it increasingly difficult to maintain power without becoming ever more tyrannical.

> *Politics in the Age of Power*
> Exton Land
> 2031 O.E.C.

X

THE YOUNG WOMAN arrived at the suite portal, which did not open automatically at her approach. With a frown, she stepped aside and tapped the contact button beneath the small screen set into the left portal support panel.

The light under the screen flashed amber and settled into the green, but the screen remained blank.

"Yes?" The disembodied voice was a male, youthful sounding baritone, with a slight edge.

"I am Lyr D'Meryon. I had an appointment for 1430."

"Your pardon, Ms. D'Meryon, but a previous interview has not been completed. If you would be so kind as to wait for just a moment. When the light flashes again, please enter."

With that, the green light went out.

"What . . . what are you getting yourself into?" she asked herself. Then she shrugged and stepped back.

Should she walk to the other end of the corridor? Or stand and wait? What if the light flashed while she was turned in another direction?

If only the specs for the position hadn't been so intriguing . . . but the independence that had been spelled out between the lines was rare for any foundation, much less for the smaller ones of the type who would consider relatively junior administrators.

She glanced down at the reddish glimmers of the corridor glow tiles, then back at the screen. The light remained dark.

Next she hitched up her portfolio under her left arm and walked to the other side of the portal. The panels on the right were featureless, and she looked back at the screen on the left side. Still dark.

She bit her lower lip.

Even before the interview, she'd put hours of effort into filling out the application, which had arrived after she had expressed an interest in the position.

The original display had been simple. She recalled that clearly enough.

FOUNDATION ADMINISTRATOR
Small and independent foundation seeks full-time administrator and research coordinator. Must have background in hard and bio sciences and interest in environmental pursuits. For further information and application, contact . . .

Both hard and biological sciences, that had been the interesting point. Most foundations headquartered on New Augusta were either involved in the arts or with very specific pursuits.

Her musing almost distracted her from the flashes of the portal screen.

She hoisted the portfolio under her arm and approached the portal. This time it irised open as she walked toward it.

Once inside, she understood the reason for her wait. The small area was but a single room, served by two portals at opposite ends, presumably on different corridors. The narrow office contained two consoles, three severe straight-backed chairs, one console recliner, and a small loveseat.

Standing by the console recliner was a slender figure garbed in a black privacy cloak with a peaked hood and a black mask.

"You'll pardon the privacy, Ms. D'Meryon, but the need for a continued confidentiality is one of the reasons for our search and one of the principal reasons for specifying the qualifications we need."

Gesturing vaguely toward the arrangement of chairs and the loveseat, the man sat down.

Lyr was convinced that the man, although soft-spoken, had some sort of military background from the alertness of his carriage. She seated herself in one of the straight-backed chairs.

"While the Foundation has a worthy purpose, it would not be appropriate for some of the anonymous backers to become known. Others do not wish public recognition of any sort."

"Might I ask the goals of the Foundation? And its name?"

"The Foundation's title is the OER Foundation, and the Founders have never seen fit to disclose what the initials represent. The goals are modest, basically to endow research in certain biologic and ecologic fields. Center primarily on development of self-perpetuating reclamation, biological stabilization processes."

The black-cloaked man's masked face remained shadowed as he cleared his throat softly and continued. "Why were you interested in this particular position?"

"For a number of reasons. . . ."

The standard questions about her background, her qualifications, her interest in science, all took nearly a standard hour.

Every question was politely phrased by the inquiring

figure, and while the light was soft, by the time that first hour had passed, Lyr felt as though the interview was approaching an inquisition.

Finally, too late, she suspected, she interrupted.

"What does that have to do with the job? You have obviously verified all my qualifications, my references, and my background. Is this intensive reexamination merely to verify my interest or my ability to endure? What is there about this Foundation that requires such painstaking evaluation of its possible administrator?"

"Are you sure you want to know that?"

"That's an odd response. My first reaction is that you're up to something illegal or exceedingly unpopular. Are you?"

"No. Popular reaction right now would probably be boredom. Intellectual reaction would probably be positive. But we're an odd Foundation. Not interested in publicity. Not interested in glory, or space in the faxnews. Don't want an administrator who is. Need someone who shares our goals, someone who will pursue them and who doesn't need public acclaim to be happy on the job."

"Can you assure me that what you are pursuing is legal?"

"I can assure you that it is legal on New Augusta and throughout the Empire. Wouldn't want to speculate about other legal codes or mores."

"Fair enough." She paused, then hurried on before the man in black could speak. "The publicity angle is strange, I'll admit, because most foundations want publicity either to gain contributions or to reflect favorably on the founder. But it's not strange enough for all this secrecy. As for the goals, other than some very general guidelines, which would be impossible to follow without more detailed information, you haven't really stated a single concrete objective that an administrator would find usable. So what do you want? What are you really pushing for?"

"Before I answer that, and I will, what do you want

from this job? Not the polite phrases. We're beyond that. What do you really want?"

Lyr took a deep breath.

"In one word—meaning. In two words—responsibility. And if I get three—money."

"We can deliver all three, in greater quantities than you expect. But there is a price, a high price. Perhaps higher than you would pay."

"My life?" She pursed her lips. "You can't be that melodramatic."

The interviewer laughed once, a short harsh sound. "Scarcely. Not in the sense you meant. The position could easily be a lifetime position. That's one reason for the in-depth nature of the application, the interview, and the reference checks. We also have done a background check."

Lyr's mouth opened in a small o.

The interviewer continued, politely ignoring her surprise. "The administrator will have sole operating authority. That authority may not be delegated, although you may hire administrative assistance and other services as necessary and financially responsible."

"You are asking for a bond slave, not an administrator."

"The starting salary is sixty thousand Imperial credits annually, plus expenses and living quarters."

Lyr didn't bother to keep her mouth from dropping open.

"What unpaid other 'services' do you want? Is this offer open only to attractive young women?"

"The sarcasm doesn't become you." The gentleness of the reproach disarmed her angry cynicism.

"I don't understand. That's more than the administrators of the Emperor's Trust get paid, and they don't get quarters."

"You'll have a bigger job, and one without the overt acclaim and prestige. It may be more important in the long run."

"How big?"

"Big enough that if we go beyond this point in the conversation, and you decline, you will not walk out of here with any memory of what was discussed."

"You couldn't! You wouldn't!"

"Said it was a big job, job that requires a big person. Stakes are as idealistic as you are. More so, perhaps. Less risk from a memory blanking than from disclosure. Besides, who would you complain about? This isn't the Foundation office, but rented for the interviews."

Lyr moistened her lips with her tongue.

"My head says to walk out. My heart wants to hear your offer."

"What do you know about ecologic reclamation? About the impact of organic chemical poisonings?"

"The problems with Old Earth, Marduk, and even with New Glascow. That's why the really dangerous manufacturing processes are in deep space or on hell-planets."

"How do you clean them up?"

"You don't. You'd have to scrub the soil, filter all of the groundwater, probably any oceans as well."

"So you go along with the tacit Imperial policy of avoiding the questions?"

"Take Old Earth," Lyr countered. "The government has devoted close to fifty billion creds over the last fifty years . . . maybe more. What do they have? A few thousand square kays of marginal land and a river or two that won't poison you on touching." She paused. "What does this have to do with the job? Directly?"

"Everything. The sponsors feel that real clean-up is possible with biologic agents. Agree with your assessment so far as mechanical reclamation goes. Ancient records say biological reclamation was started once, even begun to terraform totally hostile planets, but it stopped with the great collapse. Old Earth and Marduk were avoided since there were better places to live. Federation, and then the Empire, tried to avoid the problem by avoiding organics on inhabited planets, manufacturing in space or on waste planets for materials they couldn't do without."

The man in black stood up, his shadowed eyes looking at a point somewhere behind Lyr. "Now, the inhabited systems are growing, as well as the demand for more and more consumer goods. The collapse is long past, and the commercial barons base their power on production. The trend is not obvious yet, but it is there."

Lyr felt, for an instant, an impression of age coming from the young-looking figure who moved with such quickness and grace that he had to be her own contemporary.

"And the Foundation is worried about that?"

"By the time anyone else is worried, just as happened on Old Earth, it will be too late to do anything." The man laughed. "Even if we're wrong, biological clean-up methods will make those consumer goods cheaper."

"Istvenn . . . ," she murmured. "You really do care. . . ."

"Some of the people who created the Foundation do. They wanted to encourage the discovery, the development, and the use of biological processes to reclaim chemical wasted lands, self-perpetuating and benign biological systems to maintain the ecology under the worst of stresses, and to make these processes widely available once they have been developed and field tested.

"Your job will center on the first phase, since none of these processes are known. They may be out there in the Empire, but if so, they are buried and unrecognized. As you pointed out, no one can reclaim a wasted planet like Old Earth, not even with the resources of the Empire. And already, reports of space-based contamination drifting in-system are being reported. A number of the nastier organic by-products can withstand reentry heat, particularly if they're in dust form.

"More important, with the energy costs of space

transport, virtually every industrialized system has some organic production somewhere, and as demand keeps increasing, so will possible sources of contamination."

Lyr coughed to break the other's gloomy monologue. "You paint a depressing picture."

"Don't all fanatics?" He laughed again, but the laugh was without humor, except in the self-deprecation.

"What sort of operation now exists?"

"Are you interested?"

"Yes. I couldn't say why. But I am."

"Fine. The Foundation has offices, plus financial resources, and an approved charter. You will not need to raise funds, but you will need to create the entire mechanism for reviewing and screening grant and research proposals, the procedures for follow-up and field testing."

"You're not serious?"

"Quite serious."

"Handing this over to someone you scarcely know?"

"Do you want the job?"

Lyr paused.

The man in black said nothing, just waited.

"Yes."

"Fine. You have it."

"I do?" Lyr looked at the other blankly.

"You do." He stretched and withdrew a card from his cloak, along with a small databloc. "The card has the Foundation address. In those quarters are the basic information and equipment you will need, as well as access to the consoles. Currently, the master console is locked to your retinal prints. You can change that if you wish, but it was the safest way to begin."

"My retinal prints? But . . . how . . ."

"From this point on, you control the day-to-day operations of the Foundation, its assets, investments, and its grants."

"How did you know I would accept?"

"Didn't. But it was likely. I said we did a thorough

background check on the most likely candidates. W
did. Thorough. Even to the time you told your fami
you were going to Eltar for the summer, when instea
you used the summer to raise your tuition for th
university by entering that bond-contract with Fari
El-Noursi. You used the name Noreen Al-Fatid. . .
Should I go on?"

Lyr could feel herself turning crimson on the exter
or, and the fury building on the inside.

"Take your filthy job—"

"No."

The single, quiet word, for some reason, deflated he
anger.

"Purpose wasn't to embarrass or to push. But to l
you know how thoroughly we screened you. What yo
do with your private life is for you. But you ar
trustworthy, totally trustworthy, whether you wi
admit it publicly or not."

"If I weren't?"

"You wouldn't be here."

"What if your administrator changed? If . . . the
. . . he . . . she . . . cheated you?"

"I will let you in on one thing."

"What?"

"One of the Founders is a graduate of the Corpu
Corps."

Despite herself, Lyr shivered.

The man gestured toward the portal, the one she ha
not used.

"Once you get settled, I'll be in touch to fill in th
details. But remember you are the OER Foundation
Without you, it is merely an assembly of assets. Fo
your own peace of mind, I'd suggest you tell you
friends and acquaintances that you were lucky enoug
to land the spendthrift trust of a well-connected Imper
ial functionary.

"By the way, there is an emergency call function i
the console. It cannot be tracked. No good if someon
is standing by you and has a stunner to your head, bu

ne normal security systems should prevent that. Emergency function is more for substantial policy questions where you would like guidance or to talk over the *thrust* f future decisions. Not for nuts and bolts questions . . ."

The portal opened.

"But . . . I don't understand. . . ."

"You will . . . once you look it all over. . . . You vill. . . ."

Lyr stood alone in the empty corridor, shaking her ead, wondering. She looked down to find her portfoo, still unopened, under her left arm, and in her right and, the small square databloc and the Foundation ard.

After locking the databloc into her beltpak, she tudied the address on the card.

"Hegemony Towers . . ."

She shook her head, nearly forgetting the address. low had he found out about El Lido and Farid? She ad forgotten that summer as quickly as possible, even hough the contract had been the only way she could ave finished the university after her father's death and nother's suicide. She still shuddered at the thought . . . nd the thankfully infrequent nightmares.

"Hegemony Towers . . ." She repeated the address, s if to drive away the memories.

Certainly a modest but respectable address in one of he business parks north of the capitol.

She shrugged, as if lifting a weight from her shoulders.

"Off to Hegemony Towers . . ." And to find out what she had volunteered for.

Not understanding why, she hummed happily with each step toward the drop shaft at the end of the long corridor.

XI

"HE'S REQUESTED THAT his orders be changed to maintenance, out-Base station."

The Vice Admiral for Logistics and Administration looked up from the hidden console screen, pushed back a short and straggly gray hair, one of the few he retained for impressions, and nodded. "Did he say why?"

"Standard language. For the good of the Service and for a broader exposure."

"Where's the most out-of-the-way place where there's an opening?"

"Standora. Base Commandant."

"Could he mess things up much there?"

"Admiral, that's not the problem," replied the Commodore, who stood across the console. "We've checked his profile. He can run anything, probably better than ninety percent of the Service's senior officers."

"So why is his folder red-lined? Political problem with the Court?"

"Not exactly. Remember New Glascow? Where the official explanation was that the Emperor suddenly decided to dedicate more resources to rebuilding Old Earth and when he created Recorps and diverted two cohorts of combat decon dozers for effect?"

"Where the Duke of Triandna's yacht spread the word?"

"That was the official line. . . ."

"And the unofficial one?"

The Commodore looked over his shoulder before

50

realizing the portal was closed behind him.

"Commander Gerswin hijacked the *Sanducar*, borrowed the yacht without asking, and delivered the arc-dozers in person, claiming that the Emperor had donated them to Old Earth. The message torps and all the publicity were touches he orchestrated . . . but no one could ever totally prove it. . . ."

"Not prove it?"

The Commodore nodded slowly.

"That good. . . . I see. And how do you know?"

"My cousin was the navigator on the *Sanducar*. None of the officers ever made another rank, except one. She was wounded fighting them off."

"Your cousin?"

"Unfortunately . . . no. He's a cernadine narcie on Duerte."

"So you think Gerswin's up to no good?"

"I don't know. But he's the type that always has a purpose."

"How long has he been on the fringes?"

"Fifteen standard."

"Maybe he's tired. Even someone like him has to be running down. Send him to Standora. Five year tour. Or double tour. Surely we'll close the place by then."

The Commodore kept his face expressionless. He did not argue. When the Vice Admiral decided, the decision was final.

"Yes, ser."

The Vice Admiral smiled. "I know you don't agree, Medoro, but the C.O. of an out-of-the-way, nearly unused naval refit yard isn't going to upset the Empire. How could he? The place is nearly obsolete. It only handles scouts these days, and it wouldn't be there except to funnel currency to the locals under the terms of the Sector agreement."

The Commodore nodded in return and stepped back off the Furstan carpet, his heels clicking as they touched the tiles.

Then he turned.

"If it makes you feel better," added the Vice Admiral, "you can code a memo to the file on your misgivings. I'll even review it."

"I just might, Admiral."

"Always the cautious one, Medoro. Remember, caution saves worlds, but it doesn't make them."

XII

THE SCREEN LIT as Lyr acknowledged, and the cloaked face of her interviewer appeared.

"Have you had a chance to study the accounts in detail?"

"Yes." Her voice was cold. She had been waiting to question him.

"Questions?"

"Who is empowered to draw on the Special Operations Account? For what? Then there's the Reserve Fund, and the way the system is set up I can only tell what goes into it, not what it's for, and the charter doesn't specifically mention it."

He raised a cloaked arm and gloved hand.

"Answers? Or do you want to resign?"

"Resign? Who said anything about resigning? I'm administrator of the Foundation, and I don't know where more than thirty percent of the funds could go, or why."

"Very well."

"Very well, what?"

"Let me explain. You are the administrator. You are not the Trustee. The Trustee is empowered to draw from the Special Operations Fund. Everything he draws will be reported, and the system will give you an itemization. That will allow you to comply with the Imperial record-keeping requirements."

"I cannot draw on that fund?"

"That is correct, not unless you have a special need and ask the Trustee to transfer funds to your accounts. Remember, you alone control the disposition of seventy percent of the Foundation's income and more than half its assets."

Lyr frowned. "Only half the assets? The Trustee controls the other half?"

"No. Thirty percent of the assets are in the Forward Fund, with half their income being returned in addition to current income."

"I know that."

"—and the other half being invested in Forward Fund assets, which are currently a mixture of first line Imperial Money Houses."

"That's not the best investment policy."

"If you have a better one, present it, and have the system put it forward for the Trustee to evaluate."

Lyr worried at her bottom lip with her teeth.

"Let's get back to the unanswered questions. Why the Special Operations Fund? Why the Forward Fund?"

The man in black's shoulders slumped, as though he were sighing, although no sound was conveyed by the screen.

"The Special Operations Fund was set up by the Founders to allow sufficient funds for the Trustee to carry out the aims of the Foundation. If you will reread the bylaws, those funds can be spent on anything which is legal under the law, including, if necessary, the living expenses and transportation of the Trustee."

As he looked straight into the screen, Lyr shivered as she saw the hawk-yellow of his eyes. She would know the man by them, should they ever meet when he was not in privacy clothing, and she had to ask herself why he chose a disguise that did not conceal his most prominent feature.

"The Forward Fund is set at thirty percent of assets

for one simple reason. That is the maximum allowed under current Imperial law. At some point in the future it is anticipated that large capital grants will be required. To expend those funds requires a proposal by the Trustee *and* the approval of the administrator."

"*Capital* grants?" asked Lyr with the horror of the financial professional who avoided use of capital whenever possible.

"The goals of the Foundation are to pursue biological technology. What if extensive laboratory or production capability could not be obtained without actually building it?" He waved a cloaked arm. "Premature at the moment. Job now is research. Later, the capabilities."

Lyr kept worrying her lower lip. The answers made sense. And she certainly couldn't object to the Trustee, anonymous as he might be, who was also her superior, having access to less than a third of the fund income when he reported to her what was spent.

That left one unanswered question.

"What about the Reserve Fund? That's nearly twenty percent of the assets, and I have no control there at all."

"Reserves may be converted by the Trustee without your approval, but only for the purchase or acquisition of buildings, facilities, permanent transportation equipment, or property."

"Does that give me any control?"

"Only indirectly. The more the Trustee spends, the less he has. The more he spends, the more you control. Call it a balance of power."

"Sort of. But he could replace me at any time."

"He could. And the Founders could replace him. Or the Empire, if he ever should break Imperial law."

Lyr stopped worrying her lower lip. She still didn't have the satisfaction she wanted, but she had some answers, and some implications that were even more far-reaching. The assets of the Foundation were far greater, far greater, than she had been led to believe when the unknown hawk-eyed man had interviewed her and given her the job. And the emphasis on long-range contingency planning for capital grants and expenditures indicated a more action-oriented mentality behind the Foundation than was usually the case.

She looked at the screen. Was the man in black a Founder? Or the Trustee? Who were they? Imperial family? Court? Commercial? Or an Ethics Conscience Fund set up by a manufacturing consortium?

"Any other questions?"

She realized she had said nothing, caught as she had been in her own thoughts.

"Uhhhh . . ." The nonsense syllable escaped her, and she clamped her lips shut. What else could she ask?

"Nothing. Not yet."

"Check with you later."

The screen blanked, without even a good-bye.

Lyr frowned, almost biting her lower lip. Was she being co-opted? *What* was she managing? Or more precisely, for what end was she managing the Foundation?

"You worry," she said, wanting to express her feelings aloud, "but you don't have a thing to point to. Except that the people who set this up don't want to be publicly identified. Have you been asked to do anything shady? Haven't they been overly concerned about insuring that all the legal formalities are complied with?"

She looked at the blank screen, then at the blank walls. In the operating plan for the year was an amount reserved for decorating the office, however she wanted. An amount large enough to do it quite nicely, even extravagantly, although she could certainly reduce that if she wanted. Altering the plan was well within her discretion, but she suspected it had been a polite way of letting her know that she was welcome to decorate as she pleased.

"You already have more control over your job than many of your contemporaries will have in their whole careers."

She stopped the monologue, ran her upper teeth side-to-side over her lower lip.

She knew one other thing. Without a better reason, a great deal better reason, she wouldn't walk away from the money, the title, and the mystery. Not now, maybe not ever.

But she worried at her lower lip as her hands dropped to the console keyboard and the financial projections.

XIII

HIRO'S FEET WERE beginning to hurt. The new C.O. had insisted on walking through every single hangar and viewing every single stasis dock. Every single one, including some Urbek Hiro himself had never seen in his ten years at Standora.

Hiro had tried to steer the senior Commander around the Delta complex entirely, which shouldn't have been all that difficult since the only ground level entry was through the back of the last hangar in the flitter repair section.

Senior Commander MacGregor Gerswin had just pointed to the portal and said, "To Delta complex."

It had not been a question, and Captain Urbek Hiro had just nodded.

Unlike most new Commandants, Commander Gerswin had either committed the entire plan of the base to memory or was personally familiar with it. Neither possibility appealed to Hiro.

Three steps behind the senior Commander, the Captain shook his head.

The senior Commander frowned, and for the moment appeared nearly as old as a senior Commander should. His hand jabbed at the pile of assorted metal parts in the corner of the dusty hangar.

"And that?"

"Sort of an unofficial spare parts inventory, Commander." Hiro repressed a sigh. He had hoped the new chief would be as easygoing as the last. According to the records, and to his HQ sources, senior Commander Gerswin had close to a century in Service, and was *the* senior Commander of the I.S.S. With that sort of record, Hiro had expected a silver-haired, lightly wrinkled man ready to enjoy a graveyard tour.

Commander Gerswin looked more like a thirty-five-year-old, fast track deep selectee, but one of the medical techs had informed Hiro, off the record as usual, that the senior Commander was indeed the senior Commander.

"Captain Hiro. Correct me if I'm wrong, but some of these parts belong to Beta class scouts. The I.S.S. hasn't had a Beta class scout in service since before I joined."

"Yes, ser. I'll have them removed."

The Commander patted Hiro on the shoulder. The Captain couldn't stop the quiver.

"No. Don't remove them. Might find them useful. But not in a heap. Have them sorted and categorized, those that are serviceable."

"What . . . I beg your pardon, ser?"

"Captain Hiro. I don't like messes. Not terribly fond of people who try to cover up. But Standora is nearly a junkyard. You know it, and I know it. Rather have a museum than a junkyard. Least that's good for something."

Hiro shook his head again, so imperceptibly it was scarcely visible. The senior Commander made no sense at all. He avoided thinking about it by lifting his eyes from the discolored plastone floor to the open hangar end. Outside, the sun had disappeared behind the thick gray clouds that usually formed by midafternoon of every day.

The new Commandant's laugh—like a series of short barks—shook Hiro's disintegrating composure further.

Across the hangar one of the idle techs had lifted her head from the unused console where she had been dozing. As she saw the silver triangles, she came to her feet and began to wipe off the console with brisk strokes. The fact that it had no screen did not deter her sudden enthusiasm.

"Look at that, Hiro," added the Commander in a softer voice. "People need something constructive to do."

Hiro didn't like the idea of something constructive to do at all. Not at all. But he smiled, as he had learned to do so many years earlier.

"I also don't like being humored, Captain."

Hiro could feel the sweat beginning to trickle down his back. What in the Emperor's mangy name had they sent him? And why?

"I understand, ser. I understand."

The senior Commander did not respond, instead stepped up his pace through the hangar, heading for the empty stasis docks outside.

XIV

GERSWIN CHECKED THE time. 2303 standard Imperial.

Easily, almost lazily, he moved to the locker and began pulling on the black uniform stored in the back of the bottom drawer.

When he was finished, he studied his image in the mirrored back of the locker door, aware that even his own eyes wanted to avoid the indistinctness of the full-fade black uniform. Only his eyes were uncovered.

After palming the light stud, he eased into the narrow space between the portal frame and the wall, letting his eyes adjust to the darkness, and waited.

Shortly he could hear the muffled feet of the four, slow step by slow step, as they approached his temporary quarters.

He grinned in the darkness.

Click. Click.

The portal irised open, and a dim sliver of light pierced the room, followed by a searing yellow glare.

Thrummm! Thrumm! Thrumm!

Three stunner bolts, wide angle, blanketed the small room.

"Mange!"

"Gone!"

Rather than leaving, as professionals would have, the four crowded in through the portal.

Gerswin noted the heavier bulk of Hiro as the last inside.

Striking with the silence of unseen black lightning, Gerswin garroted Hiro with his forearm, while knocking the Captain's knees and legs from under him. The quick, brute-strength maneuver left the heavy Captain unconscious in seconds.

Gerswin dropped the maintenance tertiary and dispatched the pair next before him with alternate hands.

"What—"

The cry of the fourth man died as Gerswin's elbow crushed his throat.

The senior Commander, still scarcely breathing heavily, tapped the portal shut, relocked it, and tapped the light plate.

The three dead men—Morin, Zorenski, and Vlaed—all had stood close to a head taller than Gerswin. The hawk-eyed Commander nodded, rearranged two of the bodies. Next, Gerswin pulled the unconscious form of Hiro around so that the maintenance Captain was propped against the side of Gerswin's bunk.

"Uhhh . . ."

Last, Gerswin picked up the stunner, already set to the setting that was lethal at short range. Lifting Vlaed's body, he stood, supporting the dead man in front of him, and waited for Hiro to react.

Hiro's eyes opened, and he grabbed at the side of the bunk. He looked, wide-eyed, at the dead man, who with open eyes had a stunner leveled at him, then scrambled toward the weapon.

Thrummm! Thrumm!

Gerswin changed a few patterns in the floor scuffs, avoiding all four bodies, and removed the black uniform, easing himself into a robe, and wiped the butt of the stunner he had used on Hiro clean before he finally unlocked the portal.

Brinnng!

He leaned down and picked up a second stunner and stood against the wall waiting for the response to the alarm.

"Ser?"

The security rating decided against touching his weapon as he measured the C.O. leaning against the wall and looking at the carnage on the deck.

"Captain Hiro came charging in here to warn me about an attack. Before he could make me understand what was happening, those three"—and Gerswin gestured toward the three bodies beyond Hiro —"charged in. Hiro took them all on, but they got him."

"Yes, ser. If you say so, ser."

"Not only do I say so, D'Ner," Gerswin said, picking the rating's name off his tunic, "but that's exactly what the retinal images will show, and what all the evidence will indicate."

Not only that, reflected Gerswin silently, but the disclosure that the Commandant had discovered the illegal diversion of funds from the Imprest Fund and the selling of unused maintenance spares would certainly bolster the fact that the three were guilty of attempted murder, or would have been, had not the courageous Captain Hiro stopped them.

Hiro, of course, had been careful to keep himself above the illegalities.

D'Ner saluted. "Yes, ser."

Gerswin looked down at the four, then back at D'Ner.

"Let's get this taken care of, D'Ner. We've got a base to run, and one that's supposed to repair ships."

"Yes, ser."

D'Ner's shiver was not lost on the Commandant, who smiled at the security tech.

"Think about it, D'Ner. For what earthly decent purpose would three like those be dressed in dark clothes and sneaking into my quarters? And why would they be carrying stunners?"

D'Ner bit his lower lip, then looked up. "When you put it that way . . ."

Gerswin shook his head slowly. "Tell me, D'Ner . . . how long has Technician Morin been holding off the completion of the repairs and improvements to the regular Commandant's quarters?"

D'Ner frowned. "I don't understand, ser."

"Not up to you, D'Ner. Up to the Board of Inquiry. But you deserve to know. Put it in question form. Could this kind of attack take place if the Commandant's regular quarters had been ready? With all the security checks?"

"No . . . no, ser."

"Why weren't they ready? Did it have anything to do with the fact that Morin was in charge of the day-to-day work?"

It did. Hiro had put Morin in charge, which had been one of the things that had alerted Gerswin in the first place.

"Never thought about it. . . ."

"Well . . . damage done already. Lost a good officer . . . and I owe the Captain a great deal. Hope the Board

of Inquiry can get to the bottom of the whole thing.'
He let his voice turn cold as he finished.

D'Ner shivered, glanced at the cold eyes of the
Commandant, as if to say he was not sure whether he
would rather face the Commander or the Board of
Inquiry, then glanced out the portal as he heard the
steps of the security reserves.

"In here . . ." The security technician's voice was
faint, but firm. "In here."

Gerswin handed the stunner to D'Ner. His face was
impassive.

XV

Who are the men who own the skies?
A tall man, a thin man, a mean one.
A man who has no heart, and one who has no eyes.
A man who laughs, and one who never dies.

Do no women own the skies?
A tall one, a thin one, a mean one?
A woman who has no heart, one who has no eyes?
A laughing woman, or one who never cries . . .

. . . you cannot own the skies and stars.
You cannot prison them with bars . . .

And yet, a steel-crossed heart,
with ports that never part,
with daggers from his eyes,
has let the Captain hold the skies.

And who will melt the steel away?
Who will steal the daggers' day?
Who will split the clouds in two,
and with her heart the stars pursue?

Fragments from *The Ballad of*
the Captain (full text lost)
Songs of the Mythmakers
Edwina de Vlerio
New Augusta, 5133 N.E.C.

XVI

THE LIEUTENANT WALKED quickly, as if he were trying to outdistance Gerswin.

"Just ahead, Commander. Just ahead."

Torn between a sigh of exasperation and a smile of amusement at the young supply officer's nervousness, Gerswin kept his face impassive.

"All the security systems in place, Hursen?"

"Yes, ser. Checked them this morning." The dark-haired man did not look back as he followed the walkway through a right angle turn and toward the massive open stone archway.

Through and over the archway, the wide sweep of the rejuvenated but antique Commandant's quarters dominated the crest of the low hill.

The hill itself had been raised at the "suggestion" of Standora Base's first commanding officer, in order to allow him to view the entire Base from his quarters.

The two men halted before the archway, an archway

that concealed the low level personnel screen that ringed the entire grounds, gardens and all.

"You have to go through first, Commander. The screen is keyed to you."

"Just me?"

"For now. You could add anyone you wanted. Did you have anyone in mind?"

Even as the words escaped the lieutenant's mouth, Gerswin could see the young man swallow hard, as if he wished to take the words back.

Gerswin could not quite hide his grin, nor the smile in his voice.

"Don't worry, Hursen. There isn't anyone like that."

The smile left his face as he considered the import of the words. No one like that—no, there wasn't. Not now.

Caroljoy was dead. Dead, for all the memories, and so was their son, the one he had not even known. Three memories of her—once scarcely out of girlhood, for all her warmth and wanting. Once as a Duchess, aging, but still warm and vital. And once as a dying woman, not even in person, but captured in cold print and Foundation incorporation charters.

He shook his head. Twice. Only twice had they been together in a century. And twice had not been enough.

He had spent more time with some casual lovers. And those casual affairs had sometimes been too much, far too much.

He shook his head and looked up at the all too imposing quarters he would occupy, quarters that were obviously left from the days of earlier Imperial expansion, days when the energy had been abundant and cheap, and when every base had been another attempt to recreate the glory of the Empire's rising sun.

Like the day itself, Gerswin reflected with a wry twist to his lips, the Empire had moved into its afternoon.

"Commander?"

"A moment, Lieutenant. A moment."

When he stepped through the archway, he did not

immediately key the release to allow his supply officer through, but paused and surveyed the formal garden to his right, and the clipped green velvet of the lawn as it sloped down and away from the pathway that hugged the artificial ridgeline, as it led to the wide stone steps that waited to greet the Commander.

On the other side of the quarters, he recalled, was the truly imposing main entrance, designed to accept groundcars of size and splendor. Even if none had been seen at Standora Base in more than half a century.

The formality recalled Triandna to him, clear as the single time he had been there, clear as that day he had seen Caroljoy the second time and learned he had lost the son he had never known.

"The Emperor's Cross . . . for this? For what it stands for?" The senior Commander remained unmoving in the sunlight of the early afternoon.

"Commander?"

The plaintive sound in Hursen's voice jerked him back to the present, where he stood in a pleasant garden before a large, but not ducal, military home.

"Sorry, Hursen. Just . . . remembering . . ."

He took several steps back to the stone archway and coded the momentary release that dropped the screens for the younger officer.

"Come on in."

"Thank you, ser." Hursen cleared his throat, once, twice, then finally spoke again. "You were here before, ser?"

"No. Just reminded me of something that happened a long time ago. A long ways from here."

"I imagine you've seen a great deal, ser."

"Hardly, Hursen. Hardly. Sometimes it amazes me to find out how little I've seen."

He turned and began to walk slowly down the stone walkway toward the small but well-restored formal garden, with the dark green of its low hedges, and the intermittent splashes of small flowers.

Had Caroljoy known he might have rated such quarters, would she have considered contacting him after she discovered she would have his child?

He shook his head once more, slowly and with a faint smile.

The Lieutenant Gerswin he had been could not have competed in the same universe as the Duke of Triandna. In life, they had inhabited separate worlds, and not even death, whenever it might come, would change that.

Death? Hardly yet, he thought with another quirk to his lips.

His steps picked up as he marched toward the house. So much time for self-pity and reflection, and no more. Neither sadness nor self-pity would help reclaim Old Earth . . . or Standora Base.

"Come on, Lieutenant. Let's get on with it."

He did not smile as he sensed the puzzled expression on the young supply officer's face. Instead he took the stone steps two at a time.

XVII

"THE SMALL HANGAR at the end? Those are the museum pieces, ser."

The I.S.S. pilot laughed. "Museum pieces? You have to be joking."

"No, ser," answered the technician. "When the Commander got here, he said that since we were only fit to work on museum pieces, we should at least make them the best there were. Was before I came. Each year, we restore another old one from the scrapyard. Make it fully operational. Off-duty time, but it gets to you."

The pilot—young, female, blond, square-jawed
—stared at the technician. "You're serious?"

"Ser . . . why don't you take a look? The hangar's
open to the public, too. Got headquarters to classify it
as a public exhibition. Must get a couple hundred
visitors a day."

"All right. Nothing else to do."

As the young officer strolled down the plastarmac,
she could feel the technician grinning behind her back.
She wondered if the man told the same tall tale to all
the transients at Standora.

Still . . . the hangar was less than half a kilo, and she
had little enough to do until the emergency repairs on
the *Dybyykk* were completed.

"Standora . . . for Hades sake." She shook her head.
The place should have been closed down years ago.

That was what the Operations officer had said.

She glanced at the arrayed hangars, all clean, and the
clear tarmac that stretched to the "museum" ahead.
While the base appeared less busy than many, it did not
appear deserted or run-down, nor did its personnel
conduct themselves as if they had been consigned to a
dying installation.

She glanced inside the hangar to her right, then
glanced again. The grids positively glittered, and the
hull inside seemed the focus of a full crew.

This the junkyard of the fleet, supposedly? What
other ships had been sent here recently? From the Fleet
Dispatch log, she couldn't remember any.

Her steps brought her to the hangar at the end closest
to the main gate toward the local community.

A sign a meter square caught her eye.

IMPERIAL   SMALLCRAFT—HISTORICAL
DISPLAY

None of the craft displayed here are currently in
Imperial Service. For historical and academic
research purposes, all displays are fully functional
and in complete working order.

She read the caption twice before entering the hangar.

Once inside she had to blink, for she had been expecting the hushed, dimly lit recesses of a museum. Instead, the lights were those of a first class repair installation, clear illumination from both direct and indirect sources.

The plastone underfoot was the clear blue of a newly constructed hangar, and outside of the faint hint of metal and ozone, the air was fresh.

From where she stood inside the hangar entryway, she could see eight smallcraft, the largest of which was an ancient corvette.

Another look around the hangar revealed details she had missed. Both entrances, the one from the base and the one from the other side, open to the locals, were guarded by I.S.S. techs. Not by Imperial Marines, but by armed technicians who wore regulation side arms and whose uniforms matched almost any Marine's for sharpness.

Beside each craft was a small stand with a vidcube display to explain the background of the particular boat or ship. And at the far north end of the hangar, suspended from the overhead, were the crossed banners of the Empire and the I.S.S.

Each of the displays appeared as ready for lift-off as the outside caption had claimed.

The pilot headed for the one she recognized from the tapes, a Delta class flitter, which had been retired less than a decade earlier, and which seemed to be the most modern of the craft displayed.

She grimaced as she approached, realizing that the canopy was seal-locked, as it should be if the flitter was indeed operational. She climbed the steps to the platform to view the controls. At least she could get some idea whether the flitter was indeed functional.

"Lieutenant?" A voice intruded upon her observations.

She turned to see a senior technician at her elbow.

"Would you like to try the controls?" He did not wait for her answer, but turned to the seal and made some adjustments. The canopy recessed, and the climbsteps extended from the hull.

"Why—"

"Commander likes to have pilots see what ships used to be like. Can't open them to everyone because they're all hot. He does most of the test flights. Makes sense. Only one checked out in most of them."

"Checked out . . . all of them hot? Even—"

"Even the old black scout, even the Federation Epsilon corvette. If it doesn't work, then it's not on display. We've got some in the work area below. May take years to get in shape. Big project is the *Ryttel*."

The lieutenant dropped suddenly into the padded accel/decel control shell.

"The *Ryttel*?"

"No one could bear to scrap her. Been out in the serveshells for two cees."

Her hands touched the controls, controls that felt new, as recent as the shuttles and flitters of the *Dybyykk*.

"These don't feel old."

"They're not. They work. Commander insists they all work. Every one is absolutely stet with the original specs, except in cases where the original specs were changed in Service to improve operations."

She touched the power readout plates. Ninety-eight percent power. Again she shook her head for what she felt was the hundredth time.

"I don't believe it."

"Not many do. Commander says it shows what we can do." The tech paused. "Just close the seal when you're done. Set to relock."

The pilot shifted her weight to get the feel of the shell, and of the flitter, letting her fingers run over the controls, trying to set up a scan pattern with the different positions of the board instruments.

Even without the power assists on, without the full

panel lit, or the heads-up display projected, the flitter felt new, felt ready to lift clear of the hangar.

At last she took her hands from the stick and thruster controls, unfastened the webbing, and eased out of the cockpit. With a final look at the interior, she touched the closure panel and stepped back onto the platform as the canopy slid into place with a muffled *clunk*.

Straightening her tunic, she turned and took the steps back down to the hangar floor.

She wanted to see if the old Federation's Epsilon class corvette felt as new as the Delta flitter had, knowing in her heart that it would.

Before she reached the wide steps to the viewing platform, she could tell her assumption had been correct. Not a single scratch marred any individual plate, leaving the full-fade finish more perfect than any she had yet seen. Her eyes wanted to twist away from the corvette, to forget it was there.

Licking her dry lips once, she glanced around the rest of the hangar, surveying the six craft she had not yet approached.

What could he do if he had a real ship to work with? she wondered.

Then she laughed. The Commander, the mysterious Commander both techs had mentioned almost reverently, did have a real ship to work with. He had the *Dybyykk*.

If his crews were half as good with the cruiser as with the antique wrecks they had reconstructed, the Captain wouldn't need to go on to New Glascow.

The lieutenant turned back to the corvette, concentrating on the details such as the placement and finish of the heat drops, to avoid having her vision twisted.

From the corner of her eye she could see the same senior tech moving toward the stand.

She knew she would have to check out the controls of the corvette, and perhaps the Alpha shuttle . . . if not the scout in the far corner . . .

XVIII

FROM: C.O.
       H.I.M.S. *DYBYYKK*
TO: 12 FLT HQ
       LOG/SUPP(CODE 3B)
SUBJ: REFIT STATUS

1. *DYBYYKK* ARRIVED STANDORA
   DEC/12/2100/76.
   STATUS: DELTA ARO BTTL ACT

2. SPECIFICS   DRIVES: OMEGA WITHIN 10
                          W/O REPAIR
                SCREENS: OMEGA
                SYSTEM INTEGRITY: DELTA

3. REPAIRS/REFIT COMPLETE SEC/07/0900/77.

4. *DYBYYKK* DEPARTED STANDORA
   SEC/08/2100/77.

5. SYS/CHK/STATUS: ALPHA DRIVES: ALPHA
                                     PLUS
                         SCREENS: ALPHA
                         SYSTEM
                         INTEGRITY:
                                 ALPHA

6. OTHER: (A) REFIT UNNECESSARY THIS
                   TIME
              (B) *STRONGLY* RECOMMEND
                   GREATER UTILIZATION
                   STANDORA RP
              (C) REQUEST REPLACEMENT LT
                   A.L. INGMARR/ I.S.S./PLO/2:
                   MEDICAL LWP(MAT/DET
                   DUTY STANDORA)

XIX

THE NEWBORN HAD only cried once, enough to clear his
lungs, and, placed on his mother's stomach, had immediately tried to go to her breast.

Both the mother and the nursing tech pushed him
gently into position, somewhat awkwardly because
neither had much experience in the matter.

The I.S.S. surgeon completed her work, focused on
the sterilizers, and gave the mother a quick jolt from
the regen/stim tube, all according to the tapes she had
studied and studied for the past week.

The infant resisted when the surgeon lifted him away
from his mother for the prescribed checks, reflexes
—respiratory and neural—but did not cry, though his
eyes were wide.

His look bothered the surgeon, but she completed the
checks as surely as she could, and returned him to his
mother's breast. Then she entered the results on the
health chart, a standard Service chart suitably modified
for the newborn, whose reflexes had topped the scale,

and who plussed the green for neural potential.

Dr. Kristera repressed a sigh. Standora wasn't the best place for a newborn, not with the background contaminants from the facility, and not with the lack of dependent care facilities.

The mother, stretched out on the light-grav stretcher, cradled the tiny boy at her breast with her right arm.

The doctor could see the sucking movements, and both the gratitude and tiredness on the mother's face.

"Why?" murmured the surgeon to herself. To have had the child could not have been a spur of the moment decision, not when having a child had to have been a positive choice before the fact. And the interruption in the young lieutenant's career as an I.S.S. pilot wouldn't help her promotion opportunities, since it would be more than a year before she could leave detached duty for accel/decel related duties—*if* she chose to stay in Service and if she chose to leave the child.

The I.S.S. surgeon looked again. Carefully, she approached the mother and child. "How do you feel?"

"Tired. Tired." Her smile was wan. "But glad."

"How's your friend?"

"Hungry."

The surgeon bent down, trying to get a better look at the boy's eyes, which opened for a moment, as if the newborn had sensed her approach.

The baby's eyes were not blue, but yellow-flecked green, a strong color intensified by the short blond fuzz that would become hair. Dr. Kristera had to stop herself from pulling away from the intensity of the newborn's look.

"He's . . . strong . . . ," she temporized to the mother.

The pilot nodded, closing her eyes.

The surgeon straightened and took the mother's pulse. Strong. The pilot was in excellent condition, had kept in shape, obviously, even though the birth had cost her more than any single high gee maneuver in the operations manual.

The surgeon stepped back as the nursing tech returned.

Maintenance stations were not equipped for childbirth, and for some reason the mother had rejected adamantly the local civilian health care. The C.O. had granted her request to use base facilities.

The surgeon wondered if his permission were yet another part of his efforts at upgrading Standora. Already, the load on the docks was increasing, after decades of neglect.

"You can go now, doctor," suggested the nursing tech, a stocky mid-aged woman.

The I.S.S. surgeon nodded and turned, worrying at her upper lip with her lower.

What was it about the child?

The blond hair was uncommon at birth, but certainly not rare. But the eyes . . . it had to be the eyes.

She wished she had more background for O.B. work, but who expected much in the Service, particularly away from the main staging and training centers?

All babies had blue eyes at birth. Or dark ones. Didn't they?

Who had eyes like that? Like a hawk?

She sucked in her breath.

"It couldn't be . . . it couldn't . . ."

She remembered who had eyes like a hawk, eyes that missed nothing. How could she have forgotten? How could she have possibly forgotten? Was that why he had given his permission?

Mechanically, Dr. Kristera began to peel off her gloves. She shook her head.

Who ever would have thought it?

Shaking her head slowly, she began to remove the rest of her operating room clothing.

XX

Screee . . . thud!

The mass of metal that had once been a pre-Federation scout came to rest in the makeshift cradle in the middle of the small hangar.

The man in the gray technician's suit, a repair suit without decoration or insignia, watched as the salvage trac eased back out into the gray morning. His hawk-yellow eyes scanned the black plates and fifty meter plus length of obsolete aerodynamic lines.

The pre-Federation scouts had been a good thirty percent longer and more massive than present scouts, with the attendant power consumption, but they had one impressive advantage from his point of view. They had been true scouts, able to set down and lift from virtually any world within thirty percent of T-type parameters.

Not that the jumble of metal, broken electronics, and missing equipment before him was really a scout. But it had been, and would be again.

"You MacGregor?" asked the trac operator, who had returned with the clipack after stopping the salvage trac outside on the tarmac. The shuttle port outside the hangar door served the few commercial interests of Standora and the small amount of native travel.

"Same."

"Need some authentication."

"Stet." The man in the technician's repair suit produced an oblong card.

The trac operator inserted the card in her clipack, which blinked amber, then green.

"That's it." The salvage operator glanced over at the long black shape and shook her head. "What you going to do, break it down for higher value scrap?"

"Client wants her restored."

"Restored? That'd take years, thousands of creds."

"You're right."

"Why? No resale. Black hole for power use. Wrong construction for a yacht."

"Prospecting."

"If you say so."

The salvage operator was still shaking her head as she left the hangar for her cab.

The technician, who was not exactly a technician, cranked down the hangar door. At one time, when Standora had been on more heavily traveled Imperial trade corridors, before the increasing power consumption of the newly colonized planets had pushed jump-travel for commercial purposes into fewer and fewer ships and trips, all the hangars had possessed luxuries such as individual conditioning units and powered doors. As the commercial travel had dropped, so had the amenities.

The long-term lease on the hangar barely covered the taxes and expenses to the owner, but the lease terms provided that any upgrades in the facility would revert to the owner at the end of the twenty year contract.

According to the logs that had accompanied the mass of metal that had once been a scout, the official name of the craft had been the *Farflung*.

While the hull contained the fragments of drives, generators for screens and grav fields, all the communications gear and the minimal weaponry associated with scouts had been removed before the auction. That was fine with him, since weaponry mounted for use was illegal and since he intended to use the equivalent of equipment associated with more impressive craft.

He laughed once as he turned back toward the raving cradle. The power consumption from what he planned for the main drives and screens would really have stunned the salvage operator.

As she said, it would take time.

But time . . . that he still had.

Time—while the devilkids struggled half a sector away at the mechanically impossible task of restoring Old Earth. Time—while Eye and Service headquarters watched him and wondered how soon he would begin to age and die. Time—while the ghosts of Caroljoy and Martin nibbled at the warmth provided by Allison and Corson.

Yes. He had time. For now.

XXI

His steps were measured as he came through the stone archway. His black boots, not quite polished to the sheen expected of the Imperial Marine he was not, barely sounded on the stone steps of the rear entrance to the quarters.

"Good evening, Commander." Ramieres nodded at the senior officer respectfully, but did not leave the cooktop.

Gerswin sniffed lightly, appreciating the delicate odor of the scampig. "Evening, Ramieres. Smells good. As usual."

"Thank you, Commander. I do my best."

The Commander smiled. The rating was the best

Service cook he had run across in his entire career, and better than a score of the so-called chefs whose dishes he had sampled over the years.

He knew he would miss Ramieres when the younger man finished his tour in less than three months.

"How long before dinner's ready?"

"For the best results, I'd rather not hold it more than another thirty minutes, ser."

"Try to make it before that. See how the upstairs crew is doing."

Ramieres did not comment, instead merely nodded before returning his full attention to the range of dishes and ingredients before him.

Gerswin swung out of the huge kitchen through the formal pantry and took the wide steps of the grand staircase two at a time.

From the faint scent of perfume to the additional humidity in the upstairs hall, he could tell that Allison had just gotten out of the antique fresher that resembled a shower more than a cleaner.

She was sitting in the rocking chair—another antique that he had found and refinished for her—with Corson at her breast. His son's eyes widened at the sound of the door and his footsteps, but the three month old did not stop his suckling.

Allison wore a soft purple robe that complimented her fair complexion and blond hair.

"Interrupted your dressing?"

She nodded with a faint smile. "I always dress for dinner like this."

Grinning back at her, he sat on the side of the bed next to the chair.

"Are you going to stay home tonight? Or go out and play with your new toy?" Her voice was gentle.

He forced the grin to stay in place. "Thought I'd spend the time with you and Corson."

"That would be nice. He's had a late nap, and I think that he will have to have dinner with us."

"He about done?"

"In a minute. He's like you. There's not much in
between. When he's hungry, he's hungry. And when
he's not, he's ready to tackle the world." Allison
brushed a strand of long hair back over her left ear.

Since she was no longer on high-acceleration duty,
she had let her hair grow far longer than when they had
met, during the refit of the *Dybyykk*.

He watched as her eyes studied the greedy man-child
as he fed.

"Hungry?"

"I am. He eats so much that I can eat just about
anything."

"Corson?" he asked quietly.

She laughed a soft laugh. "Why ask? You know he's
always hungry, the greedy little pig." She paused. "Like
his father."

Gerswin quirked his lips.

Abruptly the baby's mouth left his mother's nipple.
He turned his head and eyes toward Gerswin.

"See? When he's done, he's done."

The mother, who had been and remained an I.S.S.
pilot, swung her son onto her shoulder and began to pat
his back gently.

"I'll do that. You get dressed."

"You don't want me dining in my finery here?"

"You'd shock Ramieres."

"I doubt that. The fact that you might let me appear
in anything this revealing might shock him."

Gerswin leaned forward and extended his arms.

In turn, edging forward from the rocking chair,
Allison eased Corson into his father's arms.

The Commander stood and inched the boy baby
farther up onto his left shoulder, holding him in place
with his left hand and patting his back with his right
hand.

A gentle "*brrrp*" rewarded his efforts.

"You do that so easily. It amazes me that he's your
first."

Gerswin did not make the correction. He had never

held Martin, had never even known Martin had existed until well after his first son's death. And perhaps he had had other sons or daughters—that was not impossible, although he did not know of any.

His lips tightened, and he was glad he was looking out the window, facing away from Allison.

How would he know? Much as he attracted women, he also drove them away. How would Allison feel two months, two years from now?

Gerswin repressed a shiver. She had already picked up that he had intended to work on the old scout after dinner. Now . . . how could he?

She had obviously come back to the quarters after a full day in the operations office, determined to look good for him and to spend the time with both Corson and him. So how could he leave?

He forced his face to relax as he turned toward the dressing area where Allison was pulling on a long and decidedly nonuniform low-cut gown.

He could feel Corson's fingers digging into his shoulder, could feel the small body's heat against his, and the smoothness of his son's skin as he bent his head to let his cheek rest against Corson's.

Gerswin let the sigh come out gently, silently enough that Allison would not hear.

"How do I look?"

"Exquisite."

She frowned. "You make me sound like a piece of rare porcelain."

"Not what I had in mind." He grinned, not having to force the expression as much as he feared.

"I know what you had in mind. But I'm hungry, and Corson won't be sleepy until after dinner. *Well* after dinner."

"Then we shouldn't keep Ramieres waiting."

"No. Not tonight, at least."

Gerswin ignored the hint of bitterness and reached out to brush his fingertips across Allison's cheek.

She grasped them, pressed them to her lips, and smiled her soft smile.

"Shall we go, Commander dear?"

He nodded, and the three of them made their way down the grand staircase toward the dining room, which would dwarf them.

XXII

LYR TABBED THE portal. Halfway into the Foundation office, she realized that someone was sitting before her console.

Without breaking stride, she grabbed the pocket stunner and raised it with her right hand, coming to a halt as she squeezed the firing stud.

Thrummm!

Thud.

The console recliner spun into the console as the intruder flashed to the left before she could readjust her aim.

Thrummm!

Crack!

The stunner flew out of her hand as the intruder, clad in some sort of black that twisted her eyes away from him, swung her around and caught her in a grip that felt unbreakable. She tried to catch a glimpse of his eyes, but he kept her firmly turned away from him.

She attempted to shift her weight, to stamp his feet, to get her elbows into play . . . anything. But none of her self-defense tactics seemed to work. Screaming was useless within the total soundproofing of the office.

Thrummm!

This time the stunner bolt hit her legs, and she felt them collapse under her, although the intruder contin-

ued to support her weight. She decided to stop th
pointless struggle and see what developed as her assail
ant, who scarcely seemed any taller than she was
bound her hands behind her and set her on the singl
settee.

"Stop being ridiculous." The light baritone voic
sent a chill through her. She had met him before. Th
question was when, or where.

"Ridiculous? When there's an intruder using m
console?"

She tried to twist her body to catch sight of his face
but he had kept one hand on her shoulder, and withou
any control of her legs she could not override his ligh
grip.

"Exactly. Are you the only one empowered to use th
console? Do you shoot and then ask questions?"

"Only the Trustee has the right to use this equip
ment. And he's never—"

"Ah, Lyr. I interviewed you, give you instructions
and you don't even recognize my voice. Even if it ha
been a few years, I expected better."

She shivered. Had he been the interviewer? And had
the interviewer actually been the anonymous Trustee?

"You never said you were the Trustee. Am I sup
posed to ask every common thief, 'Oh, pardon me, are
you supposed to be here?'"

She tried to squirm around to face him, but he had
not let go of her shoulder.

"Ha!" The single harsh bark resembled a laugh.
"Point. Point for you."

"I would like a bit more than points."

"Who else could have given you the access codes?"
His voice softened. "And how could anyone have
gotten through your defenses without a trace unless
they knew the system?"

She was silent for a moment. Finally she responded.
"You honestly expected me to think about that when I
saw an intruder?"

"Perhaps that was expecting too much."

His tone made her feel guilty, and then angry as she rejected the guilt for being human in her reactions.

"I quit! Right now!"

"If you wish . . . but I won't accept your resignation until we're through talking."

"I told you. I quit."

"Fine. But we're still going to talk. You're not going anywhere under your own power for a few minutes, at least."

Lyr said nothing.

"While your financial management has been excellent, outstanding in fact, I have not been as pleased with your grant policy. Came to suggest some changes."

"I followed the guidelines, exactly as outlined."

"Lyr," answered the soft voice with the hint of iron behind it, "what is past is past. No time to argue. Only to change."

"I'm not arguing." She worried her lower lip. "What were you doing here?"

"My job. I have access here whenever I want. Access built into the system. If you changed that, which would be most difficult, your own employment would have been automatically terminated."

The hard sound of his last sentence gave her the impression that more than her employment would have been terminated.

She could smell him, like the faint scent of wild grasses, although only his hand rested lightly on her shoulder. She ignored the scent, pleasant though she found it.

"You never did say what you were doing here."

Instead of answering, he picked her up from behind as if she weighed no more than a small child and carried her the half a dozen steps across the antique carpet to the swivel chair. He placed her in the seat in front of the console. His arm reached across her and tapped the keyboard, his fingers even faster than hers would have been.

"Revised Grant Guidelines"—that was the title tha lit up on the screen.

"If you hadn't decided to work in the middle of th night—"

"It was only 2110."

"—you would have found them waiting for you in the morning. As you have on a few other occasions."

"That was you?"

"None other."

"Why all the secrecy? Who are you? Why don't yo want anyone to know who you are?"

By now Lyr was not angry, but furious. She'd nearl stunned her real employer because he'd believed in sneaking around with cloak and stunner, and she could have risked her job and life if she'd toyed around with the wrong parameters in the Foundation's information and control network. To top it off, he had handled her—her!—as if she were a child, mentally and physi cally.

"You're angry."

"I am angry. You're right. This time you understand I am very angry." She forced herself to space out the words, to keep her voice low and even.

"I owe you an apology."

"You owe me nothing except back pay. I quit. Re member?"

"Didn't accept your resignation. Yet." He paused "Offered an apology. What else will it take to get you to listen with an open mind? To remember that the Foundation is not your private fiefdom?" He laughed softly. "You've already reminded me that it's not mine."

"How about some honesty? I know. You've never lied. But there's too much hiding, especially now. Anonymous calls over the screen I can take, but not anonymous intruders sneaking around my office. I'll think, *think*, about reconsidering once you've shown me who and what you are."

"Still better you don't know. For you. For the Foundation."

"I'm beyond someone else deciding what's better."

"You're sure?"

"Sure enough to quit on the spot."

"You're right about one thing. I haven't been totally fair."

"No. You haven't. You expect me to guess what you want or what the Founders of the Foundation want, then you change the rules without even telling me why." She sighed, once, twice. "But you're right in a way, too. You know I don't want to quit. But I will."

"Unless?"

"First, untie me. Then we'll talk. Then I'll decide."

He said nothing, but she could feel him bending over her, and his hands touched hers. His were warm against the coldness of hers, with their impaired circulation. The bonds fell away.

She gripped the arms of the swivel and straightened herself. She did not turn around.

"I would like to see you, face to face, but I don't want to jeopardize my life or my future by doing so."

"Let's talk first. I'll try to answer your questions, and leave the decision in your hands when we're done."

"In my hands?"

"After I've answered your questions, you decide. Fair?"

"Fair enough."

"Your first question. Why the secrecy?" He paused, as if to gather his thoughts. "Most important. The fewer people know the Foundation exists and what it does, the better the chances for its success without interference. Two people is about the maximum for keeping a secret. You and me. Second, in my own obscure way I am extremely controversial. So controversial I believe considered as possible Corpus Corps target. Third, what you do not know, you cannot reveal. More important, cannot be hurt for it."

Again he paused. "There are other reasons. Those are the most important."

"Secrecy implies that there is opposition. That indicates there is a purpose behind the avowed goals. What is it?"

Lyr could sense him behind her, but kept her eyes in front of her.

"The purpose behind the goals? I may have one, but that's not the same as the Foundation. The Foundation is set up to do exactly what it is doing. To try to develop biological techniques for improving or reclaiming the environment. Low cost ones. Not that the research has to be low cost, just the eventual techniques."

"You're convinced about that?"

"I know that. I wrote the goals."

"What about you? You said your goals weren't the same as the Foundation's. What are they?"

"My goals? Not sure they affect what you do." He sighed. "But you'll claim that they do. And the Foundation needs you. So . . ."

The silence drew out.

"I appreciate the vote of confidence, but you were right. I am interested in your goals for the Foundation."

"In a nutshell, I have a strong personal and vested interest in the successful application of the Foundation's techniques. Call it, if you will, the only way I can reclaim my heritage."

"Sounds rather dramatic."

"No. Just truthful."

"What else?"

"That's it. The Foundation has to be successful. That, or some other entity, or me personally. Need bio reclamation techniques. Believe me or not, that's it."

Lyr could sense the exasperation behind the words, an exasperation that indicated truth, if not the whole truth.

"Did you set up the Foundation?"

"No. I know . . . knew . . . one of the Founders."

"Would you tell me who?"

"No. Condition of being Trustee. Not to tell anyone."

"Where does the incoming funding in our blind
account come from?"

"It's an account which channels dividends, interest,
from a large portfolio. Totally legitimate."

"How would I know?"

"The firm handling the account is Halsie-Vyr."

"The Halsie-Vyr?"

"Yes. Think about it. The Imperial Treasury verifies
our receipt of funding by matching our blind account
number against the one to which Halsie-Vyr deposits.
Treasury insures that to make certain taxes are paid.
Information stays confidential."

"How could it?"

He laughed. "What I asked. Star in the sky principle.
Last time there was a public report, five years ago,
Treasury reported 100,000 blind trusts with assets over
ten million credits. Safety in numbers. Who could
match? Depository bank only knows that Halsie-Vyr
deposits and that deposits are posted to another account number in another bank. Treasury doesn't care,
so long as they get their cut."

"Cynical, aren't you?"

"No. Creating the Foundation wasn't my idea. Presented to me as sort of legacy. Came unasked and
unanticipated."

"You have another occupation, then." Her statement
was more seeking verification than inquiring.

"Yes. That's why the Foundation needs an administrator of independence and nerve."

She almost turned to catch a look at him, but stopped
herself, looking instead at the knotted Targan wall
hanging in the right corner, just beyond the portal. Its
curves seemed to fade into oblivion, yet twisted back
upon each other with abrupt changes in the thread
colors.

"What was wrong with my grant policy?"

"Too conservative. Need to take chances. We'll lose credits. Know that, but best chances lie with research-ers and professors outside the clear mainstream. Some-one not tied to orthodoxy. The kind others say, 'He', brilliant . . . strange . . . never know where he's going. That sort of thing."

"How do I tell who's unorthodox and who's frac-tured?"

"Design a questionnaire as a condition of grant application. Make it simple. 'How do you propose to solve your problem, Honored Scientist?' 'What science or evidence do you have to support your theorem?' If you make it too complicated, too orthodox, the really creative types won't play, and you'll get lots of second-raters who are first rate at filling out forms."

"I think I get the idea. How do I know, with a limited scientific background, what's good?"

"After you've read several hundred, you'll know."

"Are you willing to waste all those creds while I learn?"

"Won't be wasted. Not if you learn. Some things can't be done any other way."

"The Foundation . . . you really are looking for a pure research solution, aren't you?"

"No. Looking to support research that will lead to practical solutions. Simple ones."

"How simple?"

"Spores that break down chlorinated organics. Plants that reclaim poisoned land. Biological solutions that primitive or resource-poor cultures could use."

"Primitive cultures haven't poisoned their lands," Lyr objected.

"Not yet. Not in the Empire. Foundation has to look forward and back. Could use Marduk, if we could reclaim it."

"Don't tell me—"

"No. No one knows how long ago that was."

Lyr rested her head in her hands. Her legs were shaking as the muscles contracted involuntarily, trying o rid themselves of the paralysis imposed by the stunner.

"Nothing makes any sense. You don't make sense. I can't even ask questions that make sense. You won't answer the ones that would help me understand."

"Such as?"

"Who are you?"

"How about starting with what I am?"

"That's a start."

"Mid-grade officer in Imperial Service. Technically, I can serve as a trustee of an Imperial chartered foundation, but cannot permanently administer a trust."

"How can you keep who you are a secret?"

"I don't. Same star in the sky principle. My name is on the Foundation charter. Charter lists are not subject to public search. The bureaucrats who monitor foundations and trusts are not the same bureaucrats who monitor officers of Imperial Service."

Lyr wanted to turn and grab him, shake him, or stamp her foot . . . or something. The more he answered, the less she knew.

"So why shouldn't I see who you are?"

"Decision is in your hands. Finished asking all your questions?"

"What questions have I missed?"

"Is there a danger to you from knowing who I am? Do you really want to know, or are you angry that you've been kept in the dark?"

"I am, but that won't be why I decide. Is there a danger to me?"

"Thought there was. Not so sure now. Probably more danger to me than you."

"Why?"

The Trustee did not answer. Finally she could hear him take a deep breath.

"Because I'm out to change the galaxy."

"You sound too sensible to be that crazy."

"Wish I were. If the Foundation is successful, could change popular perception enough to upset the Em-

pire's economy, perceptions, and power base. Migh
not, but it could."

"How? Even if we publicized grants, who would care
about reclaiming a poisoned spot here and there with
plants instead of machines? That's assuming we ge
these grants to a workable state."

"Look beyond the near orbit. Techniques that let you
clean up chemicals are the same techniques that can be
used to make them. Bio techniques, when they work
are usually cheaper, less energy intensive. Right now
less efficient. But we could change that."

Lyr frowned. He seemed to be assuming that the
Foundation would be successful, as if there were no
doubt at all.

"You're assuming a great deal."

"Could be." He laughed. "Maybe the fact that the
Foundation is the only one supporting biological technology means we're the only crazy ones. Maybe I'm just
paranoid."

Lyr frowned again, but said nothing.

"Any other questions?"

"I'm sure I have dozens. I just can't think of them."
Her leg twitched involuntarily and threw her off balance.

His hand touched her shoulder as if to keep her from
pitching sideways.

"Thank you."

"Any last questions?"

"No." Her lips were dry, and she licked them once,
then again. "I'm probably wrong, but I just don't think
I could stay here, not unless I have some better idea of
who and what you are, what you look like."

"All right. Will you consider staying, then?"

"I'll consider it."

His hand squeezed her shoulder gently, and he
stepped around the swivel and stood before her, next to
the screen.

She looked up.

The familiar hawk-yellow eyes caught her attention

irst, that and the hint of darkness behind them, a
darkness that hinted at a man far older than the one
who faced her. She studied his face, the sharpish nose,
the unlined and smooth skin, thin lips, and the short
and blond curly hair cut military-style. He had neither
beard nor mustache.

While his chin was not pointed, it narrowed in a way
that almost gave him an elfin look, had it not been for
the penetrating power of his eyes and the strength of his
nose.

Once more, she tried to focus on his body, but the
black of the form-fitting singlesuit he wore kept pushing her eyes away from his form and toward the floor or
his face.

He noted her confusion. "It's a full-fade combat
suit."

"You aren't . . ."

"No. Just something useful."

She licked her lips again. His face, even with the
hawk eyes, looked familiar, but she could not say why.
She had never met him, outside of the interview years
ago, that and the scattered screen contacts. That she
knew; yet he seemed familiar.

"No horns. No black cloud." He smiled.

"No recognition, either," she countered.

"Didn't say you'd recognize me. Said the ability to
recognize me might be dangerous."

Lyr cocked her head to one side. For all the clipped
sentences, the shortened words, his speech pattern had
a touch of a lilt, an odd tone that she had never heard
before. She wondered why she had not picked it up
earlier, even though there was no doubt now that he
was the man who had interviewed her. The unique
hawk eyes were enough to confirm that. Perhaps the
screen speakers did not reproduce the lilt, underlying
his speech as it did.

"Shall we dive for the event horizon?" she asked.

He raised his eyebrows in inquiry, but said nothing.

"Who are you?"

He shrugged. "If you insist . . . MacGregor Gerswin at your service."

"I don't recognize the name, either."

"Never said I was famous. Glad to know I'm not." He took a step to the side. "How are your legs?"

Lyr tried to lift her right foot, could feel the effort but the leg did not move. "Better, but I still can't move them."

"Shouldn't be too long." He spread his hands. "Now that you've unmasked me . . . what next?"

"I don't know."

"Still want to quit?"

"Common sense screams that I should, but I wouldn't want to force anyone else to go through one of your employee searches, Ser Gerswin."

"What can I say?"

"Don't. Just be thankful I'm as crazy as you are. But," and her voice hardened, "don't sneak in again and change the files without at least warning me that you might be in the area. And fax me directly without that damned hood and mask."

He laughed. "I'll do both, unless I can't reach you. Promise me you'll look before pulling your stunner."

"I promise."

A frown crossed his face. "I should have left some time ago."

"Another woman. I knew it."

He shook his head. "Duty, so to speak. I have . . other obligations. I will stay in touch. How is your leg?"

"The feeling's back."

"Good." He nodded, bent, and picked up a small case from beside the base of the console, a case she had never seen, for all the time it had apparently lain there.

With a salute, he turned and was gone.

So quickly had he departed that Lyr shook her head to make sure he had indeed gone. What else had she missed? Besides everything?

MacGregor Gerswin? Was he in any of the lists?

She bent over the console, nearly losing her balance

gain as her legs twitched. Feeling had returned to
both, along with the faint sensation of needles jabbing
at her skin.

"Might as well search while you wait," she said softly
to herself. She did not trust her legs to bear her weight
yet.

No MacGregor Gerswin appeared in any of the New
Augustan Imperial Government directories, not even
an M. Gerswin.

Imperial Service? Which one?

She tried the Marine Directory.

Nothing.

Aerospace Defense?

Nothing.

Retirees?

No such listing.

Interstellar Survey Service?

"Individual names and assignments are not available
for security reasons. An alphabetical listing of names is
available with rank and communications locator code.
Do you wish to continue search?"

She tapped in "Yes."

"Gerswin, MacGregor Corson, Senior Commander,
455 NC 466/OS."

That was all.

Lyr shook her head tiredly, conscious of the fatigue
in her legs as the stunner wore off. It had been a long
day before the evening's events.

"Just a senior Commander. Not even a Commodore?

"But he never claimed anything," she answered her
own question.

She tapped the screen and erased the inquiries. She'd
have the time. Cursing and damning herself for a fool,
she knew she would have the time.

XXIII

WHAT FORECAST THE fall of the Empire?

Was it the increasing development and resource requirements of the associated systems, pushing inevitably as they did for use of those resources for more local needs? Was it merely a turning away from the Imperialist nature of the Empire? Was it a repudiation of the growing corruption manifested in New Augusta?

Was it the development of the totally impartial Galactic Communications Network by the fanatically honest Ydrisians, whose peaceful intentions were never doubted and with whose fairness the biases of the Empire contrasted so unfavorably?

Was it the growing awareness of social change, manifested Empire-wide in such movements as the Ateys, the Droblocs, the Aghomers? Or was the Empire merely one of those accidents of history that lasted so long as it did because it took fifteen centuries for its people to discover that it had really never lived?

The Last Great Empire
Ptior Petral, IV
New Avalon, 5467 N.E.C.

XXIV

Lyr D'Meryon stepped out of the electrocab and into the warmlights of the entry tunnel.

To her right was a towering figure—a doorman—whose weight and bulk might have qualified him for the Imperial Marines' Front Force.

She hesitated, then began a series of quick steps toward the portal, where she presented the card that Commander Gerswin had left for her. Was he the Trustee or the Commander to her?

She didn't know, but apparently the invitation was his apology. At least she hoped that was all it was.

The portal accepted the card, but did not return it as it opened for her.

Inside, the lighting was brighter, though fractionally, and the tiles were replaced with carpeting. She looked again as her eyes took in the decor. The foyer where she stood was about the same size as her private office and was floored in dark wood, over which laid an individual carpet with a central design, in turn bordered by a more geometical design, both woven in a harmonious blend of blue and maroons.

"Administrator D'Meryon?"

The voice came from a short, gray-haired man who stood by the tall wooden table flanking the exit from the foyer into the next room.

"Yes?"

"Your patron has arrived already and is expecting you. If you would follow me?"

Lyr inclined her head in assent and followed the man

95

through the archway into a dining area, dimly lit, wit
the tables arranged in a circular pattern, each in its ow
paneled recess to create a sense of full privacy withou
closeness.

The dark and heavy carpeting, the wood paneling
and the crisp white linen all gave the impression of
time from history, of a place removed from the her
and now.

Commander Gerswin, in a formal gray tunic an
trousers that resembled a uniform, stood as she neared

She almost smiled, more in embarrassment than i
pleasure, as his eyes came to rest on her. She wondered
if he saw through people the way he seemed to when h
looked at them.

"Lyr. Pleasure to see you."

"I appreciate your asking me, Commander." He
tone was as cool as she could politely make it.

He nodded in response, but said nothing until sh
was seated in the comfortable armchair opposite hir
at the square table.

"Would you like something to drink?"

"Squierre and flame."

Lyr did not see the waiter until the Commande
looked up over her head and repeated the order.

"Straight fizz," he added.

She surveyed the room as well as she could from he
chair without turning around, and waited.

He waited.

And the waiter returned with both drinks, set then
down in the appropriate places, and departed withou
saying a word.

"Owe you an apology. Perhaps more. Start by sayin
I apologize."

The directness of his words took her breath away
She took a sip of the squierre before answering.

"It's not that simple, Commander. You don't ask m
to an obviously expensive private club, say, 'I apolo
gize,' and assume that everything is forgotten an
forgiven."

"No. I know that. So do you." He paused. "Have t

start somewhere. Foundation needs you. I need you."

"Fine. I'll accept that. But it means more trust on our part. Why don't you start by telling me who you really are?"

He shrugged. "You know a lot already. Broken-down and passed-over I.S.S. Commander. Pressed into public service in my off-duty time. One reason why I need you." After sipping the nondrug, nonalcoholic drink, he waited for her response.

"That doesn't compute. Broken-down Commanders don't end up as sole trustees of powerful foundations, unless they're related to Court families or the Imperial family."

"I'm not. I'm originally from an impoverished and forgotten outer system. Used the Service to improve myself, but, as ambitious officers will do, ran into difficulties with High Command. Finis to promotions."

"It couldn't have been too bad or you would have been cashiered or had to resign."

"Delicate orbit. Some pushed for that. Public opinion ran my way, and High Command backed off."

Lyr smiled wryly. "And you're just a poor, broken-down Commander? If they backed off because of the publicity, you must have had an extremely high profile."

"Wasn't like that at all. Would have been inconvenient for the Service to deal with me."

"The more you say, the more mysterious it gets. But you offer no substance. No glorious battles from years in the I.S.S. It sounds more like a series of screen-pushing assignments in headquarters."

"Ha!"

The single barked laugh startled Lyr, and she set down her goblet too hard, hard enough for the liquid to splash and dribble down the outside of the crystal. She dabbed at it with the napkin.

"I take it you have done more than screen pushing."

"A bit. Rated skitter and flitter pilot. Had command of a cruiser for two tours."

"Which one?"

"Fleurdilis."

"The *Fleurdilis*? The one that discovered the bearlike aliens? The . . . Ursans?"

"Same one. Yes."

"Yes?" Lyr's face screwed up into an inquiry. "Yes to what?"

"Was the C.O. at the time."

"Oh . . ." A slow smile crossed her face. "I suppose I owe you a bit of an apology, Commander."

"No."

"Yes, I do. I've been thinking of you as more of an administrative officer, a man who postures more than acts."

"All men posture," snorted the Commander.

"Some have reason. And I can see why High Command left you well enough alone for whatever else you did."

The Commander nodded with an odd expression on his face, one which Lyr could not place.

"Did you actually engage in hand-to-hand combat with an alien, the way the faxers showed?"

"Combat, one on one, but not so romantic as the newsies recreated. Pretty grubby. Should have been able to avoid killing him, her, it. Wasn't good enough for that. Turned out all right in the end. Better than the Dismorph first contact."

Lyr took a sip from the goblet.

"What about you?" the Commander asked.

"Me?"

"Know your background, and you're a good administrator. Can tell that from what you've done with the assets, new investments, even the protection of the few early research returns. Why do you do it? What do you want? More money? More time off? Or more knowledge about . . . anything in particular . . ."

She set down the goblet and frowned, then worried her lower lip.

"Think about it. We'll come back to that. Time to pick out your dinner."

"As your guest, Commander, I'll defer to your taste. I'm not terribly fond of red meat. Other than that, anything is fine. Whatever you think best."

The Commander looked at the silent waiter, whom Lyr had not heard approach this time either, then cocked his head to the side momentarily, as if trying to remember something.

"The lady will have the flamed spicetails, the bourdin cheeses, the house salad, and the d'crem. I will have the scampig, the cheeses, the salad, and lechoclat."

The waiter vanished.

"You eat here often?"

"When I'm in New Augusta. Not all that often. Car—one of the Founders proposed the membership, I suspect. Took it. It's helpful."

"Helpful? That's an odd way of describing it."

He shrugged, then picked up his glass for another sip.

She emulated his example, but set the goblet down as the waiter reappeared with the two salads.

She glanced up from the salad to find him studying her face.

"Lyr? If you could do something entirely different, what would it be? Where would you go? What are your dreams?"

The laugh bubbled up in her throat even as she tried to swallow the remaining drops of squierre in her mouth.

"Phhhwwwww . . . uuouugh . . . ucoughhh . . ."

He stood, but she waved him away, dabbed her chin with the cloth napkin, coughed twice more to clear her throat. Finally she managed to swallow.

"Dreams yet, Commander. Please . . ."

This time she held up her hand before he could interrupt.

"Dreams? Commander, you must be joking."

"No joke." He laughed once, the hard bark that chilled her, that reminded her that for all his direct-ness, the directness that bordered on uncouthness, he would be a dangerous adversary. For anyone.

"I'm sorry," she added in a softer voice. "But the question was unexpected. You really don't know, do you?"

"Unexpected? Why?"

Lyr frowned. Should she tell him? Subtlety wasn't likely to work, one way or another.

She sighed. "It's like this. You said once that there were more than a hundred foundations with greater possible endowments than OER. It's more like fifty—"

"That's now. Because of your efforts."

"—and they have one thing in common. That's a lack of initiative. My job isn't good. It's the best in my field. That's why I'll stay unless you force me out. You handed me something that no one ever expects, much less at my age, and said, in effect, and despite all the mystery, go and do your best. And you didn't second-guess every investment and every fund transfer. So I've done my best."

"Very well," added the Commander.

She stopped and worried her lip. "So you see why I have to laugh at your asking about dreams. I'm worried about your forcing me to leave a dream, and you're asking me about a dream beyond a dream. You don't want me to leave, do you?"

"No. Your work is just beginning, now." His voice softened on the last word.

She saw his eyes lose their intensity momentarily as he repeated quietly one of her phrases.

"A dream beyond a dream . . ." Then his eyes were back on her, boring into her. "Humor me. Give me a dream beyond a dream."

Lyr looked away, damning herself for revealing too much, feeling like she had worn nothing to the table.

"Do you have dreams beyond your dreams?" she countered quietly.

"Sometimes. Sometimes I dream of rolling hills covered with grasses, and streams sparkling from mountain rocks." He looked up. "Land . . . so . . . poor . . . where I grew up . . . no green grass." He looked away and took the last gulp of his fizz. "What about your dream, Lyr?"

She did not answer, but took a sip, a small sip, of the squierre, ignoring the salad before her, and stared at the white of the linen on the table as she let the warmth trickle down her throat.

"If I couldn't do this . . . I'd have to get away. Some place like Vers D'Mont . . . with mountains but culture. I haven't been there, not even on my salary, but you asked me to dream. People, but with privacy. I—" She stopped, watching him nod as she spoke.

"A small cottage?"

"A chalet, on a hill, not a sharp peak, but one where you could see the high mountains, and the valley below, with a lake. A chalet that had balconies on all sides."

The Commander continued to nod as if her fancy were as possible as sitting across the table.

"But that's impossible!" she burst out, then lowered her voice. "Why encourage an impossible dream?"

"No dream is impossible. Wasn't encouraging, but inquiring."

"But why?"

"Dreams are important." He said nothing to amplify that, but took a last bite of his salad, then sat back as the waiter placed the scampig before him.

Lyr nodded at the man to take her unfinished salad.

"What are they?" She studied the question-marklike objects on the porcelain plate.

"Spicetails. Seafood delicacy. My second favorite dish, but should I tell you that?"

She smiled in response to the Commander's gentle self-deprecation.

"I'll try them anyway."

The longer the meal went on, the more confused she became as to the Commander's motivations. His attitude was not apology, exactly, nor seduction, nor exactly interest, though he continued to ask gentle questions.

"Do you have other interests . . . hobbies . . .be-

sides numbers? . . . Would you travel widely? . .
Your family? Were you close? . . . Whom of the public
figures do you admire the most?"

Those questions she could not avoid, she answered
gently and as briefly as possible, not forgetting to enjoy
the dinner.

The cost of the meal had to have been astronomical.
The setting, the cutlery, which was worked sterling
silver, the antique porcelain, the linen, the use of
well-trained help—they all pointed to an establishment for the extraordinarily affluent.

And yet, the man across from her, while born a
leader, had obviously not been born to wealth. For all
his Service training and accomplishments, he was only
a Commander.

Or was he?

Even when she had left the Aurelian Club, headed
back to her own more than comfortable apartment, the
hundredth floor of the Murian Towers, she could not
decide.

He was more than a Service Commander, she knew.
But what?

XXV

SCF-EC-4 (Sector Red, CW-3)

SCF-EC is a spectral type G-2, population 3 anoma-
ly. Seven planet system, four inner hard core/crust.
Planets three and four within T-compatible life zone.
Planets five and six are gas giants. Planet seven is
captured comet accretion satellite with irregular
orbit . . .

Planet three possible for future intelligent NH life. Wide spectrum, classification range O/N, WAL, LP/MP, FSR . . .

Planet four limited organic classifications N/N, SMS/MS. CrB. Site of nonidentified intact Class I artifact (See Aswan, legends section, and SCF-EC-4 —Engineering/Structures) . . .

> *Chartbook, Sector Three*
> Commonality of Worlds
> 5573 N.E.C.

XXVI

BOTH CIRCUIT BLOCS remained black.

With a sigh, the man in the working tech's jumpsuit set them aside and stood up.

Each aspect of rebuilding the courier took more time, more credits, and more equipment than even he had anticipated. He reset the test probes, and reattached the cube blocs. His fingers played across the tester's console.

This time, the circuit bloc on the right turned crimson. But the one on the left remained black.

He sighed again and stood up, glancing across the hangar at the incomplete structure in the graving cradle, the structure that he hoped would someday be the ship he needed.

His eyes strayed to his wrist and the comp-timer there.

2230—far too late already. Allison would be asleep, assuming that Corson was not giving her trouble. But

Corson seldom did, despite his intense interest in the world around him and his already too active efforts at crawling.

Corson, and Allison—there was never enough time for them, not with the demands of being Standora Base Commander and the invisible deadlines for completing the courier that crept up toward him.

How could he tell Allison that he had to finish the ship before his last tour at Standora? She thought he had all the time in the universe.

Caroljoy had thought that, too.

Perhaps they were right, but he could be killed as easily as any other man, and would be, once the Empire discovered his plans. On that basis, he had little enough time, and no one in whom he could confide.

Allison, wrapped up in her moments of joy, and in Corson, could not understand the desperate need of a distant and antique planet forgotten by all but the myth tellers, the historians, and one Imperial senior Commander.

Caroljoy, who had understood, had also opted for her moments of joy in her son. But she had left him the means and, indirectly, yet another pressure, to pursue his obsession.

"Obsession?" he asked himself wryly.

"Obsession," he conceded as he placed another circuit bloc into the tester, ignoring the tightening in his guts as he felt the night inch toward morning, as he could sense the loneliness radiating from a large house on a high hill.

The third circuit bloc flared crimson, and he smiled, using his lips only, as he placed it inside the screen relay he was reconstructing.

"Only five more," he muttered as he selected yet another bloc from the case of scrapped components he had obtained through the Ydrisian free market.

He shifted his weight as he began once more to work the testing console, probing the minute circuits before him to insure their integrity and functions.

Taking a deep breath, he settled back into the routine. Select, set up the test patterns, scan, and test. Select, set up, scan, and test.

He hoped Corson was sleeping well.

And Allison. And Allison.

XXVII

"CONGRATULATIONS, ADMIRAL. CONGRATULATIONS."

"Appreciate it, Medoro." The newly sworn Admiral of the Fleet surveyed the palatial office, the wide armaglass windows that overlooked New Augusta from the hillside that the I.S.S. had claimed generations earlier, and the small group of Imperial courtiers, functionaries, and subordinates who waited at the far end of the high-ceilinged room.

He repressed a smile as he glanced back at Medoro. The senior Commodore, who had served as Chief of Staff for the last two Fleet Admirals, obviously would lose no time in pressing his own agenda. The Admiral nodded at his Chief of Staff. "It's time to play politics, I gather."

"It's always time to play politics, Admiral."

The Admiral let the smile come to his lips. "Always and forever, from now on. Right, Medoro?"

"If you want a long and healthy tenure, ser."

Medoro's tone was light, but the Admiral caught the bitterness of underlying truth. The most senior officer of the Service took a step toward the white linens of the over-laden table where the official "informal" celebration of his swearing-in would commence.

"Any space for truth?" he asked the Commodore, almost as if the question were an afterthought.

"Only if you are careful, ser . . . and now is not the time to begin . . . Admiral Keraganis is the one on the far right . . . next to him is Admiral Fleiter, head of logistics and personnel . . . and behind him is Rear Admiral Thurson, Information Services—"

"That's basically the Service rep to the Eye Council right?"

"He does sit as liaison to the Council, currently."

The Admiral refocused his attention on the officers approaching as he moved up to the table area.

"Congratulations, Admiral Horwitz," boomed out the man Medoro had identified as Keraganis. "Look forward to working with you. Heard a lot about you especially the way you handled the original Ursan contact. Brilliant strategy."

Horwitz inclined his head. "Thank you. Just fortunate to have the right people in the right places. I look forward to having the benefit of your unique experience, and your distinguished advice will certainly be welcome."

"Glad to see you again, J'rome," broke in another Admiral, a silver-haired and thin man who stood a half head above the others.

"Marsta! Didn't expect to see you. When did you get here?" The Fleet Admiral sidestepped Keraganis, favoring him with a pat on the shoulder that he hoped would get the point across that Keraganis was not working with him, but for him, and around the end of the laden table.

He stopped before reaching his friend.

"All of you, it's a happy occasion. Please enjoy the food and the company. Dig in."

Immediately several junior Commodores and a senior Commander, appearing rather out of place among the senior officers of the I.S.S., took refuge in the food

"J'rome. Didn't expect to make it, but we wound up the Rim maneuvers almost a week ahead of schedule. For once, everything worked. Smart idea that Alexandro had, insisting on premaneuver checks at Standora."

"Alexandro? Standora?"

"C.O. of the *Dybyykk*. He had some emergency work done there a year ago. Better than any Service yard yet, he insisted, and since no one else out that way could fit the squadron in, I agreed. Took a week more than we thought, but it cut the down time on station by twice that. So I'm here."

Horwitz frowned. "Standora? Why is that so familiar?"

The Rear Admiral laughed. "How could you forget? Gerswin? He's the Commandant at Standora."

"Gerswin is still around? He was ancient at the time of the Ursan contact."

"Doesn't look it, but I understand he's on his last or next-to-last tour—"

"Congratulations, Admiral Horwitz," broke in another voice. "Marc Fleiter, here. Logistics and personnel. I just wanted to meet you informally before we get together officially, and I wanted to let you know how much I look forward to working for you."

Horwitz repressed another smile. Fleiter was sharp, and had seen Horwitz's reaction to Keraganis's attempt to put the Fleet Admiral down.

"Good to meet you, Admiral Fleiter. I'm sure we will do well together, and I appreciate your interest."

"Not at all, Admiral. Just wanted to say hello, and I apologize if I intruded."

"No problem . . . no problem."

As Fleiter stepped back and away, and as Horwitz and Marsta were left alone momentarily, Marsta smiled a brief and rueful smile.

"Watch out for that one, J'rome."

"Sharp, isn't he?" Horwitz responded. "And dangerous, I suspect," he added in a lower voice. "But not the most dangerous one."

"Who's that?"

"I think it was Gerswin. Too bad he got mixed up in that Old Earth mess. Or maybe it's a good thing he did."

"Admiral Horwitz . . ."

The new Fleet Admiral turned to greet the next in the stream of well-wishers.

Admiral Marsta nodded and turned toward the fruit.

XXVIII

THE EMPTINESS STRUCK the Commander as soon as he stepped through the portal into the foyer, with its real slate tiles that had been left from the days when the Base had boasted a Commodore in residence.

Boots clicking, the slender officer in working grays glanced into the salon, into the living room, into the formal dining room, and into the kitchen that was twice the size necessary even for the entertainment needs of the Base Commandant it served.

Empty—the main floor rooms were empty.

A dozen quick steps carried him up the wide formal staircase to the second floor, opposite the room she had used as a nursery. The standard crib, which had been presented to them by a local acquaintance, stood empty; the handmade quilt the boy loved, gone with him and his mother.

The I.S.S. senior officer crossed the small room and checked the closet. No clothes remained.

With a sigh, he surveyed the room once more.

Another deep breath, and he left, heading for the master suite, knowing she would be gone, and that the room they had shared, briefly it seemed, would be immaculate, and vacant.

In the wide hall outside the old-fashioned doorway, he paused, not wanting to burst in, nor wishing to find what he knew he would discover.

His eyes traced the perfectly squared panels of the wood. Finally he reached and touched the handle. The door swung inward at his touch.

For a moment, an instant, everything seemed normal. The crimson trimmed gray quilt still covered the outsized bed. A solideo cube still graced the bedside table on the side where he slept. Late afternoon sun still poured through the western windows of the sunroom and spilled through the archway into the bedroom itself.

His fears were confirmed by the other absences—the bare tabletop on the right side of the bed, the empty space on the wall where the portrait of the three of them had hung, the missing daccanwood box where she had kept her uniform insignia.

With slow steps he reached the closet, opened it, and saw his own uniforms on the right, and the emptiness on the left.

He turned, paced back and forth three times along the foot of the bed, almost as if she were still there, always back before him, her long legs curled under her, Corson at her breast, listening to him tell her about the day.

His eyes flickered to where she usually sat, then back to the floor before he realized that a white square lay across her pillow.

The Commander pounced upon it, so quickly an onlooker would not have believed the speed with which he moved, and studied the script, the nearly childish lines with the large loops and clear and precise letters.

My dear Commander—

It is time to go. My resignation has been accepted. While it will hurt, it would hurt so much more later, when Corson and I would become a wall between you and destiny.

Already, you pace the floor at the foot of the bed at night. A thousand projects are on your mind, and you are torn between us and what you must do. I can see the fury building, though you have never been other than gentle.

The Service owes me a last trip home, and that is where we will head. I do not expect you to follow. This is *not* a hidden plea to show how much you care. I know nothing could stand in your way if you chose to find us, and I have hidden nothing. All that can stop you is your own good sense.

Please do not come after me. I would rather have eighteen months of wonderful memories than a lifetime of resentment. I bear you only love. Both you and having Corson were my choices. Most would say I was foolish. Now, perhaps, I should admit that I was. That is past. I have Corson, and to keep him, in any real sense, I must resign. I have, because he is too wonderful to leave.

For his sake as well, we must leave. No matter how brilliant and talented he grows up to be, he would always stand in your shadow. Because he is you, and your son, he will need his own light.

In time, I will lose him as well. Already he resembles you. That is why time is precious, and why I will give him what you never had. He may not be the great man you are and will be, but I trust he will find the universe a more loving place.

It is strange, how you inspire love. You do not want to accept it. As you accept it, you become outwardly more gentle. But the furies inside you build. Istvenn help the universe should you ever unleash them.

I can say no more. I love you, but I love Corson more, and, for now, he needs that love. If you love him, if you have ever cared for me, let us be, Commander dear.

The formal notecard in hand, he straightened and let his steps take him into the sunroom. From the wide

indows, he looked downhill toward the empty shuttle
eld.

She and Corson had taken the *Graham* back toward
e Arm, back toward Scandia and its tall conifers and
cky islands.

Scandia . . . the name even sounded like her.

He shook his head and turned away from the vista.

She had liked the view from the Commandant's
uarters. How many times had she sat in the swing
hair in the late afternoon, after she had gotten home,
orson cradled in her left arm, just looking out?

"Destiny . . ." The single word seemed to cast a
hadow on the sunlit carpet.

Was he that driven? Was it so obvious that those who
ved turned away? Or did they really love him at all?
Vere they just drawn to him for some other reason?

He laid the notecard on the arm of the swing chair
efore he left the sunroom, before he looked through
he rest of the quarters for the two he would not find,
or any trace of the pilot, woman, and officer who had
ved him, and of his son, whom he had known so
riefly.

The sunbeams played across the weave of the Scandi-
n carpet he had bought for her, illuminating the soft
olds and browns in the silence.

XXIX

SENIOR WEAPONS TECHNICIAN Heimar scanned the list
n the screen again. Shipment four—standard heavy
cruiser replacement pack—was listed as having been

picked up by the *Bernadotte*'s tender.

Heimar checked the orbit schedule and frowned. According to New Glasgow orbit control, the *Bernadotte* had closed orbit less than four standard hours ago. The pickup time had been more than ten hours earlier.

The technician compared the screen list to the hard copy receipt. Then he called up the code section. The authentications were identical.

Finally he turned to the impatient Major.

"Your shipment is listed as already having been picked up. It's not here, either. That rules out screen error."

"How could it have been picked up?"

"That's what we'd like to know."

Heimar tried not to show the shaking he felt inside. A standard weapons pack for a heavy cruiser consisted of a dozen tacheads and four hellburners.

One pack was apparently missing, properly logged out, apparently properly picked up by a cruiser tender with the right identifications, the right codes, and loaded by Heimar's own crews.

The only problem was that the tender couldn't have belonged to the *Bernadotte*.

Would the Commander be upset? Would he? Heimar shuddered. Although it had not happened in his watch, his men had obviously been the ones suckered, and Heimar did not want to be the one to notify the Commander.

He reached out and slapped the red stud on the console. Then he waited, but only for a few seconds.

"Commander, this is Heimar, at off-load. The weapons officer of the *Bernadotte* has some information that you should know."

Heimar stepped back and motioned the Major to the screen.

He stared at the dome above, thinking about the murky atmosphere outside, the nearly unbreathable air, wishing he were anywhere, even there, besides on duty and in reach of the Commander. It had never

appened before, not that he knew. Sixteen nuclear
arheads gone—disappearing from a tightly guarded
mperial system, disappearing without even an alarm
eing raised or anyone being the wiser.

Heimar had heard the rumors about the great dozer
eft of a half century earlier, or whenever it had been,
ut that had happened in orbit, not planetside.

But twelve tacheads, and four hellburners? He bit his
ps. It wouldn't be as bad for him as it would be for the
ommander, but that wouldn't make it any easier.

"HEIMAR!"

He stepped back to the screen to explain what he had
iscovered.

XXX

THE MAN STEPPED inside the building's foyer. Although
he wind whipped snow with the force of needles along
he broad expanse that would be a boulevard in the
hort summer, he wore but a light gray jacket and
lack, calf-high boots. Hatless, he showed blond hair,
ike the majority of Scandians. Unlike theirs, his was
hort and tight-curled to his skull.

Once inside, he shook himself, and the light dusting
f snow fell onto the wide entry mat. Three steps took
im to the directory block, where he confirmed a suite
umber before taking the low stairs behind it two at a
ime to the second story of the three-floored building.

The office he wanted was at the rear northern side,
nd, as he walked through the open archway he could
mmediately see a panorama of the lake at the base of
he hill on which the building stood. Below swirled

drifts, and frozen white covered the lake. The wind sculpted drifts ran from the stone wharves and the docks of the town on the right, and from the tree slopes of the park on the left out into the indistinctness of the white north.

"May we help you?"

The young man who spoke was black-haired—the single dark one of the five in the office—and clean shaven.

Before answering, the visitor studied the other four, two men and two women. All five wore collarless tunics, trousers, and slippers. He glanced to the rack at the side, where parkas and heavy trousers hung above thick boots.

"Looking for Mark Ingmarr."

"That's me," laughed the darker man, who stood more than a head taller than the slender visitor. "You are . . . ?"

"Corson . . . MacGregor Corson."

"You mean Gerswin?"

"Said Corson. Meant Corson."

The two women exchanged glances, but said nothing.

"If that's the way you want it . . ."

"That's the way I want it."

"You called earlier." The tall man's tone was flat.

"That's correct. You are an advocate . . . an attorney?"

"I told you that."

"Satisfactory. Need your professional ability."

"What if I don't want to give it?"

The visitor looked up at the heavily muscled young advocate. "You don't have to. Find someone else. You would be better."

Ingmarr stared down at the other, found his eyes caught by the hawk-yellow intensity of the smaller man's stare. For an instant, it seemed as though he were trapped in blackness. He dropped his eyes, breaking the contact.

"I'll talk about it," the attorney conceded.

He pointed to a console and two chairs in the far

corner, half concealed behind a bank of indoor plants.

The man in gray took the right-hand chair, the one farther from the console.

"What do you want?" asked the advocate.

"A modest trust. Designed to receive funds from a blind account in the Scandian Bank. Should include certain provisions for education, an alternate to the trustee, and a termination and succession clause."

"That's rather general."

"The beneficiary is about seven standard years old. I'm acting for his father's family. His mother felt that his father was not the most stable of individuals. Mother left with son when the boy was less than a year old. Father couldn't do much. Family feels son should be provided for, particularly education. Half the trust would be his ten standard years after he reaches statutory majority. The other half goes to his mother, ten years after he reaches majority, or after he would have. Should he not reach majority, his half would be used to endow scholarships in his name at the university."

"What if the boy's mother doesn't want the money?"

"We can't prevent her from not using it, but the funds would be his at some point regardless."

"You seem rather determined."

"It is both the least and the most that can and should be done under the circumstances."

"Rather a strange way to put it."

The shorter man shrugged. "Strange situation."

"Why didn't you have the bank set it up? You wouldn't even have had to make a long trip. They could, you know."

"Some things require a personal touch." He handed Ingmarr a sheet. "This contains the securities that will compose the trust, as well as the specified asset composition for incoming cash flows."

"I'd have to advise against too much inflexibility."

"Only the investment parameters are inflexible. The categories, not specific choices."

"You said a modest trust . . . this looks to be more than that."

"In addition to the listed securities, the initial credi transfer will be fifty thousand credits. Annual pay ments will be in the neighborhood of about five thou sand credits for roughly the next ten years. After that the trust will be expected to be self-sustaining."

Ingmarr looked at the list and touched his console his eyes darting back and forth between the informa tion he called up and the securities listed.

The man who called himself Corson watched i silence.

"For Scandia, this is much more than a modest trust much more, ser . . . Corson. This would set . . . the boy . . . up comfortably for life."

"Not wise without conditions. Mentioned those ear lier. First, may not collect even any of the interes unless he finishes primary studies. Second, not more than half the interest until he finishes graduate level Third, he may not *ever* acquire control of the principal capital until he is commissioned as an I.S.S. officer or completes the full Nord Afriq survival course."

"But if he cannot collect without the schooling—"

"Sorry. Should have made that clear. Trust pays school expenses directly, as necessary. Any excess income is reinvested, unless he needs it for living expenses, but he or his mother must submit records, like an expense account, to the trustee."

"I think I understand your interest and reasoning, ser . . . Corson."

"One final stipulation. He is not to be informed of the trust until he completes primary studies, or until ten years after majority, whichever comes first."

"At that time, do you want him to know the source of the trust?"

"I would leave that to the trustee and his mother. She could also tell him that the money was left for him by a distant relative. An eccentric old Imperial officer. That might be best, but that would be her choice."

Ingmarr frowned. "Any other conditions?"

"Not unless you think there should be."

"All right. Let me get started on this, if you don't

mind. We'd all feel better if it were completed and you could get on with . . . could get on with . . . whatever . . ."

"I understand."

The outsider leaned back in the chair and transferred his sharp glance to the snow-drifted lake and the gray-clouded skies and the fine sheeting snow that appeared more like fog.

He could tell the taller of the two women kept looking at him, although he did not need to turn to check, and his keen hearing could pick out some of the phrases.

". . . same eyes, same curly hair . . ."

". . . but her brother?"

". . . he knows . . ."

". . . scary . . . when you think how old . . ."

". . . fascinating though . . ."

Ingmarr continued to work with the legal terminology on the console, apparently oblivious to either his client or the rest of the office.

After a time, the stranger straightened in his seat and removed a thin folder from inside his light jacket, which he had opened but not removed. He checked the contents, then left it in his lap and returned his attention to a line of skiers moving smoothly across the lake toward the town with practiced strides.

"Ser Corson . . . if you would like to check this out . . . and fill in the necessary names and details."

"Fine."

The outsider slipped into the seat in front of the console, eyes running over the displayed text.

Ingmarr noted the ease with which he operated the equipment, changing pages, cross-indexing, checking references.

"No problem . . . except here. Think you should add something about, 'with the approval of the mother, Allison Ingmarr.'"

The man in gray stood back from the console, still holding the folder that he had brought.

"All right." Ingmarr sat back down and made the

changes, scanning through the text to insure that hi
client had supplied all the necessary information.

The smaller man stepped up as Ingmarr looked up
from the screen.

"You'll need these."

"Which are?"

"The portfolio securities. In Corson's name."

Ingmarr took the folder without opening it.

"Let me run out the copies of this for authentication
and registration."

The stranger nodded and half-turned toward the
winter scene outside.

As Ingmarr touched the last stud on the console, he
stood, laying the folder on the flat top of the equipment. He moved away from the console. Looming over
the stranger, he cleared his throat and flexed his shoulders as if to assure himself that his muscles were loose.

"Who are you, anyway? As if I didn't know."

"I told you. MacGregor Corson."

"I don't believe that for an instant." The Scandian
reached out for the smaller man with a huge right hand
and grabbed him by the shoulder.

"Let go." The words were quiet.

"Who are you? Why are you here?"

Thud.

Ingmarr stared up from the carpeted floor into a
yellow, hawk-eyed glare. He appeared stunned.

"Doing my best to hold to her wishes. Without
disinheriting him. No more questions."

Each word, though whispered, seared. Ingmarr stiffened, but did not get off the floor.

"You! . . . never believed . . ."

"Get the trust finished. Sooner the better." The
stranger's light baritone voice was calm.

"Agreed," conceded Ingmarr, rubbing his hand and
then his shoulder. The smaller man had handled him as
if he were a doll, and for the first time, he was
beginning to understand his sister, her tears, and her
fears. And her reasons for having to trust the man.

Ingmarr stood up slowly and repeated himself.
'Agreed."

Both men ignored the whispers from the other side of
he open office as they moved toward the printing
station in the middle of the office.

". . . like a child . . ."

". . . so fast . . ."

". . . has to be *him* . . ."

Outside, the wind picked up, and the snow fog
thickened until the gray light resembled twilight rather
than midafternoon.

Inside, two women shivered in thin tunics while a tall
man continued to massage a sore shoulder, and a
shorter blond man began to authenticate a legal docu-
ment.

XXXI

GERSWIN LOOKED OVER at the innocuous set of plasteel
shipping containers that filled the small aft hold of the
Caroljoy. Twelve bore labels indicating they were high-
speed message torps, and four bore labels indicating
long range torps.

Not that the labels were totally inaccurate, mused the
Commander. Someday they might have to be used to
send a message of sorts, but he had obtained them now,
when it was still possible, without too much difficulty.

The maiden voyage of the refurbished former scout
had gone well, well indeed, although it would have
proved difficult, if not impossible, to have traced the
supposed private yacht through three separate identi-

ties, two military, and four systems, not including Scandia. That diversion, on the return trip, had been for other reasons, later than he would have wished, but accomplished nonetheless.

His eyes lost their sharp focus for a minute as he recalled the snow-covered firs of Scandia, and, more distantly, a pair of eyes as clear as a cloudless winter morning. He shook his head to bring himself back to the small hold.

Gerswin checked the hold locks once again before extricating himself from the hold and climbing back into the former crew room. Loading the shipping crates from outside through the exterior cargo lock, an armed tender lock converted for his purposes, had been far easier than inspecting them from inside the ship. Small as the aft hold was, the forward hold was even smaller, containing only emergency stores and an emergency generator and solar array.

There was less crew space under Gerswin's internal redesign than in the ship's original configuration. As a scout, the former *Farflung* had carried a four man crew under tight living conditions. Gerswin had reconfigured the newly and officially registered *Caroljoy*(IPS-452) as a single pilot ship, with emergency capacity for two passengers on short hauls.

The drives were not those of a scout, but of a small corvette, with total power cross-bleed between the corvette screens and gravitics. The extra power and range had come at the cost of habitability and because Gerswin had installed higher quality control and communications systems—the lower weight and improved reliability offset by the considerably higher price.

The Commander sealed the hatch beneath him, which resembled another tiled floor square of the cabinlike section of the ship, which contained the fresher, wall-galley, and bunk. He stood, surveying the trim and efficient interior.

"Stand down mode, full alert," he ordered.

"Stand down mode, full alert." A voice, feminine, but impersonal, answered the Commander.

He sealed the locks behind him, and stepped out into the hangar, which, as he had rebuilt the *Caroljoy* from scratch, he had turned into a maintenance facility capable of handling all but the largest of private yachts. The equipment within the hangar could also have serviced virtually all Imperial scouts and corvettes, although that capability remained the secret of the Commander.

He had not kept secret from his subordinates that, after Allison's departure, his sole vice was his "hobby"—building a private yacht from surplus scrap for his eventual retirement.

Some of his officers had even visited the hangar and the *Caroljoy*—at suitably arranged times when the disarray was maximized—and while all were impressed by the Commandant's personal expertise, they shook their heads sadly behind his back at his tales of spending all his savings on his project.

None knew that the *Caroljoy* was already spaceworthy. He had not registered her until after he had returned from the maiden voyage. While the fact that his ship was spaceworthy would leak out sooner or later, both the registration date and his officers' memories would reflect a much later first launch than the reality.

Gerswin smiled wryly at the recollection of some of the looks as they had seen the scout in the graving cradle, looking as if it would be forever before she lifted.

His steps carried him across the hangar toward the outside lock and the groundcar that would carry him back to Standora Base, back to the empty quarters of the Commandant. Back to a short night's sleep before another day of shuffling priorities, fleet repairs, and the fragile egos of ship captains who had heard that Standora Base could perform miracles and who all wanted to be first in line.

The Commander shook his head as he thought of the sixteen slender missiles sealed in the *Caroljoy*'s aft hold. Just as he hoped he would not need them, he

knew he would, although he could not say for what
Not yet. But that time would come, had to come, as the
Empire began to crumble and the commercial barons
began to grab for more and more.

Not yet did he need them. But to reclaim Old Earth
he had no doubt he would need them, and that he
would have little or no time to obtain them by the time
he needed such power. By then, too, the source of the
weapons might have been forgotten.

As he slipped from the hangar, he automatically
scanned the area, but the private shuttleport was quiet
as usual.

He guided the official groundcar across the
plastarmac and toward the south gate of Standora Base
more than twenty kays away.

XXXII

THE SENIOR OFFICER accessed the private personal line,
fed in the privacy links, and scrambled.

The screen colors swirled, then settled into the even
lines of text provided by the agency.

"Quarterly Report—Corson Ingmarr."

The title was scarcely larger than the text that followed, but the Commodore devoured each word, line
by line, of the ten pages that had been transmitted by
torp, each page costing as much as a set of undress
blacks.

At last he keyed the report into his own personal files,
though he doubted he would reread it, not for years,
since he could remember the last reports verbatim.

Finally, he shut down the small console, the single

piece of furniture or equipment in the rambling quarters that he could truly say was his own, along with the private comm relay he had leased with it.

Most of his creds had gone into the *Caroljoy*, along with the discretionary funds allowed him under the Foundation bylaws, although his personal investments were still considerable, since he had attempted to fund the restoration out of income, rather than capital. The fact that his assets were more than comfortable was not surprising, not considering his years in Service, and his few personal needs.

He stood, blond, slender, despite the loose-fitting light suit he wore, and walked around the console and out of the paneled room that bore the archaic term of "library," though there were neither books nor tapes within or upon the wooden shelves.

The room echoed with his steps, and light-footed as he was, their echo recalled the tapping of other steps. She had never liked the library, and Corson, of course, had not been walking when she had taken him.

"Why do you do it?"

The words did not echo as he left the room. The issue carpeting in the front foyer insured that, and his steps were silent as he climbed the wide steps to the second floor. Only the Commandant's quarters had two stories, with the wide staircase, but then the quarters had been designed with entertaining in mind, back in the expanding days of the Empire, when energy had been more abundant, and before the rights of the occupied and the colonized peoples had been taken quite so seriously.

Most nights, the Commodore did not mind the quiet and the isolation.

Most nights . . . except for those when he thought about a curly-haired blond youth skiing across frozen lakes parsecs away.

Most nights . . . except for those when he dreamed about another curly-haired blond boy scuttling in terror from flaring torches through a tunnel, toward a light filled with king rats and landpoisons.

He shook his head as he entered the bedroom, n~~ot~~
glancing at the overlarge bed he had never replace~~d~~
when she had left.

Not that he always slept alone . . . but none had ev~~er~~
asked or hinted to spend another night. Not that he w~~as~~
ever other than gentle . . .

XXXIII

ALREADY THE VISITORS' stands were filled to overflowin~~g,~~
though the seats had been designed to hold more tha~~n~~
five times the Base complement. Civilians from Ste~~r-~~
den were continuing to pour through the main gat~~e.~~

The woman who would be the next Commandan~~t~~
stood behind the reviewing stand and surveyed the a~~d~~
hoc parade ground, the rows and rows of I.S.S. techn~~i-~~
cians wearing silver and black dress uniforms crease~~d~~
to perfection, the thousands of Standoran civilian~~s~~
wearing their best brikneas, the crisp white and gree~~n~~
dominating the stands.

She wanted to stamp her foot, to stand on th~~e~~
podium when her turn came, and to bellow that sh~~e~~
could do more than anything Commodore Gerswi~~n~~
could ever have done. She knew it was childish, that ~~it~~
might not even be true, but seeing the wistful look i~~n~~
the technicians' eyes, she still wanted to. Instead, sh~~e~~
looked down at the spotless gray-blue plastarmac an~~d~~
took a deep breath.

Despite the Base's reconstitution as one of the bus~~i-~~
est and most efficient refit yards in the Empire, the ligh~~t~~
breeze bore only the faintest tinge of ozone, and non~~e~~

of metal and oil. Underlying it all was the scent of trilia from the formal gardens planted around both the tech and officer quarters, and from the hedgerows that flanked the small squared sector for accompanied personnel.

A cough at her elbow brought her head up.

A young Captain, wearing the crossed ships of a pilot on her breast pocket, stood at the Commander's shoulder.

"Commander H'Lieu?"

"Yes, Captain?"

"I believe the ceremony is about to begin."

The senior Commander turned away from the crowds that flanked the reviewing stand, with a smile that could have been described as wry, straightened, and looked toward the steps of the reviewing stand itself.

She would sit on the left side of the podium, on the left of the crossed banners, for the review. Then the Commodore would say a few words before turning over his sword. She would take the podium to say a few words, then return his sword, and then change places with him to review the departure parade as the new Commandant.

All in all, a civilized and ritualized turnover of administrative authority. The only problem was that Headquarters had never told her that the man she was replacing had made himself into a living legend, both to the personnel he commanded and to the locals.

She had reviewed the Base procedures, seen the audit reports, and interviewed a few key people—quietly, of course. All gave the impression of a competent and dedicated Commanding Officer, fair, impartial, and knowledgeable. But the records and procedures still did not show how he had turned the Base around, nor did anyone seem to be able to tell her.

Yes, the man worked hard. Yes, he had improved operating procedures. Yes, he had instituted outreach programs with the locals. Yes, he insisted on absolute accuracy and perfection. Yes, he insisted on discipline and order.

She pursed her lips and dismissed her misgivings. Putting her hand on the railing of the temporary stairs she glanced over at the visitors' stands. She could no recall a local community ever showing up for such a mundane affair as a change of command, even for a C.O. who had spent an unprecedented three five-year tours as the Commodore had.

"Impressive, isn't it?" asked the Captain. "Even the locals practically worship the ground he walks on."

The senior Commander snapped her head back without commenting and stepped up to the landing.

The Commodore was already there to greet her. She remembered the piercing eyes from a meeting on New Augusta years earlier.

"Welcome, Commander H'Lieu. Good to see you again."

"A pleasure to be here, Commodore." From the landing she could survey the entire area, and she let her eyes do that. "You obviously command a great deal more than Standora Base."

He chuckled, a self-deprecating sound, and then met her eyes. Both their brilliance and intensity were too much, and she eyed the raised stage with the two empty chairs, the podium, and the backdrop with the crossed banners of the Empire and the Service.

"I pleaded with the exec for something simple, but as you can see, lost."

Face to face, she realized that she stood taller than he did, but that wasn't the way she felt.

"Commodore . . . Commander . . ." The Captain's voice moved them apart and toward their seats.

As the Commodore stood before the crowd, the rustlings stopped, as did the background conversation until there was a hush.

The sound of the ancient trumpet calls echoed back from the hangars at the bugler below. As the notes died away three squads of technicians snapped into motion

The tech drill team's silent performance was marred
y neither mistakes nor by excessive length.

Commander H'Lieu glanced at her timestrap and
ealized that the performance had taken well less than
n standard minutes.

As the drill team returned to position, the ranks of
rrayed techs began to move, marching by units before
ie Commodore, who still stood at attention, perfectly
raight and yet perfectly relaxed, while giving the
npression of total alertness.

The Commander stopped herself from shaking her
ead. The man looked less than forty stans, yet he'd
een at Standora for fifteen, and, if the rumors and
cords were correct, had more than a century in
ervice, which was possible, certainly, but totally un-
eard of.

The continued hush bothered her. In her own thirty
lus years of Service, never had she heard such sus-
ained quiet, almost as if it were a funeral or memorial
ather than a mere change of command.

Her eyes swept the parade ground, the crowd of
upport personnel, and the visitors. No frowns, no
iughs, no signs of fear, but no signs of celebration.

When the last detachment had stepped past the stand
nd back into position, then and only then did the
'ommodore move, in quick steps, to the podium.

He offered no salutations, no jokes.

"All things must end, and all things must begin.

"My time here must end, and the time of Command-
r H'Lieu must begin. Standora Base is respected,
ppreciated, and, I believe, a worthwhile place to be.
'hat it is all of these things is not because of a
ommandant, and not because it merely exists, but
ecause the whole is greater than the sum of the parts.
!ecause together we can do what none can do sepa-
ately.

"No man, no woman, no child . . . stands alone. Nor
ave we. Together we have accomplished much. In this,
must include those who were stationed here and who

have since departed, as well as those of you who hav
remained. Times and people have changed, b
Standora Base remains. Change is a necessity fo
excellence, and excellence has been your greate
achievement.

"With Commander H'Lieu, I expect you to buil
upon that excellence, for much as we have done, muc
remains to be done. We have forged strong working tie
within the Service, within the Empire, and wit
Stenden, its people, and have begun to work well wit
the Standoran government. But that work must co
tinue.

"Never forget that your success is built upon mor
than machines, on more than discipline. It is bui
upon the spirit. In the end, that spirit can move an
change planets. That spirit alone can achieve exce
lence, and understand its price and responsibilitie
And for that spirit, which you have demonstrated yea
in and year out, must all of you be commended.

"In my leaving, my departure, you lose a comman
dant, and you gain a new one. But your spirit you keep
May it always be so."

The Commodore bowed his head momentarily in th
silence that held, if possible, deeper than before.

"And now"—and he lifted his sword—"I offer m
command and sword to Commander H'Lieu." H
turned. "Commander H'Lieu?"

The Commander stepped forward to the podiun
marveling yet at the understated eloquence of th
Commodore and beginning to ask herself, for the fir
time seriously, how she could follow the example h
had set.

She stood opposite him, accepting the sword he ha
offered, then laying sword and scabbard on the hal
table on her side of the podium.

What could she say, knowing that her lengthy re
marks at least by comparison, would have been totall
inappropriate?

"Thank you." Her words came slowly. "Unlike you,
have not had the privilege of working with Commodor

Gerswin. The example he has set is one to which anyone could and should aspire.

"I am not Commodore Gerswin. We are different people; we have different backgrounds. However, I share his striving for excellence and his belief that such excellence can happen only when we work together.

"Beyond that, the Commodore has said what must be said, and I wish him well. I look forward to continuing his tradition and working with and for you all."

She stopped, deciding against any flowery conclusion, and bent to pick up the plain sword and black scabbard.

"Commodore, while I accept the responsibility you have passed to me, your sword is yours. May it always be so."

The Commodore stepped forward to take back the sword. Then they exchanged places, and both faced the command and the crowd.

Still . . . silence lingered across the upturned faces.

After a long moment, nine notes sounded from the trumpet, in three groups of three, and the reverse parade began as the two senior officers presided over the retreat.

This time as each squad passed the reviewing stand the Commodore received a salute from each. The squads did not reform on the parade area, but continued down the plastarmac to the nearest hangar, into which they disappeared.

When the parade area was at last empty of military personnel, except for the corner sentries, nine more notes sounded from the antique trumpet.

The Commodore broke the spell by twisting toward the new Commandant.

"Nice touch with your acceptance. They'll like it, and you'll come to believe it, if you give them the fairness, the discipline, and the hearing they deserve."

She inclined her head toward him stiffly.

"It is rather difficult to follow a living legend." She pointed toward the civilians who were now filing out

toward the main gate. Even from the reviewing sta[r]
she could see that several were wiping their eyes.

"Hasn't always been so. Won't be." He patted h[is]
shoulder. "You'll make it, probably a lot farther tha[n I]
did."

"Did?"

"Resigning. I have a few things left to do, and I ne[ed]
the time to do them." He paused. "Shall we g[o?]
Captain Ihira is waiting to show you to your office a[nd]
quarters."

"You're out?"

"Out and packed. With the ceremony, my resign[a-]
tion is fully effective."

"Just like that?"

He shrugged. "Traveled light for a long time. Still d[o.]
Seems to work that way whether I decide to or not."

"What . . . where . . . will you go?"

"Intend to travel. Check on some research."

"If I'm not too bold . . . Commodores are well pai[d,]
but not for extensive travel."

"Been careful. A small bequest. Position with [a]
group . . . and there's the *Caroljoy*."

She could not have missed the accent on the nam[e.]

"The *Caroljoy*? A ship?"

"Patchwork of sorts, but certified and speedy. Kee[p]
me more than busy."

"*Caroljoy* . . . unusual   name . . . understan[d]
your—" She broke off the sentence.

"No . . . wouldn't have been right to name it aft[er]
someone still living. She made it all possible, and [a]
great deal more that I never knew." His eyes seemed t[o]
mist over for a few seconds, and he stopped speakin[g.]

"Who was she?" asked Commander H'Lieu softl[y.]
"She must have been rather special."

"Special?" laughed the Commodore, and there wa[s]
an underbite to the self-mocking expression. "Lik[e]
saying Old Earth was special. Or that devilkids ar[e]
unusual. She was a—" He stopped again. "Getting ol[d,]
I guess, because I'm tempted to talk too much. Leave [it]
at that. She was special."

"I'm sorry," apologized the Commander. "I didn't mean to pry."

"You didn't. You asked, and I did not have to answer." He grinned. "But I'm just a relic on the way out, with time on my hands."

Commander H'Lieu could not help grinning back at him. "You're scarcely a relic, and I doubt seriously that you will ever have time on your hands."

"Perhaps not, but I won't have my hands full the way you will. Especially if High Command finds out how good your people really are. Then some senior Commodore, a *real* Commodore, not a preretirement Commodore like me, may decide to take over Standora Base."

"You think so?"

"Unless you make Commodore first." His tone was light, and the shadows that had crossed his features minutes before were gone, gone as if they had never been.

Captain Ihira was waiting at the base of the now nearly empty reviewing stand for them.

The Commodore returned the Captain's salute, crisply. He turned and was gone.

Commander H'Lieu swallowed twice before speaking.

"Lead on, Captain. Lead on."

XXXIV

G. Kyra J'gerald, Bio. D.
Department of Environmental Biologics
University of Suharta

Faith, New Hope Code FNH-Red-Sec 3 - RT
DL

Dear Dr. J'gerald:

The Foundation has reviewed your proposal for th
development through genetic substitution and accele
ated environmental stress of "fuel globes" suitable fo
use in vehicles as a nonpolluting fuel source.

Your proposal has been approved for a Class II gran
for a maximum of seven Imperial years, as you pr
posed. Class II grants are reviewed annually, and fund
are disbursed for the following year upon successf
completion of the annual review. If the final specimen
meet the criteria outlined in your prospectus, an
function as you have outlined, an additional sum wi
be paid, equivalent to the total amount of the seven
year grant, either in a single payment or annually fo
ten Imperial years.

The attached contract contains all details. If yo
agree to the proposal, please authenticate and retur
three of the copies. On receipt, the Foundation wi
disburse to the account you have specified the fir
year's funding.

Failure to make specific annual or semiannual re
ports will constitute breach of contract. Failure t
undertake the work, for reasons other than illness, wi
be taken under advisement and treated under bot
local and Imperial law.

We wish you the best.

Sincerely,

Lyr D'Meryon
Administrator

* * *

Narla Div Kneblock, Bot. D.
Drop D-100
Full City, Urbana Code FCU-Blue-Sec 2 - RT
BG

Dear Dr. Kneblock:

Thank you for your proposal to create structural and building materials through the accelerated genetic selection and cultivation of deciduous T-type flora (trees).

Unfortunately, this work has largely been perfected, and the Foundation is not in a position to expend funds for incremental improvements at this time. Since we may not have fully understood all the implications of your proposal, if you have amplifying material, of course, we would be more than pleased to review that in light of any updated submission you choose to resubmit.

Again . . . thank you for your proposal, and for your interest in improved biologics.

Sincerely,

Lyr D'Meryon
Administrator

*   *   *

Restra Ver Dien
Professor of Sanitary Engineering
University of San Diabla
Ghila, New Arizona Code GNA-Green-Sec 1 - RT
HY

Dear Professor Ver Dien:

Thank you for the update in your annual report on your progress in modifying water sylphweed to provide the dual function of water purification on a commercial scale and to precipitate toxic and nontoxic contaminants in a reusable mineral form.

In view of your success with water purification, the Foundation is pleased to extend your grant another two Imperial years to allow you the additional time necessary to develop the precipitation capabilities in selected sylphweed strains.

An addendum to your contract is attached. Please authenticate all copies and return three to the Foundation immediately. Upon receipt of the copies, the Foundation will disburse the first of the four additional payments provided for in the addendum.

Looking to your success,

Lyr D'Meryon
Administrator

XXXV

All planets have life. Somewhere . . . somehow . . . there is life. It may be in hibernation forever, created when there was heat, sleeping until moments before a final conflagration. It may be buried in sheltered ravines, or float in high clouds over burned-out lands, but there is life. With one exception.

That exception is Marduk.

Picture a T-type world, with an old red sun still close enough to maintain life, half-covered with oceans, and circled by three small moons.

The seas are crystal violet, and when the waves crash on the rocks, the droplets coating the stone sparkle with the shimmer of blood red diamonds in the sun.

The clouds are white, towering, with a hint of purple.

The sands are purpled silver, and bare, as bare as the dark brown-purple of the mud flats that stretch where there should be marshes.

Where there should be forests stretch only

kilometers of purpled clay. Where there should be
grasses roll on kilometers of purpled bare hills
that slowly ooze toward the depressions where
rivers should run and do not.

No spires grace continental divides, but aimless
heaps of weathered crimson and maroon stone,
some buttressed from the bedrock, some lying
loose.

The planet promised life, and there was none.
All the explorers found was death.

N'Doro—dying in his shuttle. Crenshaw
—screaming for death for days in the Service
wards at Bredick. The crew of the *Copernick*
—found dead to the last soul in orbit. The list is
long, longer than it should be because the planet
should, by all rights, have supported life.

The deaths bolstered the argument that there
had to be life, for what else besides unknown
viruses or alien organisms could kill so many so
terribly?

The answer, when it came, was disappointing.
Chemicals—just chemicals. Every virulent chemical known to intelligence existed in the oceans
and lands of Marduk. Every stable synthetic concocted by the late masters of Old Earth had been
concocted earlier by the departed masters of
Marduk. Concocted and left for the universe to
find.

If it is violently mutagenic, teratogenic, carci-
nogenic, oncogenic, or toxic, Marduk has it.

And for some, Marduk held a certain
promise . . .

> *ANNALS*
> Peitral H'Litre
> Bredick, 6178 N.E.C.

XXXVI

THE OER FOUNDATION administrator checked the item
ization from the Special Operations Account again.

"Unique power source (obsolete) for non-tech plane
—C/r 1.5 million. Special equipment transport (one
time charge)—C/r 4.5 million."

No explanation on the official accounts, just the
figures. The Commander, and she thought of him as the
Commander despite his preretirement promotion to
Commodore, had spent more than a third of his annual
operations budget on just two items. If they were
audited by the Imperial Revenue Service, she'd better
know what they represented.

On the off-chance that he had had an explanation
but didn't know how to code it, or wanted to leave that
to her, she checked the "notes" section, which was
sealed except to her personal key.

Wonder of wonders, she thought. There was an
explanation.

"The unique power source is an obsolete atmospheric pulse tap. Couldn't buy an equivalent source for less
than ten times this, but gadget is good only on a planet
with an atmosphere and without intelligent life with a
metal based technology. Somewhat limited, but fine for
my outspace operations. Even have a place to put it
Will reduce the power costs for the ship. Could be as
much as eighty percent less."

Lyr nodded. It sounded crazy, but if he was right,
and about equipment he had always been right, the cost
would be absorbed in less than a standard month. His

136

nergy bills ran nearly C/r 10 million annually, and that
vas what he drew from the Foundation. From his
rivate sources, who knew what he was paying?

"The one-time transport charge is what it cost for a
ne-way disposable jump hull to carry that and some
ther equipment to base. Didn't want to charter a
reighter, though it would have cost half as much, for
bvious reasons. Hope you can figure out a way to
xplain this."

She worried at her lower lip once more.

Some things he was so secretive about, as if the
impire really cared about the doings of a Foundation
romoting biologics research and use. The secrecy, she
vas sometimes convinced, might cause more problems
han the mission.

She frowned, but finally settled on the standard
lassification of equipment freight charges, with a
ew codes and supporting figures that should get her
hrough all but the most thorough of audits, if one
vere even requested.

In more than twenty years, she had been requested to
ppear before the Imperial Revenue Service twice.
Once had been for a grant to Sadukis University, which
ad been diverted to support the candidacy of the
Jniversity Chancellor for delegate—unknown to the
JER Foundation.

The second time had been because the receipts to
nd assets of the Forward Fund had exceeded, for a two
nonth period, the thirty percent maximum require-
nent. That had been her fault, because of a rather
pectacular increase in the value of some Torinian
onds that the banking community had written off as
vorthless.

Still worrying at her lower lip, which was always
happed despite the moisture shield cream she used
eligiously every night, she began to input the informa-
ion.

If the Commander, in his capacity as Trustee, were
ot so obviously committed to the Foundation and its
aims, she would have been more worried. At times, his

single-minded pursuit of improved biologics scared her, and now that he was pushing the implementation of the basic research and research into actual applications . . .

She shook her head. If she knew more, she would only worry more, and there was more than enough to worry about with the research grants and the accounting legalities.

XXXVII

"THE ASSIGNMENT IS a standard one—the father and the son. The baron, if one could call him that, and the heir. That means the timing must coincide."

"Explain."

"The father has his own yacht, and can pilot it himself. He is surmised to have a hidden base, probably in an uninhabited system. The son lives with the mother and her clan, separated from the father. But he remains the only heir."

"Then there is a preferred order."

"Exactly. Father, then son. The client did not specify the order, but preliminary investigations indicate that the father is the more formidable of the two, and would be even more so if alerted by—"

"The action against the son."

The woman nodded. "You understand."

"If the man travels so freely, how can one predict where he will be?"

"That takes patience. He does have a philanthropic connection in New Augusta and must travel there

ccasionally. That is the sole predictable factor in an
xtremely irregular and unpredictable schedule. He has
ever made less than a trip a year, often two or three.
Ve have taps on the torp center and on the clearance
ector in Imperial control. Those should give us ad-
ance notice, but you will have to take up residence in
Jew Augusta.

"From there, it should be routine. Routine, but not
asy."

"On New Augusta?"

The woman lifted her shoulders. "It cannot be
voided. The commission was large, and not to be
urned down."

"How much of a bonus?"

"Double your normal."

"I assume the rules for actions on New Augusta have
ot been changed by the Guild."

"They have not."

"Then energy and projectile weapons remain forbid-
len?"

"Correct."

The heavyset man glanced at the floor. "You are sure
his is the best way to accomplish this contract."

"Are you questioning the Secretariat?"

"No. But a man who could be called a baron and is
ot, who pilots his own space yacht, and all that
mplies, who is strong enough to have captivated, even
or a time, a Scandian woman, that sort of man will be
lert to such things as accidents, poisons. That
neans—"

"I know what that means. That is why you were
ssigned."

The heavyset man's hands moved toward the long
knife concealed in his trousers.

"He is said to have some familiarity with hand
weapons, including knives."

The man smiled. "Some familiarity with knives.
How interesting."

"The details are in the envelope."

The man picked it up, but did not break the sea knowing that exposure to air would destroy the mater al within minutes, as intended.

"Once you have begun, send the signal. The secon upon completion."

"Understood." He nodded and turned to go.

As he stepped through the portal from the sma office into the main corridor of the commerce clearin house, his face was composed into the look of boredor common to many small businessmen, a look perfectl within character, since eighty percent of the time h was in fact a small businessman specializing in th brokering of odd lots of obscure jellies. The twent percent of his time devoted to the Guild, howeve demanded one hundred percent loyalty and provide eighty percent of his not insubstantial income.

For all his bulk and blankness of expression, hi boots scarcely sounded as they touched the corrido tiles and as he moved toward the central exchange.

XXXVIII

GERSWIN SIPPED THE liftea slowly as his eyes travele from one side of the small dining area to the other While he did not fully appreciate the intricacies of al the varieties of teas, perhaps because to him all their tastes were strong, he found liftea the most pleasant and far more enjoyable after a meal than the alterna tives, particularly cafe.

After all the years since the *Torquina*, he still failed to appreciate cafe, and he knew he never would.

He shook his head wryly, thinking about it. Cafe had to have been invented by a failed chef, one who wanted all remembrance of food seared out of memory by its bitterness.

With the hour as late as it was, only the smallest dining area of the Aurelian Club was in use, but the staff was as helpful, as quick, and as alert as if the Duke of Burglan were in attendance.

Gerswin did not know what influence Caroljoy had employed—or had it been the Duke himself—to procure his membership in the Club. Realistically, he assumed that it had been their influence, although that had never been confirmed one way or another.

He had just received the simple card, stating that he had been proposed for membership, and that, after consideration, his name had been accepted.

The rules were even stranger than the acceptance.

No member could ever invite more than three guests at once, and there were no bills or charges. Restraint in use of the dining facilities was expected, but no such restraints were necessary for the use of the library or the moderate exercise facilities. Extravagant use of the facilities constituted grounds for revocation of membership.

Members were expected to propose one or two qualified individuals for membership at some time, and such proposals were to be accompanied by the entire membership sponsor fee. If the individual proposed was found unsuitable, the club retained the fee, which would be applied to the first suitable individual recommended by the member. The sponsor fee was 250,000 credits.

As he took another sip of the liftea, Gerswin wondered how many people were willing to spend that for a friend or worthy citizen. At some point he probably would, but currently he had no candidate he thought suitable—except Lyr, and he shied away from the idea of proposing her for membership in his sole club. He might anyway, but not for a while.

Two other tables were occupied, the one direct
across the open central parquet flooring from him an
one two tables to his left. At the opposing table sat
woman, alone, in a severe dark purple tunic.

While he did not know her, she was either wealthy (
powerful in her own right, since guests were not permi
ted without members, and spouses were considere
guests.

At the table to his right were three individuals, tw
men and a woman. Their conversation was politel
modulated, with neither whispers nor low jovialitie
suggesting that the subject was whatever commerci;
interest they shared.

After more than twenty years of membershi;
Gerswin knew less than two dozen other members b
sight, and he doubted that many knew him.

"More tea, ser?"

"Yes, thank you."

He had asked Lyr if she wanted to accompany hi;
after they had gone over the annual reports he wa
required to authenticate, but; despite the wistful loo
on her face, she had declined.

"Damon has been pressing me for months to go wit
him to the free fall ballet, and I agreed. Next time, d
give me more notice, Commander. Please."

Gerswin shook his head. For all his long range plan
for the Foundation and his own enterprises, his mar
agement of his own personal schedule and life had bee
less than exemplary.

Two sons, one dead long before he had even know
he had a son, and the other as lost to him as if h
scarcely existed.

His lips tightened as he pushed away the thoughts o
Corson, of the boy no longer a boy, who had inherited
as indicated in the cubes he received and reviewe
quietly, his mother's height and father's strength.

Was he right to have let Allison raise him alone?

"And what would you have done? Carted him al

ver the Galaxy? Settled on Scandia?"

He took another sip of tea.

Just because he had answers to all the questions did ot mean he could lay either questions or answers to est.

The woman in purple had entered shortly after he ad, but had sampled a salad of some type, two mugs of afe, and now stood to leave. Her face was familiar, and ae former Commodore suspected she was a govern- aent minister of some portfolio, just from her carriage.

The conversation to his right continued, with a trace aore intensity and a fractionally reduced volume, as if ae trio was getting to a critical point in negotiations.

Gerswin sat back, decided that he might as well eturn to the shuttle port for the trip to the orbital tation. New Augusta was one of the handful of systems rohibiting deep space ships or, for that matter, any on-Imperial shuttles from entering the planetary en- elope.

The *Caroljoy* was docked in a magnetolocked posi- ion off station three beta.

Gerswin frowned. At some point, he suspected, it vas going to be far too dangerous to travel to New augusta in person. The time was coming when he and yr would have to work out other arrangements. Either hat or he was going to have to develop a series of lternative personas with enough depth to pass all mperial screening.

When it became more obvious who he was and what ae was doing, if he continued as successfully as recent- y, he would doubtless develop both government and ommercial opponents. He hoped that point was years r decades away.

He almost laughed, but repressed it, knowing how nocking it would sound in the dignified confines of the ristocratic Aurelian Club.

Instead, he eased himself out of the comfortable hair and around the table, nodding to the waiter.

"Very good, Commodore. Hope we will see you mo
often."

Surprisingly to him, the term "Commodore" was n
used with the condescension he had heard in the voic
of even the staff of more than a few commercial baror

"Never can tell, but thank you."

He took a last look around the circular room of le
than ten tables, and at the group of three at the sing
occupied one remaining. Neither the woman nor t
two men looked up from their discussion.

"Would you like transportation, Commodore"
asked the submanager at the front desk.

"Yes. That would be fine."

He might as well be heading back to the shuttle por

While he waited for the electrocab, he studied t
main foyer, pacing quietly from one side to the othe

Unlike many clubs, the Aurelian Club had no pi
tures of individuals anywhere, nor any listing of of
cers, nor any posting of rules. Gerswin wrinkled h
forehead in concentration. Thinking about it, he cou
not recall any written captions anywhere within tl
Club, except for the signatures on some of the pain
ings, a few of which he recognized as originals f
which any number of collectors would have bid sma
fortunes.

"Transportation, Commodore."

"Thank you."

Gerswin went through the double portals quickly.

The electrocab was a shocking silver, radiating a lig
of its own bright enough to make Gerswin shake h
head.

The outside doorman saw the gesture and smiled.

"Not exactly tasteful, ser, but at this time of evenin;
they're mostly out for the nighters. This is conservativ
for that crowd."

Gerswin raised his eyebrows, but said nothing as h
stepped into the back seat.

"Destination?" The inquiry was mechanical.

Gerswin tapped the code for Shuttle Port Beta into the small screen.

"Thank you. Please authorize the sum of ten Imperial credits."

Gerswin used the Foundation card for the fare, since the purpose of the entire trip had been strictly for OERF reasons.

The electrocab hummed from the Club portal and after less than a hundred meters dropped into the high speed tunnel that slashed diagonally under the city and toward the shuttle port.

He closed his eyes as he leaned back in the seat, but his thoughts did not come to a similar rest.

Should he continue his detailed tracing of the grants issued by the Foundation? Was commercialization the only way to produce the products he needed on a wide enough scale? If so, how soon should he start trying to implement such projects?

What about Corson? Was there a way to channel some of his considerable income from his own investments over the years to his son? Was it wise, given the trust fund already created? Would too much money without a purpose leave the boy, the young man really, adrift? Or make him a target of the unscrupulous?

What about Lyr? Was he being fair to her in piling more and more upon her? Were additional salary and appreciation sufficient?

"Destination approaching." The mechanical voice of the electrocab was almost a relief. Why was it that New Augusta triggered so many questions? Was it the memory of Caroljoy? Or was it that New Augusta symbolized what he must oppose and had not?

He sat up, eyes flicking toward the window to take in the increasing illumination as the vehicle slowed and completed the climb to the beta concourse.

As he stepped out into the even flow of bodies heading to or from the various shuttle gates, Gerswin wished he could have worn full-fade blacks. The sheer numbers handled by the Imperial shuttle ports always made him uneasy. Numbers could conceal so much.

His hands flicked to his belt, where the knives and sling leathers were still in place. He began to scan the crowd while his steps carried him toward the less crowded section of the port that served private ships and travelers.

Most of the crowd were commercial or in-system travelers, which was the case at most ports throughout the Empire. Few indeed could afford the high cost of either a private ship or interstellar passage.

The majority of travelers were human. He caught sight of a single Ursan, flanked by an Imperial Marine honor guard, and two Edelians, looking more like walking sunflowers than the sentient beings they were.

While he should have faxed ahead, he had not, assuming that the shuttle to station three beta would lift on a recurring and regular schedule. The departure portal was closed, with the message board flashing.

"Next shuttle to beta three in fifty-five standard minutes. Please insert your access card for your shuttle seat. Ten seats remain."

Gerswin took his permanent squarish pass from his pouch and inserted it.

The message board changed to fifty-three minutes and nine seats remaining.

Satisfied that he could do no more for the moment, he turned to head back to the main terminal lounge for a place to sit down. His steps clicked on the hard tiles, the sound echoing through the predawn lull of the nearly deserted section of the port terminal.

A scraping sound, barely a whisper, rustled ahead of him, as if someone had brushed the archway to the public fresher three meters ahead of him on his right. The clarity of the faint sound bothered Gerswin, and he edged his steps toward the far left-hand side of the five-meter-wide corridor.

As he drew abreast of the fresher entrance, he saw the shadow of a man, presumably about to leave, but the shadow did not move as the retired Commodore continued onward.

Gerswin glanced over his shoulder as he entered the main lounge area, with its circles of padded seats mostly vacant. Behind him walked a heavyset businessman carrying a black sample case, his expression blank, as if his thoughts were systems away.

Gerswin sat down in the middle of a three-seat row, facing the direction from which the businessman had come. In turn, the heavy, brown-haired man slumped into a seat perhaps three meters away and to Gerswin's right. He did not look at Gerswin, but opened the case in his lap and pulled a folder from it.

A smile quirked the devilkid's lips.

For whatever reason, the man was looking for Gerswin. His build ruled him out as a Corpus Corps type, which meant he was either an intelligence operative for some out-system government, for an out-of-the-way Imperial bureaucracy, or a private operative contracted to find Gerswin.

Gerswin dismissed government intelligences immediately. Out-system governments would not send operatives into New Augusta, particularly after obscure and retired Commodores, and all the Imperials had to do was to monitor his reservation on the shuttle and wait for him at the lock to his ship.

Since the man had required a clear look at Gerswin and a comparison of facial profiles, that further supported the fact that he was representing a nongovernment source. And since the operative was on New Augusta, whoever hired him had money.

Gerswin pursed his lips.

The Guild?

That meant trouble he had not anticipated this early.

The Commodore sat relaxed, waiting, letting the minutes pass as he watched the watcher without obviously doing so.

Finally Gerswin stood and stretched, then ambled toward the still open dining area. Coincidentally, his

path would take him by the seat occupied by h
hunter.

The man unhurriedly closed his case and stoo
adjusting his tunic, and fiddling with the case itself. H
turned as Gerswin neared, and his face screwed up as
in recognition.

"Commander Gerswin?"

Gerswin looked puzzled in turn, but said nothin
although he stopped where he stood.

"Don't you remember me? Lazonbly, from th
Valeretta?"

"Can't say I do. But what could I do for you?"

Gerswin wondered how far he could push before th
operative panicked.

Lazonbly stepped closer and shook his head, as if h
could not really believe it was Gerswin. "You haven'
changed at all."

Gerswin smiled. "Who's paying the Guild for this?"

Lazonbly blinked, but only once. "I don't believe
understand."

"Lazonbly died in Feralta ten years ago. The Guil
has accepted a contract on me. I'd like to know wh
your client is, not that you'd know."

"I'm afraid I don't understand, Commander."

"Very good. Very good. You realize I know you can'
use long range energy weapons here. Standard knife o
laser cutter?"

Lazonbly moved his arm, showing a glint of blue
"Laser cutter, Commodore. Shall we go?"

"At least you've dropped the pretenses." Gerswir
stepped back so quickly that Lazonbly could not reac
without appearing obvious. "As you wish. Toward
which dark corridor?"

"The public fresher serving beta three. You first."

"How about side by side?"

"You first." Lazonbly's voice remained jovial.

"Rather not." Gerswin eased back slightly as he
disagreed.

"Commodore, don't force the issue."

"And what do I have to lose? You don't want your kill recorded on the public monitors. You've obviously taken care of the monitors on that corridor. So why should I go with you?"

"Because you think you might have some chance of getting away." Lazonbly shifted his weight in an attempt to move closer to Gerswin.

"And you're willing to gamble on that?" asked Gerswin.

"No gamble."

"No, it's not." Gerswin frowned. "Lazonbly, where did you get your orders?"

"Haven't the faintest idea what you're talking about, Commodore. Not the faintest. But you talk well, especially for a man of your advanced age. Rejuvs may give you back muscle and appearance, but they don't improve old reflexes. So . . . shall we go?"

"I see you are rather hard to reason with." Gerswin smiled. He half turned and walked away from Lazonbly in even steps, toward the corridor the operative had indicated.

The heavyset man followed easily, trying to close the gap between the two without making it too obvious.

Gerswin let the other approach, glancing over his shoulder and listening for a change in breathing patterns or steps. He would rather have faced the Guild assassin down in the lounge except for one thing—the Imperial inquest, which would doubtless have delayed his departure long enough for another Guild assassin to strike.

As he walked, Gerswin slipped the leather thongs and rounded stones from his belt.

The corridor narrowed as the two men neared the three beta concourse, then made a gentle left turn.

Gerswin decided Lazonbly would move as soon as they were screened from the other monitors. He readied the thongs of the sling.

Click. Click.

Gerswin threw himself to the left, rolled, and came up with the thongs whirling.

Thunk!

Thud!

Lazonbly's body pitched forward onto the tiles, his face as impassive in death as it had been in life. The laser cutter lay centimeters from his hand.

Gerswin walked away after pocketing the round stone, not looking back. There was nothing to connect him to Lazonbly, and nothing on Lazonbly to connect him either to Gerswin or to the Guild. And there was no record anywhere of one Commodore Gerswin's proficiency with the sling weapons of Old Earth, let alone anyone on New Augusta who would deduce with certainty the exact cause of death of the Guild agent. Gerswin had no doubt "Lazonbly" was at least noted as a potential Guild agent in Imperial files.

He turned the last corner. Several other shuttle passengers now waited near the portal, obviously ready to board the same shuttle on which Gerswin was booked.

Gerswin and the *Caroljoy* were now headed for Scandia, which represented a sudden change in destination. He wondered if he would be in time, or if it were a false alarm. If so, so much the better. If not, there was not much else he could do. No one else could get there sooner, not even a message torp.

Would he lose another son he scarcely had known? He shook his head at the thought.

With less than ten minutes before the shuttle lifted, Gerswin doubted that even the Imperial authorities would be able to react in time to block off the entire shuttle port to resolve the strange incident with Lazonbly. Particularly when the tools which were doubtless in Lazonbly's case were found to have been those that disabled the corridor monitors. Either that or the entire case had melted itself down, which would certainly intrigue Imperial intelligence.

Fifteen minutes later he sat on the shuttle as it hummed toward the accelerator. His thoughts were already in orbit, already plotting the jump points for Scandia.

XXXIX

IT IS AN article of faith for the Believers that their Captain destroyed the first and only Empire without legions, without loss. A number of scholars, Elender among them, have made the case for such a sweeping generalization.

Certainly, what records were salvaged from the rape of New Augusta do contain limited references to a Foundation promoting biologics, and the fragmentary information which outsiders have been allowed to examine in detail would seem to show a definite series of links between the Foundation's research grants and the systems where the biologic innovations which brought down the Empire were first introduced and commercialized.

That biologics hastened the fall of the Empire is not the question, though some have questioned the importance of that hastening, nor is the fact that the biologic revolution foreshadowed the development of the Commonality in question. Neither, for that matter, will this commentary question whether the Captain actually developed or merely spread such biologic techniques.

This, of course, lays aside the central question of whether there was a Captain in the sense that those on

Old Earth or the Believers have consistently claimed
That is a question for another time, since *someone*, o
some series of individuals, did in fact promote biolog
ics, and that promotion was the cause of a great an
widespread unrest among the majority of systems the
associated with the Empire.

What must be questioned most strongly, however, i
the naivete that unhesitatingly assumes that such tre
mendous social and political changes were accom
plished "without legions, without loss." It i
conceivable that the initial introduction of such tech
niques may have been accomplished with minima
unrest, but the subsequent history has been, if on
wills, illustrated in the blood of the casualties.

One can only wonder, at times, assuming there was
Captain, at either the callousness or the obsession
which could have motivated him, not to mention th
personal burden . . .

> From *COMMENTS*
> Frien G'Driet Herlieu
> New Avalon
> 5536 N.E.C.

XL

Since Corson had not left Scandia yet, if the Guild
were after him, that was where the Guild operative
would be, reflected the pilot with the impassive face.

He had debated not using the orbit station and
grounding directly on Scandia, but could find no ad
vantage to doing so. He had not yet been forced to

reveal that capability of the revamped scout, and did not want to any sooner than he had to, especially with the Guild involved.

So now he sat in a rear seat in a Scandian shuttle as it dropped toward the port below.

He wished he had been able to reach Allison, but the orbit comm center indicated that her receiver had been blanked. Corson had no separate outlet. He had been forced to leave a message that he was arriving, and hoped that he was either in time or unnecessary. He was afraid he was simply too late.

His fingers drummed on the armrest, and he looked at the pale metal overhead. Scandians did not believe in passenger ports or screens in their shuttles, and he always worried about the piloting of others.

He sensed the nose lifting into a slight flare as the shuttle came out of the port turn, and he imagined the view as the pilot centered in on the landing grids, stark black against the winter white of the Scandian hills.

"Please recheck your harnesses. Three minutes until touchdown."

The shuttle pilot's voice was repeated by the overhead speaker with the metallic overtones of equipment typically Scandian—durable, long-lasting, and not designed to do a single bit more than necessary for the complete job at hand. No stereo or full fidelity capabilities for mere voice repeating speakers.

Clump.

Gerswin's grip on the armrests relaxed as the shuttle touched the grids, and one hand reached for the harness release as the other rechecked the belt knives and sling leathers. He wore no stunner for the simple reason that all energy projection weapons were forbidden on Scandia. While he had no doubts that the Guild had circumvented that prohibition, he saw no sense in wearing one only to have the Scandians secure it for the length of his stay. If he used it, then more explanations would be required.

Gerswin stood at the lock before the others had even

begun to unstrap, forcing himself to remain relaxed as he waited for the ground crew to open the double portals.

A senior Commander, I.S.S., his brown hair shot with gray, joined him, while the couple who had been sitting in front of him waited in their seats.

"You spent time in the Service?"

Gerswin nodded with a faint smile, then added, "Some."

"I thought so. You had that look on your face before touchdown."

"Look?"

"You had to be a pilot or nav type. You people all seem uncomfortable when someone else is doing the piloting."

Gerswin permitted himself a half-sheepish grin.

"Guess you can't hide it."

Clank.

"You being stationed here?" Gerswin asked, though his attention was more on the unsealing locks.

"No. I'm retiring. My wife's from here, and I decided to join her."

"Scandians do stick together," observed Gerswin before turning back to face the pleasant-faced young functionary who was standing in the lock.

"That they do," agreed the retiring Commander.

"Your entry forms, ser?"

Gerswin proferred the folder.

The woman checked the name, and her face took a distinctly sympathetic look, not even a professionally concerned one, but an expression showing real emotion.

"Commodore   Gerswin . . . uhhh . . . your . . . they're waiting for you . . . ."

"Gerswin?" asked the Commander behind him. "The Commodore Gerswin?"

The Scandian official's look darted from Gerswin to the older-looking and uniformed officer.

"Is there a problem, Commander?"

"No. Not at all. I just didn't realize . . . to have been
n the same shuttle . . ."

"I'm afraid I don't understand, Commander . . ."

"Snyther . . . Commander Snyther."

"Commodore Gerswin is not here on pleasure, un-
ortunately, and unless there's a problem, I would like
o clear him immediately."

"No, miss. Not at all. Please clear him. Please."

The woman shook her head, returning her attention
o Gerswin's documents and scanning them quickly.
he ran his pass from the orbit station through the
and scanner, and then nodded.

"You're clear, Commodore Gerswin. The Ingmarrs
re waiting right outside the debarking gate."

Gerswin felt the emptiness inside him grow. The
igns were clear enough. Too clear. The "Ingmarrs" had
o be Allison and her brother Mark.

The Guild had gotten to Scandia before New Au-
usta.

"Thank you," he said quietly, aware his face had
ecome more impassive and grim, but unwilling to
nake the effort to change it.

His steps echoed through the narrow tubeway as he
narched toward the small concourse. As he stepped
rom the tubeway, he glanced around the space in
vhich he stood. Ahead was the portal into the central
oncourse area, where doubtless Allison and Mark
vaited. The floor tiles were the same light ceramic as
hey had been on his only other visit, and the walls
vere the same yellowed cream, decorated with wood-
ramed scenes of Scandia.

"Reacting, that's all you're doing," he muttered as he
topped and stared at the pictures, stopping before
roceeding through the next portal.

"If Corson . . ." He let the words trail off, and a grim
mile creased his lips.

The woman functionary wouldn't have been a Guild
gent, because escape routes would have been closed
ff. That was no longer true once he was inside the

main concourse. And the Guild didn't forbid energ
weapons on Scandia, even if the Scandians did.

His hands checked his belt again.

He took a deep breath, sighed, and walked throug
the portal.

On the other side he scanned the entire visib
concourse, before focusing on Allison and Mark, wh
stepped forward from where they had been talking le:
than ten meters away, at the foot of one of the tw
meter-square structural columns that supported th
soaring ceiling of the terminal.

Mark Ingmarr had put on weight. While he had n
been slight or slender, he was now more than merel
solid, though short of outright obesity, and the clear
shaven look had been replaced with a square cut, fu
beard. His blue eyes were bloodshot.

So were Allison's, but her face was thin, nearly 1
haggardness, and her face was pale beneath the ligh
tan, the incipient wrinkles, and the lines of strain an
grief.

"How . . . how . . . did you know?" began Alliso
even before he was close enough for comfortable cor
versation, as if the question had been waiting for hi
appearance and could restrain itself no longer.

Gerswin's eyes flickered to Mark Ingmarr's face. Th
look behind the apparent concern was enough for hin

"I . . . just . . . knew . . . ," Gerswin answered, le
ting the words space themselves as he moved mor
toward Mark.

Gerswin looked past them, to see who or wha
remarked his arrival, and took another step, at a
angle, to Allison's puzzlement, to place himself directl
before Mark Ingmarr. He glanced over his left shoulde
as he did.

The movement was slight, imperceptible to anyon
else, but clear enough to a devilkid on the hunt.

Gerswin threw himself forward, brushing by Marl
rolling left before meeting the tiles, and turning as h
came into a crouch next to the wide structural colum

Wssstttt!

"Unnnnhhhhh."

The Commodore ignored the falling figure of Mark ngmarr and picked out the man in the quiet business unic who dropped his faxtab as if in surprise with the est of the open-mouthed bystanders. As the others egan to scatter, he moved with them.

In less than three steps Gerswin was crossing the erminal at full speed toward the Guild assassin.

The man glanced back, as if to protest, yanking his ase around so that the long edge pointed toward Gerswin.

Thunk! Thunk!

Both knives buried themselves in the assassin's chest irtually simultaneously, and his case spilled to the loor, where it rested momentarily, before smoke began o drool from the corners, as it began to consume itself.

Gerswin retrieved his belt knives, wiped them on the lead man's tunic, and replaced them in his belt.

He walked back to the center of the concourse where Allison, dry-eyed because she could cry no more, troked her brother's forehead.

Screeee!

Gerswin looked away from Allison to see the emer-gency medical cart whining down the center of the open section of the terminal toward them. He did not hake his head, but had Allison not been looking at aim, he might have.

"Why . . . ? Why?"

"Because he and you were close to me," lied Gerswin.

"That many enemies, Greg? That many?" Her voice broke.

Gerswin nodded. He saw no reason to tell her the whole truth now. Except for the Guild, his enemies lay n the future. Now that Mark was out of the picture, hey would continue to chase him, to destroy him merely from professional pride.

He stared down at the clinically dead man that the medical team had connected to three separate life support systems.

The body called Mark Ingmarr might live, but th
warped personality that had paid for Gerswin's an
Corson's deaths would not survive the treatment, on
way or another.

Gerswin sighed slowly. Once again, it had been h
fault. If he had not tried to provide for Corson, if l
had not treated Mark so cavalierly . . .

He shook his head.

Allison's eyes followed the medical team as the
moved the tubed and connected figure into the mobil
treatment center, and as the whole apparatus began t
move toward the far end of the terminal.

A uniformed figure motioned to them.

Gerswin ignored the officer and remained standin
beside Allison, not that he could say anything.

Allison ignored the officer as well, turning t
Gerswin, looking down on him once more.

"This means that Corson's—accident—it wasn
really an accident?"

Gerswin nodded.

"But why?"

Gerswin glanced down at the hexagonal floor tiles
knowing he could not tell her the exact truth, bu
knowing she would detect an outright lie.

Finally he lifted his eyes, aware that additional law
enforcement officers had surrounded the area of th
concourse where the Guild assassin had died an
where his case had melted itself down into metal an
plastic. Had the assassin panicked and fired hurriedly
Or had it been planned? Gerswin would never b
certain whether the man had fired to protect Mar
from Gerswin, or to silence Mark because he though
Gerswin's appearance meant that the Guild had bee
crossed, or because Gerswin was to be killed at al
costs.

In the long run, the reason was lost, and irrelevant.

Now, a pair of enforcement types stood behind him
and another pair waited beside Allison.

"Because death seems to strike those I love, Allison.

did not avoid Scandia because you asked me, you know."

He waited.

"I thought so. Now I know."

The silence stretched out.

"Wasn't there anything you could do?"

"I did my best. If I had tried to guard you two, that would have been like posting a sign, and it would have put you in a cage. Did you want that? Ever?"

This time Allison looked at the six-sided floor tiles.

"No. I guess it was better this way. Especially for Corson. Happy . . . never knew what happened . . ."

Despite his own resolve to be impassive, Gerswin could feel the wetness in his own eyes. He said nothing, although he could feel Allison's eyes on him, and kept his gaze fixed on the far end of the concourse, on the portal through which the emergency medical team had taken one dead man, and then another.

"But you care . . . you loved him . . . you loved me . . . and you never insisted. I don't understand. Why didn't you?"

Gerswin took a deep breath, refusing to wipe his cheeks, but his voice was like cold lead as he gave her his answer.

"Because you were right. Because Corson deserved his own life, not mine. Because you deserved your own life in the sunshine of Scandia. Because I have . . . miles . . . miles to go."

Allison touched the back of his hand, then withdrew her fingers. She looked away from him.

The silence stretched like the distance between the stars that had separated them and still did.

"Commodore?" asked a softer, apologetic voice. "Could we have a moment?"

Gerswin looked up to the tall officer who stood next to him with a sad expression.

"A moment?" he answered. "Yes. Time is what I am rich in."

At the sound of his voice, Allison took a step away

from him and toward the officer who waited for her.

Gerswin doubted he would ever see her again, but he followed the enforcement officer.

He had left Allison what he could, little as it was.

He shivered and swallowed, and the taste was bitter. But he took another deep breath, and another step. And another.

XLI

"THE GERSWIN AFFAIR . . . not exactly a shining example of our prowess, was it?"

"We did not have all the facts."

"The late client assured you that the Commodore was formidable."

"A client recommendation only."

"A *Scandian* client recommendation. Can you recall when a Scandian was prone to admit personal deficiencies or to exaggerate?"

"There are always exceptions."

"Was this an exception?"

The silence gave the answer.

"Now, with the client gone, our professional reputation remains. We took a contract, and we did not fulfil it. What do you suggest, regional chief?"

"We have two choices—either a crash search, which would be prohibitive and pointless, or making Gerswin a designated target of opportunity with a triple bonus for the successful agent. I would recommend the latter."

"I concur, but reluctantly. Given the Commodore's

ndependent and erratic travel schedules, it is the only
ealistic approach."

"What if he attempts to attack us?"

"You think that is a serious possibility? One man
gainst the entire Guild?"

"A moment ago you were cautioning me against
inderestimating the man. He has turned the tables on
wo armed agents."

"I do not doubt his considerable capabilities, as well
is his resources, but in the end even the Commodore
vill slow down as he ages. The Guild will not, and
Gerswin is not the type to hibernate, not for long.
Besides, no one has ever escaped the designation as a
arget of opportunity. Ever."

"That is true enough." The words expressed doubt
ather than affirmation. "Is that all?"

"That is all."

XLII

Cling.

THE SCREEN flickered twice, and the priority code
appeared in the upper right-hand corner.

Lyr bit her lip, relegated the information on the
screen to memory, and accepted the call from the
Commodore she thought of as a Commander, and
probably always would.

"Why a local beam?" she asked as his face appeared
on the screen. "You usually prefer guaranteed privacy."

"Prefer safety as well," responded the golden-haired
and hawk-eyed man.

"You care to explain?"

"My name has become too well-known to some fc me to travel as freely and anonymously as I once did.

She frowned at the unexpected verbosity, then rea ized that on a public link he would be somewhat le specific than normal. She studied the background which she did not recognize, but which looked techn cal, almost like the bridge of an Imperial ship.

"Where are you?"

"In orbit station. That was so I could hook into th local Imperial comm network. Once this is done, I'll b leaving."

"The lack of mobility could be troubling in th future, and my so far limited experience indicates i might pose problems for others as well."

"How would it affect the Foundation?"

She was surprised to find him grinning at her throug the screen. "Always business, I see." He frowned a quickly as he had grinned. "Limited degree. Would lik some recommendations from you. Research. If the fall outside normal business, please bill m account. . . ."

Lyr nodded.

"Remember the grant we reviewed about a standar year ago . . . one involving modified bodlerian algae Looking for information specialists in that system people who could accumulate and codify backgroun information on most Imperial systems, as well as th ability to provide perfectly legal incognitos for busines travelers."

"Legal aliases?"

"Correct. As I understand Imperial law, one may us a name not his own if no illegal intent is involved. N illegal intent would be involved. For example, if a jewe merchant has to use a courier on a regular basis unscrupulous interests could scan the passenger list for that name . . . but if accepted aliases were avail able, a merchant or dealer could use his own courie with greater security.

"If a commercial baron's agent wanted to check out a
＝w enterprise, he could do so without alerting the
'stem he was out to check. Such an enterprise might
＝ profitable. Combine that with the information back-
'ound of the type that commercial types need and
▪ve to develop themselves . . . anyway. My local
▪unsel suggests it is legal, but with your contacts in
at system . . ."

New Avalon was the system, if Lyr remembered
▪rrectly, and with the university there, it was certainly
good location for such an information processing
▪ncern.

"Doesn't anyone provide services like this?"

"Not to all comers on a cash or commercial basis."

Lyr smiled faintly. The pattern to the Commodore's
▪erations was becoming clearer.

She bit at her lower lip. Whether or not his ventures
▪plied directly to the Foundation, there was no ques-
▪n that somehow the Foundation always seemed to
▪nefit. With each of his activities, unsolicited contri-
▪tions seemed to appear. Despite his prohibition on
▪y form of solicitation, outside funds continually
▪peared to swell the capital and the income from
▪vestments of that capital.

Already she was receiving more than routine infor-
▪ation requests from the Imperial government on the
▪undation's finances and tax reports, the sort of
▪tention that was reserved, in her experience, for the
▪ore important of the charitable and academic foun-
▪tions.

She caught herself and cut off her reverie.

"What do you want me to do with the information?"

"Send it by torp to the information drop I use most
▪ten."

"That would be—"

"NO!"

She shook her head ruefully. "I'm sorry. I forgot we
▪uld be on an open wave. How soon do you want it?
▪sterday?"

The Commodore nodded.

"I'll get to work on it, and, Commander, I thin|
you'll be billed for research services."

"That's fine. Understand."

The screen blanked.

Lyr left her own screen blank, making no move t|
retrieve the material she had been studying before h|
had faxed. She had seen the man in action. For him t|
worry about his personal safety—even to mentio|
it—meant that he was more than just casually worrie|
Much more.

If he had enemies that powerful, what did it mean fo|
the Foundation?

She began to pull what her banks had on securit|
systems. After she finished with getting th|
Commander's—the Commodore's, she corrected her|
self mentally, knowing she would continue to sli|
—project under way, she would undertake a few im|
provements for the Foundation headquarters. Just i|
case.

And she needed to reinforce some of her ties wit|
Alord and his friends at the Imperial Humanitie|
Foundation, as well as those with Dimitra at th|
I.A.F.

The Commander hadn't given her any instruction|
but he hadn't forbidden it, either, and it looked lik|
they both might need the allies, information, an|
protection in the years ahead.

Her fingers moved across the console board, and he|
forehead cleared as she began to plan.

XLIII

THE MAN SMILED and swung his case up for inspection. His teeth were white and even, and stood out against the darkness of his skin, which was sun-darkened olive.

"Destination, ser?"

"Markhigh."

"Your pass?"

The traveler proffered the folder, and the port official nodded, his clearance nothing more than an affirmation of the more detailed clearance already given by the security section of the orbit station.

The olive-skinned man stepped through the portal and walked toward the monorail station platform, toward the spot where he would wait for the train that would carry him back to his small art dealership.

As he waited on the platform a man with shoulder length silver hair with a matching handlebar mustache edged up to him.

The art dealer studied the other, comparing height, coloration, and build against a mental file he carried, finally discarding all of the comparisons and relaxing slightly.

The older man had the relaxed but alert bearing of a former officer or security agent, but not the harried look of a target or the indefinable tension of a hunter. Nonetheless, the art dealer's elbow activated the slide sheath, just in case his spot assessment had been incorrect.

"Ser Giriello, I believe."

"I do not believe we have met."

"We have not. I recognized you because I ha
visited your low gallery in Markhigh. Your collection
Raiz' is rather remarkable."

"Thank you."

The art dealer scanned the platform. No one else w
anywhere near them, not that it made that mu
difference with directional pickups and focused lase
although the coating of his cloaks and tunics we
designed to give him the fractions of seconds necessa
to escape that sort of attack.

"Particularly remarkable for someone whose re
business is elsewhere."

Giriello did not answer, but readied himself an
stepped backward, as if affronted and puzzled.

"Ser . . . ?"

The ploy failed because the silver-haired man mov
with him, and Giriello found himself held in a gra
that was steellike in intensity.

"Giriello, this time—this time—nothing will ha
pen. You are to deliver a message. The message
simple. Merhlin will destroy the Guild. That's all."

There was a sharpness at the back of his neck, an
the art dealer could feel his knees buckling as the ha
pavement came up to meet him, could hear the strang
yelling for medical help. He wanted to laugh at th
hypocrisy of it all, except that the darkness wash
over him.

XLIV

LYR PULLED AT her chin as she slipped through the portals to the Foundation office.

She knew the Commander—the Commodore, she corrected herself yet another time—would be waiting. His voice had been ice-cold.

Automatically she closed the portal behind her and touched the lock stud as she surveyed the reception area and found it lit, but vacant.

The faint sound that was a cross between a whine and a hum told her that the analyzers in the tech space were operating, and in a linked fashion.

"Come on back, Lyr."

She sighed and stepped into the tech room.

His privacy cloak lay draped over one of the console chairs. He stood and pushed back the swivel where he had been working.

"I didn't expect to see you so soon again," she said.

"Didn't expect to be back so quickly. Have a problem. Not strictly Foundation, but it does impact us. Need to trust someone, and you're elected."

She opened her mouth, and he held up a hand. "I know. You have to account for everything. Perfectly legal for you to provide analytical services, provided you charge for them. Charge me the going rate, or MacGregor Corson. Charges aren't the problem."

"What is? Why did you insist on my being down here in the middle of the night?"

"Been a few other nights when you were," he observed laconically. "Running on a tight schedule. Ship

time doesn't always agree with Imperial mean time.
He grinned, and the lack of warmth in the hawk-yello
eyes sent shivers down her spine and chills through h
body. She was not certain she wanted to know anythin
more.

"What do you want analyzed?"

"Lists and destinations."

"Lists and destinations? For that you got me up—
She broke off in midsentence as for the first time sh
saw a fire in his eyes that represented anger, or a view (
hell.

"What do you want from the analysis?" she tempo
rized.

"Patterns." He sighed. "Let me explain. A group (
individuals is engaged in a highly profitable and e>
ceedingly illegal business. They use aliases, false dest
nations. Almost no possibility of determining whic
alias is a commercial traveler on honest busines:
which a philanderer, and which the deadly anonymit
of this group."

"That's not merely impossible. It would require
miracle—"

"I've contracted for a travel research contract for
shipping firm, and will be obtaining the monthly lis
ings of selected passenger destinations. Not the name:
just the arrival and departure ports. I will be adding t
that major commercial meetings, conferences, fair
reliable estimates of military personnel and deper
dents traveling on commercial ships, and other data.

"But what do you want?" she asked tiredly.

"I told you. Patterns. Probably take years, but ther
should be continuing patterns. Clear ones. You develo
the possibilities and send them to me. I'll test them an
let you know."

"I still don't understand what you want."

His eyes flared. Then he looked away, almost as if h
was afraid of hurting her, it seemed.

"Let me give you a hypothetical example. If on th
second week of the second and tenth months of th

Imperial year, there are always two passengers booked from New Augusta through New Glascow to Ydris, it means something—from whether that represents a regularly scheduled conference, a recurrent meeting, a regular fund transfer. It means *something*."

His voice softened. "The organization I am trying to locate has roughly nine hundred members on twenty planets, but ten planets are considered the key. New Augusta is the only major system not included, but remains a widely used transfer point. Therefore, anyone booked from New Augusta who belongs to this group must have come from somewhere else.

"Now, that doesn't mean I want you to exclude all others. If you can determine that the Brotherhood of Universal Peace has set patterns, let me know, and I can verify and modify. Eventually, by eliminating the obvious groups, by using the tourism stats, we should be able to eliminate everyone but the target."

Lyr shook her head. "That's *at least* a ten-to-fifteen-year project."

"Could be less. May be able to get you more and better information. Your console has the specifics, along with the beginning data base, as well as the entity to bill for the services, and the travel service for whom you will prepare the monthly report. In turn, that service will send its payment to MacGregor Corson, care of OER Foundation, and you will bill me for the balance of time and costs owed."

"What . . . that I think I finally understand, Commander. Why . . . that is another question."

"One you're probably better off not knowing." He circled around behind the swivel and picked up his privacy cloak. As he donned it, with the full-fade uniform, he transformed into a shadow, despite the clear lighting in the tech section.

"Good night."

Lyr did not shake her head. Instead she moved to the console he had vacated earlier.

"You know what he wants, don't you?" she said

quietly to no one. "You'd think that even he would
know better than to take on the Guild. Unless they
already have taken him on."

She shivered, but her hands remained steady on the
console controls.

XLV

"Whuff . . . whuff . . . whuff . . ."

The man's breath came in jerky gasps, one dragged
out after the next, as he struggled to put one foot in
front of the other. His head wobbled from side to side
in the darkness, although he did not look over his
aching shoulders.

He could hear easily enough the pad, pad, pad of his
pursuer's even footsteps. He could hear, but not believe.

None of it was believable.

"Whuff . . . whuff . . . whufff . . ."

His feet and lungs labored as he staggered along the
empty riding trail. He looked toward the heavier un-
dergrowth beside the trail, but decided against that
tactic. The searing pain that shot from his left arm
every time he moved too suddenly reinforced that
decision.

"Whuff . . . whuff . . . whuff . . ."

Whoever . . . whatever . . . chased him not only
could see in the darkness of Haldane, but could move
silently when it wanted. Whatever it was, it toyed with
him.

His more rational side told him to stop, that attack ad proven fruitless, and that flight was even less uitful, but he kept putting one leg in front of the ther.

"Whuff . . . whuff . . . whuff . . ."

How much longer he could move, let alone breathe, e did not know, only that each leg felt like lead, that ashes of hot light pricked behind his eyes, and that his outh hung limply open.

Whhrrr!

Crack!

The sound of the unknown weapon jolted his mo-entarily still legs into a shamble onward down the light incline before him.

His pursuer was invisible, silent except for the some-ime padding of feet, silent except for the occasional missile like the one that had shattered his left arm.

"Whuff . . . whuff . . . whuffff . . ."

Each breath was harder to draw, but he kept putting ne foot in front of the other. In the back of his mind, he thought flared—you're being hunted, like a fox, a arbou, like a dog.

But his unseen hunter refused to let him turn, driving im with the shadowy presence, with the silent *whrrr* of ain.

Right after he had seen the dark figure, he had harged the unknown, had actually touched the alien, if hat was what it was, for the steel muscles of the hadow figure had paralyzed his remaining good arm nd tossed him aside like a doll.

"Run . . . assassin . . ." Those had been the words issed at him.

He had not run, not him. Not then. Instead he had urned and attacked with all the skill taught by the Juild. And had been tossed aside again. Like trying to atch a shadow at night. And it had been barely night hen. Now dawn was approaching.

Each of those early rushes toward the alien blackness

had found him sprawled into the dirt, into the grass
the park.

"Whuff . . . whuff . . . whuffff . . ."

When assault had failed, he had stood his groun
Until the terrible projectiles had whirred past his hea
the second shattering his left arm.

"Run . . . assassin . . ." And the alien had hissed h
terrible message again.

He had stood—until the shadow rose from nowhe
next to him and had twisted his pain-wracked arm.

"Run . . . assassin . . ."

Whhrrr!

He had run—not wisely, but well, for who had ev
outrun him? Who had ever outrun the Hound of tl
Guild?

"Whuff . . . whuff . . . whufff . . ."

His legs were shaking. The flares behind his eyes le
him nearly blind to the path ahead. Staggering, l
managed to catch his balance, lurching leftward, the
right, until he came to the gentle slope upward, a slop
that became more steep with each meter.

"Whuff . . . whuff . . . whuffff . . . whuffff . . ."

How could you fight something that struck in dar]
ness, stronger than any man, that treated you with suc
contempt, that ran you down more easily than you ha
ever run any quarry to ground, and with seemingly le
effort?

He dragged himself another step forward.

"Whuff . . . whuff . . ."

Whhrrr!

His legs balked at the uphill effort. He stood ther
gasping, swaying like a tree about to crash into obli
ion.

Whhrrr!

Crack!

He did not feel the stone that killed him, nor see th
dawn that spilled from the eastern sky of Haldane
handful of minutes after his body had slumped into a
untidy heap on the Viceroy's private riding trail.

XLVI

THE HOODED MAN at the head of the table cleared his throat.

"And now, for the unsubstantiated information . . ."

"It's gossip time," whispered a uniformed Admiral in the corner to his nearest colleague.

The whisper was not low enough. The hooded man, the figure known as Eye, turned and looked. While Eye's expression was hidden, the Admiral wilted as if he had received a withering glare.

"Gossip, perhaps, but it has its uses. First, the Ursans are working on their own version of a jumpshift. We have a team looking into that.

"Second, an unknown group has moved against the Guild. While our sources have not been able to verify that, we have verified that there have been a number of deaths associated with individuals suspected of Guild activity. We have been able to investigate three deaths of this type and found reason to believe that the victims were also associated with the Guild."

"A question?"

"Yes."

"Why no faxnews stories?"

"The deaths have been spread over ten systems and roughly a standard year, but there is a pattern."

"Do we know who or what is involved?"

"We have a name, believed to be a code name. That name is Merhlin. Who or what it represents is unknown at this time."

173

"Do we want to get involved?"

"I doubt that is to our interests," answered t[
hooded man.

His response brought a series of low chuckles fro[
the Imperial officers around the table. One wom[
shook her head slowly.

"You disagree, Admiral Storz?"

"I would only point out that if an unknown has t[
resources to take on the Guild, not only without bei[
discovered, but without being stopped, what wou[
prevent such an organization from then applying itse[
to our agents?"

"Good point. Discovery, however, is not the same
involvement. I should have made myself clear. We a[
working to discover this group or agency. We do n[
intend to aid either party."

Admiral Storz nodded.

"Any other questions on this one?" Eye surveyed t[
shielded figures around the table in the shielded roo[
"If not, the next item is the unreleased Forseni[
communique which would require the registration [
all Imperial agents with the local Forseni[
government. . . ."

XLVII

THE MAN IN the full-fade blacks sighed.

War was hell, it had been said from the beginning [
man's recorded history, and he did not look forward [
the next phase of his war against the Guild. But th[
Guild was becoming more and more a tool of th[
unscrupulously wealthy, and the Empire did nothing[

Until he had the final product from the information he Infonet and Lyr's integrators were piecing together month after standard month, he had to continue to keep the Guild off-balance.

So far his efforts had been isolated enough to give second thoughts to individual agents, but the faxers and the other media had tumbled to the identity of the lead in less than a handful of the cases.

He shrugged.

The Infonet he had set up on New Avalon had proven a commercial success, but the mass of information he needed was still not complete. His personal wealth was accumulating faster than either ecological knowledge or knowledge about the Guild.

The Guild continued to monitor all the communications on the open bands in and out of New Augusta, and while he wondered to what degree they could pick up on his short torp messages, he found his own concerns were making even normal Foundation business harder to carry out. While Lyr could still make credits hand over fist, and while existing grants could be extended, not as much in the way of new and innovative research was getting started as he would have liked, not when he had to watch his own step every meter of the way.

This time, this time his action should give the Guild some pause.

He checked his equipment and slipped into the lift, headed for his first target in the Tower. The regional Guild councils were not quite as careful about their security precautions as the Overcouncil.

While none had arrived at precisely the same time, and while their reservations did not share common lengths, for two nights the top eight members of the Arm Council would be in the same Tower, at least theoretically.

Saverin appeared to be the one listed as Kerlieu, on the eighth level—the same Saverin once known for his proficiency in needlepoint laser work.

Gerswin stepped from the lift and walked down the

brightly lit but deserted hallway, his shiny bright priv
cy cloak with the crimson slash covering the shadows
the full-fade blacks beneath.

Saverin's portal was locked from inside, but t
Tower's locks were standard. Gerswin pulsed the ci
cuits twice, then opened the portal. He stood well ba
as the doorway irised open.

Whsssttt!

A needle flare of energy slashed across the spa
where he had been operating the portal controls a
instant before and completed a quick arc search pa
tern.

Gerswin waited until the flare died before edging
black film decoy into the laser-wielder's line of sight

Whhsstt!

Another needle of blue light burned through th
black film and into the corridor.

As the laser flare winked out, Gerswin flashed insic
the closing portal.

Whsst!

This time the blue needle came from Gerswin's lase
straight through the head of the white-haired man wit
the laser dropping from his limp hand.

Whsst!

Gerswin sent another beam through the chest of th
still falling body.

Thud . . . clank.

The laser rang dully as it impacted the har
synthwood of the suite floor.

Gerswin had rushed past the body, but his haste ha
been unnecessary. Saverin, as always, had been alone

Gerswin used his elbow to tap the exit stud and
slipped out through the portal without having touche
anything in the suite.

The weakness with lasers, reflected the hunter, wa
that they took a few fractions of a second betweer
bursts, and those fractions were all he needed. Bu
then, surprise should have been in his favor. Saverir
had reacted well, considering he should not have

.nown he was being tracked and that he had not been
.n active assassin in several years.

Gerswin swirled the privacy cloak fully back around
.imself, checking to insure that the mask was still
.ompletely in place. Although he had disabled the
.emote telltale circuitry of the Tower before he had
.tarted, he would inevitably run into guests and other
.ecording devices. Even if his tampering with the
Tower circuits had been discovered right after he had
.ompleted it, it would take a good technician more
.han a standard hour to undo what he had done, and
Gerswin planned to be out of the Tower long before
.hat.

Nonetheless, the mask remained a necessity.

Gerswin frowned as he moved down the corridor.
While he had not had trouble with Saverin, the former
.ssassin had been quick, either lucky or forewarned.

The next target, on the eleventh level, was not
.enowned for her reflexes. Margritta DiRenzo plotted
.ut assassinations through carefully arranged acci-
.ents.

A pudgy man, belly boiling out over a too-wide
.olden waist sash, stepped on the lift as Gerswin
.tepped off. A lecherous smile crossed the heavy man's
.ips as he took in the privacy mask and cloak, and he
.nclined his head in mock salute as he passed Gerswin.

The thinner man nodded in return as he turned to
.he left, away from the target suite, toward the service
.ccess. The corridor was clear as he used his equipment
.o enter the small closet and stepped inside. Once
.here, he cut aside the access panels with a cutter, then
.sed two quick movements to sever the power leads.
The corridor outside the closet turned pitch black
.efore the emergency lamps returned a dim glow.

Gerswin retraced his steps past the lift and toward
.he proper portal. He tapped twice as he cut his way
.nto the service box and used the manual controls to
.pen the portal.

"Maintenance!" he called.

"What is the difficulty?"

The woman spoke, although accompanied by a sle
der man. Both held stunners pointed toward the port
A small portable light in the room outlined their form
in a faint glow, leaving their faces dim smudges.

Gerswin remained in the shadow of the portal.

"Lost all power on this level—"

Thrumm! Thrumm!

Both man and woman dropped to the bolts fron
Gerswin's stunner without triggering their own.

Gerswin closed the portal behind him and turne
over the unconscious pair one by one. The man fit th
description of a lover of Margritta's, a sometime Guil
agent.

He looked around the room for something to com
plete the job in the proper format. The scowl beneat
the mask turned to a grim smile as he saw the ancien
projectile gun on the bedside table.

Three shots later, the job was complete.

It would be reported, at least initially, as a murder
suicide, as an accident/tragedy.

The Guild would know better, but they were sup
posed to.

Gerswin closed the portal behind him as he left. N
one along the corridor had even peered out. He sus
pected that those occupants who were in their suite
intended to stay behind locked portals, at least unt
power was restored.

He took the stairs to the twelfth level, where th
lights were on, unaffected by his actions below since th
Tower was designed with power controls set on tw
level increments. Still swirling his cloak about him, h
sauntered down to the technical access closet, where h
casually cut his way in, then through three plate covers
and burned through the main conduits for both level
twelve and fourteen. There was no level thirteen.

Although it was theoretically possible to disable al
power shunts for the Tower at one point, that one poin
was a junction center that would have required a

ull-sized laser and would have alerted not only the ower security forces, but system security types as well. 3y disabling only the levels he needed out of the way, Gerswin avoided such alerts, and delayed even the ntry of Tower security forces.

Gerswin did not intend to disable more than the two enters he had already put out.

The first suite he wanted was halfway down the allway on the left, but Gerswin did not have to worry bout opening the portal. It was wedged open.

He frowned. That meant quick action—extremely quick action—and that both Council members were probably in the Sendaris suite at the far end of the orridor.

He took the chance of darting into the empty suite nd picked up a tumbler, half-filled with something, lot that he intended to drink any of it. Then he ambled long the corridor, letting the glass slosh in his hand.

A light flashed from the corner suite of the Tower where he was headed, sweeping the corridor ahead of Gerswin.

So they had a guard.

The direct approach was still the best.

"Hallooo, there. You got power?"

"Who's there?"

"Just old Modred. Looking for Welson's suite, you know, on the corner." Gerswin lisped the words, and et his gait appear unsteady.

In his left hand were sling leathers, looking like a set of ribbons dangling from unsteady fingers. The tumbler sloshed in his right.

The light centered in on him, and he strained for the sound of a stunner whispering from a holster as he put his left arm up across his face, as if to block the glare.

"Easy . . . just looking for Welson."

"Hold it right there."

The voice was that of a bored professional, expecting no trouble from an obviously drunken partier, but ready to drop him at the slightest excuse.

Gerswin wobbled to a halt, several steps taken to ward the light, as if in an attempt to catch his balance and stop.

"You're not Welson," he accused the guard behind the light.

"Wrong suite, buddy. Better check downlift."

Gerswin could see that there were two of them, both in dark brown uniforms, the second holding not a stunner but a powergun filled with explosive pellets although it was not aimed directly at him.

"Sorry, sorry . . ." Gerswin made his voice whine with apologies as he turned and took one step, then another, back toward the direction from which he had come.

The light wavered as the guard flicked it to one side then the other. While the aim was to see if Gerswin had been trying to misdirect them, to see if he had an accomplices, it was the wrong aim.

Gerswin dropped and turned.

Whhhrrr! Whhhrrr!
Crack! Crack!
Brrrrp-Crump!
Crack!

Gerswin came out of his dive with knives ready ignoring the shrapnel cuts from the single burst of the powergun.

They were not necessary, and he resheathed them as he moved past the bodies.

The next step was anticlimactic.

Gerswin triggered the door overrides and tossed two circular objects through the portals, reversing the polarity and closing them before they had barely admitted the two grenades.

One was gas, the other antipersonnel.

Crump!
Crump!

The twin explosions reverberated satisfactorily though muffled by the closed portal.

Gerswin jammed the filters into his nostrils, but forced himself to wait two full minutes before opening e door, surveying the corridor the entire time.

Then he used the regular controls to open the portal, anding well aside.

From the entrance he could see three bodies, but he aited, listening, as the gas filtered past him into the orridor.

Finally he moved into the suite, but his speed was nnecessary. There were four figures sprawled across e furniture, and all were dead—quite dead. Three he cognized as Council members, including Sendaris imself.

He left more quickly than he had entered, spurred, as e headed down the corridor to the emergency exit airs, by the sound of a portal being forced open by omeone who had obviously not read the emergency structions. He slipped through the manual doors, esigned for power and other failures, and began the escent.

He checked the time. Less than forty standard mintes since he had begun, but too long. Much longer an he had hoped. The time, combined with the bvious awareness of the Council that someone was fter them, made up his mind, and he continued ownward and away from the last target on the four- enth level.

He who runs away lives to fight another day, reflected erswin as he reversed his cloak to the flip side, with e forest green shimmering outward. At the landing etween the third and fourth levels, he buried his face nder his arm. When he looked up and continued ownward, he wore a green face shield matching the loak.

Above him, he could hear footsteps, voices, then a cream as other Tower guests began to abandon their uites for the emergency exits. The lifts would still be perating, but those on the affected levels were not pparently stopping to try them.

A Tower employee, apparently alerted by a monitor- ng system, stepped through the first floor entrance as erswin came down the last section of stairs.

"I beg your parden, ser, but these are for emergen█
use—"

"No power on my level! Istvenn take it! Last time█
stay here! And you say that's not an emergency? Ju█
listen to all the others!"

Gerswin brushed past the man.

"No power?" stammered the young man.

"That's right. Listen. Just listen. Think I'd take *stai*█
for joy?"

Gerswin finished stepping around the man an█
around the security officer behind him and into th█
main lobby, strutting across it with every gram █
outrage he could counterfeit. He reached the electroca█
concourse without incident, and stepped inside th█
second one.

"Inverr House!" he snapped, loud enough for th█
Tower employee holding the door to step back, and f█
the surprised Tower patrons whom he had stepped █
front of to back off.

His effrontery paid off. The shrieking and clanging █
alarms began only as the electrocougar dropped aw█
from the Tower concourse.

He changed the destination, but not the color of th█
privacy mask.

XLVIII

IN THE END, a decision either begins or concludes wit█
two people. Either two men, two women, or a man an█
a woman.

In this case, the meeting happened to be between █

ιan and a woman, but it could have been between two
ιen. The head of the Guild could have been either a
ιan or a woman, since throughout its history the
ιnior assassins had picked both men and women as
ιeir chief. The modus operandi had varied little under
ιther sex.

The man wore black, as he always did on such
ιccasions, including a black face shield. The woman
ιegarded his choice of apparel as an affront of sorts,
ιarticularly in view of his disregard for her profession.

Was the meeting in person?

Not for this pair.

Each sat before a screen, neither's true countenance
ιnown to the other.

The man was who he said he was, although he called
ιimself Merhlin, and his true name remained hidden.

The woman was of the occupation she professed, but
ιot exactly the person she said she was. That deception
ιhe man suspected, but found immaterial, an attitude
ιeither she nor the woman whose place she took would
ιave appreciated had either known.

"You are the one calling himself Merhlin? The one
ιith some slight ongoing interest in the Guild?"

"That is one way to put it, honored lady."

"Assassin will do as well as any false honorific,
ιerhlin."

"Very well, Assassin."

"You wished the conversation, Merhlin, and paid for
ιhe privilege."

"I did. Thought it only fair to give you advance
ιotice of my intentions."

"That you have already done. This was scarcely
ιecessary, though we appreciate the additional
ιncome."

"Should have been more clear. Wished to deliver a
ιpecific message."

"Then do so."

"In a few moments, I will. First, a few observations."
ιe held up a gloved hand to forestall any objections.

"Observations more than relevant to the message."

"Then state them." The lady's tone had gone fro
bored to sharp.

"First, the Guild prides itself on professionalism
Second, the Guild will undertake any assassination f
a fee, whether or not the victim is a total innocent
not. Third, the Guild has gone from being a tool th
occasionally protected the oppressed to a tool f
protecting the Imperial establishment in addition
and outside the law of the Empire."

He paused.

"The Guild does not concern itself with popul
opinion."

"It should. Because it does not, and has not, and w
not acknowledge either restraint or morality, it
doomed. Should those who survive, and there may be
few, continue the tradition of serving the highest bi
der and slaughtering men, women, and children who
sole fault is that their existence stands in the way of th
powerful and the unscrupulous, the Guild will n
survive."

"Are you serious?"

"Yes, Assassin. That you should already know. I a
Merlhin. Call me Merlhin of Avalon, and tremble whe
you call upon my name. You have been warned, ar
your days are numbered."

The screen blanked.

The Chief Assassin who was not the head assassi
stared at the screen. Then she tapped a code.

"Did you get that?"

"Outspace transmission. Either has his own ship c
went to trouble of routing indirect through th
geosynch station. No way to trace him. No way even
figure out who he is."

"We know that. He's the one who's been picking o
top assassins, using their own weapons."

"Is he?"

"Why else would he go to the trouble, and th
expense? This has been going on for more than fi
years, if I recall right."

"What about his threat? Why did he even bother?"

"That's the troubling part. That implies an even
bigger effort against the Guild."

"What else can he do? We're recruiting as fast as he
strikes."

"Are our recruits learning as fast as those they
replace?"

"Now . . . you sound like *her*." The man paused.
"But what really can he do?"

"I don't know. The annual conference is coming up.
That strikes me as more than coincidence."

"So . . . ? Maybe he wanted the word spread."

"That means he knows it's taking place."

"What could he do? Destroy an entire quarter?"

XLIX

RECOMPUTE WITHOUT SUBSET TWO."

The small control room was silent except for the
breathing of the man at the control couch and the
muted hiss of the ship's ventilation system.

"Probability approaches unity. The accuracy of the
data cannot be verified."

"Stet. Recompute *with* subset two and without subset three."

The man gazed at the exterior screens while he
waited, studying the view of Iredesium in the distance.
The moon, less than a thousand kays in diameter,
housed some of the largest resort and pleasure centers
outside of the home Imperial systems, each a domed
oasis on airless stone, built at enormous costs for the
wealthy and those who played at being wealthy. Of

either, there seemed to be no shortage.

The view he watched showed the moon clearly, ha
white, half dark.

"Probability in excess of point nine. Exact figur
cannot be determined within standard parameters
error without the information contained in subs
three."

The pilot shook his head. No matter how the info
mation was juggled, the answer came out the same.

How good was the information?

Some of it had come from Infonet. Despite the fa
that he had founded Infonet and trusted the manag
ment, Infonet Class A information had a proven acc
racy pattern of greater than ninety-five percent. Give
the volume of the corroborating information, and t
independent analyses from the Foundation, which co
firmed the conclusion, the chance for the final recom
mendation to be wrong was infinitesimal.

That the AI supported the conclusion with whole se
missing was another supporting, though certainly n
conclusive, test.

Still . . . he didn't like it. When everything agree
there was a chance that everything was wrong.

Or was it that he didn't want to pay the price to finis
off what he had started? Or that he hated to solv
problems impersonally?

He looked up at the screen, touching the distanc
control and letting the view enlarge as Iredesiu
seemed to swim closer in the large screen before hin

He checked the time again, for perhaps the tent
time in the last standard hour.

Less than a standard hour before the meeting belo
came to order, and that meant less than two sta
before it was over, one way or another. Time to act, c
to fail to act.

"The same old question, isn't it?"

"Inquiry imprecise. Please reformulate."

He ignored the AI's precise statement as he pondere
the implications stretching out before him. Certainl

his opponents had shown no mercy, nor would they even understand his mercy should he grant it. No . . . business as usual, and Istvenn protect the innocent. He sighed, and stood.

"Passive detection. Report if any targets within screen range."

"Understood. Will report standard targets."

Though there was no carpet on the deck of the small ship, his steps did not click or echo as he made his way to the locker that held the space armor.

He said nothing as he donned it, nor did the AI break the silence. Finally he stepped through the small inner lock, leaving it open as he began his checks.

"Comm check."

"Circuits clear."

After the inner lock sealed, he touched the plate that would open the exterior lock, and waited. Hand over hand, he exited, clipping his safety line to the recessed anchor beside the lock plate. He moved with a minimum of excess motion to the exterior lock to the aft hold.

From a distance, any distance, an observer using optical methods would have seen nothing, for the full-fade black of the hull and matching finish of his armor created an effect of invisibility.

Once the lock opened, he maneuvered the long shape through the narrow aperture. Next came the checks of the drive ring unit he had added below the missile's normal drives.

Slowly, he edged the massive but slender shape around the hull until it pointed at the midpoint of the terminator line of the moon that the ship, the man, and the missile all orbited.

The man took a long breath, then another.

In time, he eased back the access panel and twisted the blue dial to the number "II." Next, he broke the red seal and flipped the switch beneath to the "armed" position. He closed the panel and took another deep breath.

Moving hand over hand down the narrow shape, he came to the ring drive units, where he opened a second access panel and closed one switch.

"Done," he said quietly as he edged back to the ship's lock.

When the exterior lock had closed behind him, he stated, "Course feed to Hunter."

"Beginning course feed. Course feed complete."

The inner lock opened, and he stepped back into the ship, waiting until it closed before checking the ship's pressure.

Normal.

He began taking off the armor and stowing it back in the locker.

"Commence Nihil."

"Commencing Nihil. Ignition in one minute."

He completed stowing the armor and walked back to the control station, his booted feet still silent as he crossed the hard floor.

"Ignition. Preliminary extrapolation shows Hunter on optimum course."

"Interrogative defense screens." While he knew the answer, he wanted to hear it again.

"No screens in place except normal class three precautions."

The pilot nodded. Class three screens were the standard screens against nonenergized objects, designed to divert small meteors and other space junk.

The drive units on Hunter would punch through anything but class one screens, and those were only used by ships, Imperial ships. No dome or station could afford the energy or equipment expenditure to cover that wide an area with class one screens.

"Course lines on screen two," he ordered.

"Course lines on screen two," the AI responded.

He swallowed the taste of bile in his mouth. If he could have built a wider organization, trusted more people . . .

"Then you wouldn't have to do things like this?" he

sked the empty air. "Be serious. You don't fight
anatics. You destroy them totally or you leave them
lone. You didn't have a choice. Corson—what choice
did he have?"

"Invalid inquiry. Please reformulate."

"Hades! Re—" He had almost told the AI to reformulate itself, but stopped as he realized he had no idea
what such a drastic command might do to the artificial
ntelligence.

"Istvenn!"

He bit his lower lip, not quite hard enough to draw
blood, as he watched the red line of the Hunter arcing
down toward Iredesium. He forced himself to continue
watching.

"Dampers on screens. Shield all sensitives," he
added quietly.

"Shields and dampers in place."

The command had been early, many minutes before
it would be necessary to protect the ship's equipment.

He could feel the nausea climbing back into his
throat, and he swallowed again, still watching the
screens. The red dashed line continued to drop toward
the moon.

A pale blue line flashed into place above the screen
representation of Iredesium.

"Class three screens triggered."

The pilot watched as the dashed red line penetrated
the meteor shield without deflection and continued to
dive for the target dome.

"Estimate one minute until detonation."

Ignoring the AI's statement, delivered in its impersonal feminine tone, ignoring his own urge to turn away
from the information displayed on the screens, he
forced himself to keep watching, glancing from the
visual on the main screen to the smaller representational screen, then back to the visual.

"Detonation."

For several seconds both screens seemed unchanged.
Then, on the representational screen, the dashed red

line intersected the moon's surface. On the visual
screen, Iredesium hung there, still showing half white
half black.

A pinflare of white flashed from the middle of the
moon, spreading . . . and the visual screen blanked.

"Dampers on. Impact on target verified. Detonation
height at two hundred meters, plus or minus fifty."

The man did not answer.

He had left the control couch for the fresher, where
the slim contents of his stomach were emptying themselves into a small basin.

"Probability of damage within design envelope approaches unity."

"Plan beta," choked the man from the former crew
section. "Plan beta."

He wiped his mouth and slowly straightened after
splashing his face with a handful of cool water.

"For better or worse . . ."

His legs felt rubbery, but he walked back to the
waiting control couch, still as silently as ever.

"Plot all in-system contacts on screen three."

He swallowed the bitter aftertaste and concentrated
on the full screen array.

L

THE SPECIALLY GUARDED and prepared convention hall
was nearly full.

"We have a problem."

"We have more than a problem."

"You mean the Merhlin thing?"

"Count's close to a hundred now."

"A hundred? You sure about that?"

"Two arm councils nearly wiped out . . ."

"Nobody knows who they are . . . not even Imperial Intelligence . . . say Eye himself is worried."

The hooded figure at the end of the table let the talk continue.

"Said he threatened the Council itself . . ."

The other hooded figure, sitting taller and to the right of the Chief Assassin, leaned forward.

"Is the threat that serious?" His voice was low.

"You know the answer," came back the cool tones of the woman. "It is the same answer as always. If the group called Merhlin is totally fanatic and highly skilled and disciplined, the threat has to be taken seriously. Fanatics can destroy anything. But the chances of the kind of knowledge and discipline necessary mixed with fanaticism? Not to mention the human element. We've always had warnings of any large scale movements against us, and how could anyone take on the entire Guild without an enormous commitment of personnel and equipment?

"Besides, would anyone today stoop to destroy an entire resort of five thousand people, most of them not involved with us? Even if they would, it would take nuclear weapons or a fleet-sized laser, and those are weapons the Empire has destroyed systems to keep to self."

"Order!" The command was simultaneous with the rap of the ancient handgun on the metal plate.

The conversations around the meeting hall died into a series of murmurs, and the murmurs into silence.

"The first order of business is the five year report."

The Guild delegates shifted restlessly in their seats, waiting for the routine business to pass and to hear what the Council had to say about the threat to the Guild itself.

"Delegate Beta . . ."

Like most participants, Delegate Beta did not wear a

privacy cloak, opting instead for a simple synthfle
false face and wig, combined with a voice distorter.

"The summaries are presented on the screen for yc
review. As you may recall, the screen is rear-projecti
and nonimaging, which means that your portal
equipment will not retain the images . . ." Delega
Beta launched into his summary of five years of Gu
activities and financial accomplishments.

At the conclusion he received a mild round
applause, mainly for the brevity with which the sui
mary had been presented.

"Second order of business . . . Delegate Gamma."

Delegate Gamma stood and moved toward the p
dium.

She never got there.

Sun-white light seared through the roofing of t
meeting hall, as well as through the rest of t
Iredesium Resort Complex Red, reducing all but t
heaviest metals to their basic atomic forms, turning t
square kays into a shimmering and cooling lake
molten stone and metal standing on an airless plain

LI

"WE'VE IDENTIFIED THE cause."

Eye inclined his hooded head, but said nothing.

"Class two hellburner. Surface burst."

"Where did they get it?"

"Who got it?"

"Got what?"

At the commotion, Eye raised one hand. The noise
ed down.

"Please summarize from the beginning, Commo-
ore."

"We're not entirely certain, but it appears as though
e Iredesium Red Pleasure Dome was the site of the
uild's Five Year Conference. We usually find out
veral months afterward, although they try to keep it
shed.

"The so-called Merhlin group had apparently threat-
ed the Guild with virtual extinction. We don't know
hat the Guild position was, but they didn't take the
reat seriously enough. Class two hellburner went up
n minutes after the conference started, the part that
veryone was required to attend. Casualties over six
ousand. Probably only five hundred official Guild
elegates; another two, three hundred might have been
wer grade assassins. . . ."

The Commodore waited for a moment, but there
ere no questions or interruptions.

"Definitely an I.S.S. weapon. Media faxers are al-
ady saying that it was. Delivery method unknown,
ut the tracked velocity was compatible with warship
unch. It could have come from a private yacht, but
e Iredesium complex has been choked with them this
ason—more than a hundred registered, and that's
alf of all the Imperial private ships.

"There were also three Service ships present in
stem—*Bismarck, Saladin,* and *Martel.* All their
eaponry is fully accounted for."

The Admiral of the Fleet, to Eye's right, coughed.

"Are any of the media suggesting that it was an
nperial effort to destroy the Guild?"

"No. The *Free Fax* is implying that the destruction of
uild leadership with I.S.S. weapons implies either
cit Service agreement or extremely loose controls on
uclear equipment by the Service. In either case, a
ll-fledged investigation is necessary."

"Just what we need." The sotto voce comment can from the corner of the room farthest from Eye, b neither the Intelligence Chief nor the Admiral of th Fleet acknowledged the truth of the remark or th speaker.

"Any favorable commentary?"

"The *RadRight* had an ed-blip. They said the wished the Imperial Government had acted with suc dispatch years ago."

"Wonderful."

"What is the real probability that this was accon plished by the Merhlin group?"

"One, we don't know if Merhlin represents a grou or an individual with vast resources. Two, whi Merhlin threatened to destroy the Guild and is repute to have carried out close to a hundred assassinations Guild agents in past years, we have no proof, eve indirect or hearsay, that the attack was in fact carri out by Merhlin. Three, if it was, I doubt that we w hear of Merhlin again. Nor will we if it was not. Fou now that the Guild has been reduced to several hu: dred scattered agents, the Imperial Government w face extraordinary criticism if we fail to finish the jo Five, this will result in greater economic stabili within the Empire and probably short-term expansic of Imperial spheres of influence."

"In short," finished Eye, "we have no choice but turn this terrible tragedy into an Imperial benefit. Th solves one problem and leaves two. While we ma never hear the name Merhlin again, whoever Merhlin has the capability to find out information we don't. H or she also has no compunctions about acting whe necessary. And no conscience. What do we intend to c about it?

"Second, we need someone to blame, and it can't t Merhlin. How could we admit that some unknow power can do what we can't, that they knew what w couldn't guess? So whom do we blame to get on wit the job?"

"No one, ser. We will blame the anarchists and claim
at the Guild and the anarchists collided. We have
ken steps to round up the necessary accessories, and
e will. And, in the future, enemies of the government
an be tagged as anarchists, like those who murdered
x thousand people at Iredesium."

"It might work," reflected Eye. "It might at that. But
on't collect too many dissidents. We can't have this
en as a pretext to tighter social control."

"What about Merhlin?" asked the Admiral of the
leet.

"We keep looking, quietly. I don't think we'll find
im or her. Merhlin got what he or she or they wanted.
ut people forget. Especially, they forget faceless trage-
ies. Who got seared at Iredesium? Assassins, cold-
looded killers, and playboys and joy-girls. Who's
oing to feel sorry for them for long? How can you
reate outrage about them?"

LII

Click. Click. Click.

The single set of footsteps echoed in the sub-zero
hill of what would have been dawn, had the sun not
een lost behind clouds that filtered fine snow over the
ills and frozen lakes.

Click. Click.

The footsteps halted on the smooth stone before a
narble wall. On the wall were rows of gray metal
laques, each the color of gun metal glinting in the dim
ght.

The man's eyes centered on the last three plaqu‹
picking out the names.

"Corson MacGregor Ingmarr."
"Mark Heimdall Ingmarr."
"Allison Illysa Ingmarr."

He repeated the names to himself silently, th‹
continued to stand, looking at the three names, igno
ing the long rows of plaques above them, ignoring t
blank space of the stone below them.

An occasional flake of snow drifted in from his le›
under the flat marble roof and between the square a›
smooth columns that upheld the stone edifice, but ›
paid the weather no attention.

The wind whispered, ruffling and shuffling the snc
that covered the grass and walks around the lo›
structure.

The gray of his jacket and the gray of his trouse›
gave the impression of a ghost visiting other ghosts,
spirit paying his respects to other spirits.

Outside, the fine snow falling from the dawn began
thicken, until the hills surrounding the family memo›
al were less than white shadows, though they lurked b
a kilometer from the mound on which the mausoleu›
stood.

The visitor glanced toward the brighter light of t›
east and surveyed the falling snow and the shroude
hills, his eyes seeming to burn through the white veil ›
see the slopes beyond, the trees, and the lakes beyor
the rocks. Then, as if dismissing the winter, he returne
his attention to the wall, and to the three last plaqu‹
upon it.

Finally he turned, and his shoulders dropped m‹
mentarily, and he faced the west, staring out over t›
line of footprints nearly filled by the drifting an›
dropping snow, footprints that would lead him bac›
to another shadow of the past, a ship that belonge›
to a time predating even the construction of the ce›

ries-old monument and mausoleum within which he
ood.

Click. Click. Click.

Without a word, without a gesture, the visitor walked
ack across the stone slabs of the floor, down two wide
arble steps, and into the snow, into the snow that
oaked him, that hid him and the hills toward which
e walked.

LIII

HE ADMIRAL SHIFTED his weight in the chair, waiting
r his ultimate superior to appear behind the antique
esk. His eyes took in the single Corpus Corps guard, as
ell as the sparkle to the air between him and the desk
at indicated an energy barrier.

He wiped his forehead with the back of his hand.

Click, click, click.

The man whose steps preceded him eased his tall and
nky but stooped frame through the portal and into
he recliner behind the ancient artifact that had no
creen.

"You requested this meeting, Admiral."

"Yes, sire, I did."

"Begin."

The Admiral cleared his throat as quietly as possible.
I requested a private meeting because I cannot sup-
ort my concerns with hard evidence, and because I
annot trust those who would normally provide such
ard evidence."

"You do not seem to trust our Eye Corps."

"No, sire."

His Imperial Majesty Keil N'Troya Ryrce Bartolen IV waited for the Admiral of the Fleet to continue.

"You know that a Service hellburner was employe on Iredesium. What you may not know was that single weapons pack of nuclear torps was diverted fro New Glascow nearly twenty years ago. That represen the only loss of nuclear weaponry in the entire histor of the Service. I have no choice but to believe that t hellburner used on Iredesium had to come from Ne Glascow. I also find it rather difficult to believe that private group, or even a planetary system, would kee such weaponry either unused or unadvertised for nea ly twenty years.

"Further, sire, I have to ask what group is the sing group that has challenged successfully the Eye Cor over the past century." The Admiral shrugged. "I hav no answers, sire, and my surmises cannot be verified, probably even asked as questions, but I thought yc should know."

"We appreciate your concern, and your candor. Th is an issue in which the Prince has expressed som interest. I would appreciate it, Admiral, if you woul contact Ryrce directly in the future, should you hav further inspirations or any factual support for you theory."

The Admiral wanted to wipe his steaming forehea but did not. Instead he waited.

The Emperor stood.

"We are not displeased. We also appreciate yo sense of tact. Therefore, your effrontery will not t punished, and we urge you to continue your directio of the Service with the same sense of dedication yo have so far shown."

With an obvious effort, the elderly ruler turned an departed, his feet clicking as he made his way acros the tiles toward the exit portal.

The Admiral let his breath out slowly, as evenly as h could.

LIV

GERSWIN LEANED FORWARD on the control couch and
checked the results displayed on the data screen again.
According to every conceivable test, the plant produced
thread stronger and finer than any synthetic, needed
no special fertilizers, and thrived in a wide range of
climate and soil conditions.

The field tests, limited as they were, supported
Professor Fyrio's research and contentions, as did the
limited evaluations Gerswin had commissioned from
the University at New Avalon.

Gerswin shook his head. The problem wasn't the
biology, nor the data, but that none of the commercial
enterprises or agricultural interests contacted quietly
had shown any interest in what was principally an
agricultural product suitable only for nonfoodstuff
uses.

The damned plant would make someone a fortune,
and no one was interested because there was "no real
money" in agriculture.

The man in black stared at the data screen of the
small ship, ignoring the larger pilot displays above and
before him.

"What else can you do?"

"Inquiry imprecise. Please reformulate," answered
the AI in its clinically impersonal but feminine tones.

Gerswin ignored the standard request, then tapped
the keyboard, his fingers flying across the arrayed studs.

"Set for blind torp. Route beta three. Code Delta

with databloc trailer. Lyr D'Meryon."

"Blind torp in position to receive. Ready to bl
feed."

The pilot squared his shoulders and faced the sca
ner.

"Lyr. Need some basic information. Details are
the databloc attached. Need recommended corpora
type business structure with voting control remov
from the system where the business operates. Also nee
a list of systems permitting absentee ownership. Su
pect it would include systems like Byzantia, El Lid
and Dorlian. Send a copy of the systems you come t
with to Infonet, my code, and request full backgrou
on them. I'll pick up the final from my drop there."

He paused, pursing his lips.

"Doesn't make much sense, I know, but looks like v
need demonstration ventures to prove profitability
biological products and solutions. The commerci
types accept biotech for medicine and raw material
but not for finished or semifinished products.

"Enough said for now."

He tapped the closure, and hoped that she wou
read between the words.

With a sigh, he called up the information in the Fyr
files and began to reformat what he needed for t
compressed databloc to accompany his transmission

When he was finished, he coded it to the to
message.

"Torp pack complete. Send at max two."

"Readying torp for max two path."

Nodding, Gerswin indexed the research files for t
information on protein. Somewhere, somewhere, I
recalled a project on replicating animal protein stru
ture with a common plant, a weed nearly, that had use
Amardian/T-type genetic fusion.

"Torp released on max two path."

"Amardian genetics," he tapped into the keyboard

Three cross-references appeared on screen five, t
data screen.

"In-system contact. Two eight five at one point fiv

plus three radians. CPA two hundred kays, plus or minus twenty."

"Interrogative classification."

"Tentative identification in-system ore tug, class three. Low power orbit recovery."

"Stet. File and report deviations."

He returned his attention to the screen, and to the background on Amardian genetics research.

Wondering whether he could have been more efficient with a fixed headquarters, Gerswin paused, then shook his head. He'd have long since drowned in the reports, and who else could have tracked down what was important in the long run? This way, he could make decisions, request information, and move enough to avoid terminal boredom while, he hoped, the research grants began to generate the biological techniques needed so desperately by Old Earth.

In the interim, poor Lyr drowned in the reports.

Once he finished tracking down what he needed on the meat substitute possibility, it would be time to head for Aswan to reenergize and to take a break before returning to the tedious tracing and verifying that seemed to follow inevitably from each possible lead that his own research in the grant files showed up. For each hundred approved grants, perhaps ten held some promise, and of those with promise, one or two showed either commercial or technical possibilities.

On the other hand, after nearly forty years since he had insisted on innovative grants, the research product totals had become impressive. The Foundation already had an impressive and growing income from some of those developments, nothing that yet matched the income generated by Lyr's skillful manipulations of income and assets, but he could see when that had to come, perhaps sooner than Lyr expected.

His own thread venture, if it worked out, could conceivably add a great deal, since the potential was enormous, and since the license fees belonged to the Foundation.

"Energy reserves below ten stans."

He shook his head again. Might as well head for Aswan before finishing up. While the times were currently peaceful, he hated to let the ship drop into a low energy state, or to purchase power commercially. The fewer the records about unknown yachts or the *Caroljoy* that showed for Imperial intelligence or other interested parties to pick up, the better. And the cheaper as well.

"Plot course line for jump points," he ordered as he returned the genetics research to the files and centered himself in the control couch.

LV

JORGE FUGAZEY LIKED fax screens, a fact clear from the massive console and the more than thirty screens that angled gently upward around him from his control position.

His fingers played the control studs in lightning flashes, almost as quickly as his deep-set black eyes flickered from display to display.

He did not look up as the younger man approached.

"Father . . . ," ventured the thinner man, who also had angular features and dark eyes. The son did not vibrate with the focused intensity of his sire, though most men and women would have paled beside either.

"Screen six alpha—the flashing one, Duran. Your source was correct, long past correct. He has retired from the Service, but still collects an annuity. Signifies that he is still alive. You can act—if you choose."

"Choose? What choice do I have? You have ex

pressed interest in the Daeris connection, and Helene has made it clear. Quite clear. That leaves a choice?"

The performance behind the consoles came to an abrupt halt as the older Fugazey tapped two control plates in succession.

"Never said you had to contract with Helene. Only that you choose a social and economic equal with a strong family. You chose her, without my advice."

The son shrugged. "Given the alternatives . . ."

"Study the dossier on this man, Duran. Reconsider what you must do. Do not decide before that. More there than meets the eye. Data missing that should not be missing."

Baron Fugazey watched as a red light flashed next to one screen, then another, and a third.

"Who can stand up to me, especially with your support?"

"About half the Barons in the Empire," noted the elder with a sour turn to his mouth.

"But he is not a Baron, not even a magnate."

"Titles are not everything, Duran."

The Baron shifted his weight uneasily as the number of red lights on the screens beside and behind him continued to increase.

"I have met the Honorable Alhenda Strackna Daeris, Duran," added the older Fugazey. "She crossed paths with the man once before, and neither the Strackna nor the Daeris connections were adequate. I said you had my backing, and, right now, I will not back down if you wish to continue, but I do ask that you review the files and reconsider . . . reconsider whether you must have Helene."

"I will. It won't change things, but I will."

Duran snapped his jaw shut with a quick motion and turned away too quickly to see the frown that crossed his father's face. Then, too, he had never looked to see the shadows under the eyes nor the tightness with which the angular Fugazey features were bound.

The Baron watched his son's back as the man who

was scarcely beyond his student years marched o through the portal coded only to admit immediat family.

The warnings on more than a dozen screens wer flashing red and amber by the time the Baron returne to his manipulations.

LVI

GERSWIN WAS SURPRISED to find a message torp waitin for him at the Ydris drop. Not astounded, for occasion ally Lyr had used it for information that she though pressing or of particular interest. But for a torp to b waiting at Ydris meant that she had sent more than few.

He wanted to cut short the formalities with the Por Captain to retrieve the torp, since it belonged to th Foundation, though sent by the Imperial Service, an find out why Lyr was searching him out.

The Captain, a correct lady by the name of Isbe Relyea Herris, shared the tendency toward formalit that the senior tech of the *Fleurdilis* had always exhib ited, although Isbel insisted she had no relations wh had ever served in the Imperial Forces.

"Wouldn't have it! No self-respecting Ydrisian woul ever serve for that conglomeration of bullies and apolo gists for the commercial thugs that comprise the Em pire. Yourself excepted, Commander."

"No need to except me, Isbel. That assumes I wa one of the bullies in Imperial Service."

"No assumption. Fact. Your name's no more Shail Corso than that scout's the private yacht she's regis tered, apparently registered, as."

Gerswin had raised his eyebrows, but said nothing.

"Scout's too old and too well rebuilt for the Impies to have done it. And they wouldn't think of using an *old* design. New is always better for them. You're too young to have been senior and retired. That leaves few options. You're independently wealthy, or you freelance, or both.

"You're successful, and that means experience. Wealth doesn't buy experience. Leaves age or Impie service.

"Since you're not that old, you have to have Impie service. Besides"—and her eyes twinkled—"you wear everything so properly, even shipsuits. Like uniforms."

Gerswin shrugged. "What can I say? Certainly sounds so much more impressive than my own poor background, and who am I to instruct the always correct Port Captain?"

He inclined his head. "But I do have a few matters . . ."

"I know. Any time someone sends a private torp, it's urgent or Hades-fired close. You're excused, Shaik, and cleared into Ydris again. But I'd feel more comfortable calling you 'Commander.'"

"You, Isbel, can call me anything you wish, even if it is not totally accurate."

"Break orbit, Commander." She smiled nonetheless as Gerswin collected the torp pack and arranged for the torp itself to be carted to the *Caroljoy*.

He retreated to the ship as quickly as possible.

Once back inside the scout, he dropped the torp pack into the console.

Lyr's face, straight features, and carefully combed sandy hair filled the screen.

"I still can't get used to talking to a blank screen, Commander, but I thought you ought to know what's going on. I hope you have a chance to pick up one of the torps I've sent before Baron Fugazey surprises you."

She squared her shoulders and brushed back a strand of hair.

Gerswin realized that it was gray, not silver, no dyed, and shook his head. He thought of her as alway there, and unchanging. While she might be there for long time to come, given Imperial medical technolog she was not unchanging nor immune from the agin process. He wondered if she were the type whom complete rejuvenation would benefit as he refocuse on what she was saying.

". . . first sign was a nuisance suit charging that th Foundation was employing its special status to subsi dize competition to Fugar House . . . then a rathe sophisticated attempt to penetrate the databanks . . continuing shadows on me . . . taken the liberty o hiring Kirnows as antishadows . . ."

Gerswin continued to listen as Lyr rattled off th lengthy list of attempts, all of which she seemed to hav brushed off with style and without calling much publi attention to the Foundation.

". . . That's a brief update on the situation. A mor detailed chronology is speedcoded into the trailer at th end.

"For all the furor about the Foundation, Fugaze could care less about OERF. Prove that I could not. Bu he could have tied us up in legal battle after legal battle which would have been tremendously expensive. H didn't. Once it was clear he could not get the informa tion he wanted with a given strategy, he immediatel changed tactics. My own sources, and you suggested cultivate a few, as I recall, indicate that Fugazey i employing a small fraction of his not-inconsiderable assets to obtain the information from the only othe possible source."

Gerswin knew what was coming, even before sh said it.

"The Baron has a number of contacts within th I.S.S., and it is a matter of time before he obtains th information necessary to prove that Commande MacGregor Corson Gerswin is the same MacGrego Corson Gerswin who is employed by the OER Founda

ion. After that, he will use what he can to narrow your
location. Why this is so important to him I do not
know, but his interest may be linked to an attachment
his son, Duran, would like to form with a young lady
named Helene Strackna Daeris . . ."

Gerswin shook his head. Of all the damned-fool
reasons to have someone looking for him.

". . . and from what I can determine, her mother was
a Major Alhenda Strackna, who was court-martialed
and dismissed in disgrace from her position as Executive Officer of the cruiser *Fleurdilis*, then under the
command of a senior Commander named Gerswin."

Gerswin wondered how she had tracked down all the
information as he listened to the remainder of the
message.

". . . and that's it. If you wonder how I found this
out, it was not that hard for the standard Kirnow ops to
crack the rumors from the Fugazey household. Apparently dear Helene, while attractive in visage, has not
endeared herself to anyone." Lyr frowned and cleared
her throat. "Someday, Commander . . . Commodore,
more than one of the loose ends from your past is going
to catch up with you, and since you won't give in, and
neither will some of the people you've doubtless of-
fended, the Empire will end up paying for it.

"Good luck on your latest. By the way, at last there's
some Imperial interest in the growing commercial
power represented by biologic technology. Barons
Megalrie, Niniunto, Tvarik, and others are pressing for
an Imperial Commission on the subject, and on firms
such as Enver Limited, Corso and Associates, MCG
Biologics. Thought you'd like to know. Needless to say,
the Foundation is opposing such a commission unless
it includes an investigation of the activities of tradi-
tional firms to block biologic commercialization. I
predict a stalemate, now that the Imperial Trust has
endorsed the OERF position.

"In any case, now you know most of what I do."

Her image remained unspeaking, then she pursed her

lips, licked them, and added, almost as an afterthought, "Attached is a databloc coded for entry and locked to your private code."

Her image vanished.

Gerswin touched the console.

"Record and store the information, visual and coded."

His fingers added the necessary codes to complete the entry, and he sat waiting before two blank screens as the AI went about its job.

The information had reached him before Baron Fugazey's agents had. If he had gone to Westmark, or Standora, or El Lido, or . . . he shook his head again.

Resourceful as she might be, Lyr was certainly not about to send torps and messages all over the Empire, and she couldn't send them outside the Empire, even though Gerswin moved there as well.

Too bad there wasn't the equivalent of a planetary communications network for intersystems communications, regardless of political jurisdictions. The jumpshift was the only way so far known to exceed light speed.

He snorted.

One day, unfortunately, with his expanding sphere of operations, as each of the operations he directed grew, he would be out of touch for too long. To be able to keep ahead of the Baron Fugazeys of the Empire, not to mention the I.S.S. and the Intelligence Service, he needed something he didn't have. Between the few cargo ships and the independents, one could reach the major systems, but it might be three days or four weeks.

He pursed his lips, then turned to the AI. He stopped and frowned.

Like it or not, he would have to have Lyr get the information . . . somehow . . . assuming he could also deal with Fugazey. But he would have to get Lyr started, and hoped he could survive to finish up. He laughed, a hard barking sound. If he didn't survive, the whole point was mute.

"Message for Lyr D'Meryon. OER Foundation. tand by."

"Awaiting message," the AI replied.

Gerswin sat up straight and squarely before the canner.

"Thanks for the information about Baron Fugazey. Iope I can solve his problem my way rather than his.

"Brought to mind another area that might be fruit-ul. Need some background information first. Would ou find out quietly if there are surplus I.S.S. message orps available, and at what price. If not, what would it ost to purchase or build one thousand of them from ther sources? That's right. One thousand. Any support lata you could dig up would be helpful.

"Let me know as soon as you can."

He touched the controls on data screens again.

"Interrogative analysis on the Fugazey data."

"Analysis incomplete."

Gerswin drummed his fingers on the edge of the ontrol board and continued to wait, thinking about low to organize a torp-oriented message system on a ommercial or public utility basis.

Finally, after he had mentally designed and dis-arded three schemes for a system, the AI chimed and nterrupted his reflections.

"Analysis complete."

"Put on screen four."

He straightened and began to read, left index finger egulating the speed of the summary text.

When he had completed the first run-through he was rowning, pulling at his chin. He looked at the main light controls, then at the AI panel.

He coughed and cleared his throat, then rekeyed the ummary. As he ran through it again, his eyes flickered ver the pages as fast as they appeared on the screen.

Then he leaned back in the control couch.

Lyr had done a good job, more than a good job, and he conclusions were clear.

Fugazey avoided confrontations whenever possible

and only retaliated when his enterprises were serious
threatened or if his family appeared personally threa
ened. In those few cases, professionals, the close
equivalents to the now defunct Guild, were apparent
employed, although no bodies ever surfaced.

The picture was that of a coldly sensible busines
man who used the best tools possible and never act
primarily from emotion, except where his family w
concerned.

Gerswin frowned. That meant he could not focus (
the son, who had probably caused the problem, witho
dragging in the father. Eliminating Helene would e
rage both the Fugazeys and the Daeris clan.

Theoretically, the best approach would be to co
vince both Jorge Fugazey and his son Duran th
vengeance against one Commander Gerswin was ne
ther wise nor desirable and that allowing Helene
dictate their course was particularly unwise. And I
had to do so in a way that made the point clearly, b
which left them able to save face.

LVII

THE RHINOPED SNORTED, shifting its weight from left t
right side, as if flexing the muscles that could propel i
three ton mass at close to forty kays.

At the far end of the elongated clearing, a man, sma
by comparison to the beast, in turn shifted his weigh
not taking his eyes off the rhinoped, as if to ensure tha
the red and flowing sheetmail weighed evenly across h
massive shoulders.

Well over two meters tall, the giant swung his swor

in prescribed arcs, waiting for the double bell, waiting for the sonic barrier to drop, that unseen wall that both held and infuriated the beast.

The combat was third on the card, more than a crowd warm-up, but still three events before the finale, where two firelizards, a blooded rhinoped, and a jackelion were pitted against a single man.

The giant in red mail did not have to accept those odds, since he entered the arena by choice, not necessity. In turn, the crowd cheered the animals rather than him, at least until the combat was over.

Just before the twin chimes sounded, he glanced upward, over the artificial terrain, over the synthetic recreation of the Alhurzian high forest toward that part of the spectator area bordered by the golden rail.

Whether he saw any mark of favor from the line of Barons' tables or not, he made no acknowledgment, as he recentered his attention on the snorting rhinoped.

Cling! Cling!

Thirty meters above the purple-veined replicas of Alhurzian morloch vines, the copper-haired woman with the flowing curls that glistened and the bright green eyes that flashed with cold fire sat alone at the box rail table of a Baron.

That it was the box table of at least a Baron of the Empire was clear because only Barons were permitted to purchase the inner line of tables along the high rail overlooking the arena. That she was recognized and belonged there was clear from the bowing and scraping accorded her by the staff, the depth of whose genuflections tended to be proportional to the wealth and position of those before whom they bowed.

That she was not the Baroness herself was clear from the intensity in watching the arena, for she had not yet acquired the refined indifferent cruelty born of experience, though her carriage and manners were perfect in every ostensible sense.

Three tables down, to the left, also against the railing, sat an angular-featured young man, accompanied by a younger woman scarcely out of girlhood, and by a silver-haired and slender Baroness whose veiled eyes slowly shifted from point to point, surveying everything but the action in the large arena below.

Most of the Baron's tables held one or two people, though each could accommodate eight in grand style and up to twelve in a more intimate arrangement.

In the fringe area to the left and right of the Baron's tables, where the status of the holders was in the undefined limbo of those greater than commercial magnates, but not officially recognized as Barons, a black-haired, black-eyed man dressed in black sat alone. His hair was short, but tight-curled, and while his manners were almost indifferent, the staff tiptoed nearly as deferentially to him as to any Baron.

The table belonged to Fernand H'Llory, but the man who sat there was not H'Llory, for H'Llory had never attended the spectacles at the arena and had obtained the table for the convenience of his wide range of guests and associates, all of whom were at least the equal of commercial magnates, if not more. The placement of the table afforded an accommodation between shades of status satisfactory to all, particularly to H'Llory.

The man in black was obviously from the fringes of the Empire, for he wore the black with absolute authority, certainty, and flair, defying the current unspoken convention that while women might wear black, no man of worth would do so, for black had been the color of the assassins, and they had been broken, and those who remained and followed the profession independently were obviously inferior.

The copper-haired woman clapped politely, as did most of the other Imperials, as the red-mailed man in the arena dispatched the three-meter horned rhinoped. The kill had been serviceable, but little more. He had avoided injury, but taken more than the pair of normal kill strokes required to destroy the twin hearts of the beast.

The single woman let her eyes drift toward the man in black, who had not even made a gesture toward applause. As her head turned, the angular-faced young man's eyes followed hers, although he had to strain slightly to see her actions from the three table distance.

"Who is he?" asked the angular-faced man's sister.

"I don't know. He was here last night. Black then, too."

"Gauche," the girl observed.

"By current standards," noted the Baroness.

"You approve, Mother?"

A wry smile crossed the Baroness's face. "Whether I approve or not will affect society's judgments and fads little." She turned her head. "But the man is handsome, rather, in a dark way."

The angular-faced young man frowned, his complexion paling a shade. His sister touched his arm. He removed her fingers gently, but quickly.

"What can I do? Two agents missing, and that Commodore Gerswin has disappeared, almost as if he knew they were after him. Helene has refused to consider any contract or further contact until that's resolved. She says she is sorry, but whoever her contract-mate is will have to clear that blot."

He watched as the copper-haired woman known as Helene summoned a towering staffer in cold violet formal wear, watched as she instructed him or requested something, and watched as the tall man stepped away.

He was still watching as the functionary appeared at the table where the man in black sat.

The man in black inclined his head, then shook it firmly.

"She can't do that!" hissed the angular-faced man.

"He didn't accept, Duran," observed the sister.

"That will just intrigue her more."

"Of course."

"You are too eager, Duran, too intense, like your father, though he has come to accept that failing in himself. Watch the next combat. It might be interesting."

Below, a man and a woman, each with a boar spear, bowed to the audience, which responded with an applause mainly perfunctory.

"Do you want to wager on the outcome, or the time?"

"Neither," snapped Duran, forcing himself to avoid meeting the cool glance of Helene, who had surveyed his table without seeing him or his sister and mother. "Neither."

"There will be a dance tonight. Are you going?"

"I haven't decided."

"Well," added his sister with a smile that did not hide the cruelty, "Jaim Daeris told Forallie that Helene was going. Alone."

She refrained from saying more as the Baroness's cold gray eyes caught hers.

"I haven't decided," Duran repeated. "I haven't decided."

LVIII

LYR D'MERYON MUMBLED under her breath, touched the screen controls, and surveyed the information again.

"One thousand torps. That was bad enough."

Her finger jabbed at the console controls.

"Now he wants to know about surplus in-system relay stations—and the possibility of simplified designs for both torps and stations. What does he want His own private message delivery system?"

She brushed a strand of hair back off her forehead wondering why she had ever even considered that he mysterious Commander—strange how she continued to think of him as a Commander—would settle into a more regular pattern after he retired from the Service.

Settle down? Regular? Not only could she never find him in a hurry, but the work load had more than tripled in the last ten years.

And the creds! Everything he touched seemed to generate money. The more he spent, the more it created. Plus the funds from strange names and friends, names and friends that were never explained.

Was Shaik Corso an acquaintance or an alias? She suspected the latter, but the documents were in order, and the Foundation's records had to show the latter. MacGregor Corson was so transparent, proper records or not, that she wasn't about to risk an Imperial censure. So "Corson's" contributions and expenses were listed as a subset of Gerswin's.

The Commander might complain, but the Foundation was going to be run right. Period.

She sighed, and mentally added the thought—as far as she was concerned.

She switched screens again, trying to unscramble the codes on his latest voucher, shaking her head all the time.

Where it would end, she didn't know. If it would end.

The supposedly ancient Commander still looked and acted like a man in his standard thirties, but the background she had found indicated he was well over a century old—at least.

She frowned at the thought that he might outlive her, then smiled a wry smile. She had a few more decades, at least, before she even had to worry about it.

"Ms. D'Meryon, can you check out item three on your beta?" asked the on-line tech.

"Hold one."

She transferred screens again, calling up the questioned item.

"That's an approved transportation item, deductible

under 33(a)(1). Note that in the remarks section."

"Thank you."

She returned to screen one. Satellite relay system Surplus? Where should she start there?

She frowned once more, then tapped out a numbe

LIX

DURAN STOOD IN the corner, half shielded by the i sculpture of the rhinoped, and watched the dance sweeping across the low grav of the dance floor in tir to the ancient waltz.

His eyes followed a copper-haired woman in a fo mal coppered dress that should not have compliment her pale coloration, but did, as the dance ended and she bowed to Carroll, the elder son of Baron Kellenhe and turned away, leaving the young man standing the with words on his lips left unsaid.

Duran grimaced.

At least she was equally cavalier with others, or son others.

A flicker of black caught his eye, and his head jerke around involuntarily.

The black-haired man skirted the dancing are brushing the massive forearm of a giant in red, wl whirled to confront the slender figure in black.

Duran smiled.

He did not know the giant personally, except that the younger son of a minor mining Baron, Trigarth ha achieved a certain notoriety by surviving in the arer and a certain success with women by dropping to th level of combat in the circus and succeeding.

Duran's angular features relaxed as he watched the confrontation develop.

". . . apology . . . ?" asked Trigarth.

The man in black inclined his head politely, but quizzically, as if he could not believe what Trigarth had asked.

"I think you owe me an apology." By now the hall was quiet enough for the words to reach Duran.

"I beg your pardon, but I believe I owe you nothing."

The smaller man turned, his carriage conveying his opinion of the big man, an opinion Duran silently seconded, though he would never have been fool enough to voice it.

Trigarth stepped around in front of the other, blocking his departure.

"I would appreciate that apology."

The smaller man's eyes surveyed the massive two plus meter form of Trigarth. His lips quirked, as if to sneer, then his face cleared.

"Are you trying to insist that sheer dumb mass requires respect?"

Duran's mouth dropped, as did a number of others'. Was the man mad? The wealth of Trigarth's house could pay off any death claim.

"Never . . . have . . . I . . . been . . . so . . . insulted."

"Then you have been extraordinarily fortunate. Now, if you will excuse me . . ."

Duran caught sight of Helene among the watching dancers. Even from ten meters he could see the unnatural brightness in her eyes as she watched the pair.

"I could crush you!" rumbled Trigarth.

The man in black laughed twice. Two cruel barks conveyed a sense that Trigarth was less than the lowest of the low. Then he shook his head sadly, as if to convey pity on the big noble and gladiator, and began to turn.

Duran could see it coming, watched as Trigarth lost

all control and launched hands and body toward the smaller man with a speed that caused Duran and others nearer to the pair to draw back.

Duran, his angular features tight again, waited for the stranger's dismemberment, his own reflexes keyed so that the scene seemed to play out in virtual slow motion.

Trigarth's whole body drove toward the man in black, who stood motionless for long instants. Just before hammering arms blasted through him, the smaller shifted, and his hands and body blurred as he moved.

Thuddd!

Duran gaped.

The small man appeared untouched, unmussed, and was again shaking his head sadly, this time at the unconscious figure of the giant on the floor.

Three of the staff guards arrived too late, expecting apparently to rescue the stranger's remains.

"He is unconscious, but you should find that he will be all right, except for a bruise on his jaw where he struck the floor. He must have had too much of something."

The senior guard asked something.

"Merhlin of Avalon, guest of Lord and Baron H'Llory. I will be staying as his guest for at least several days more."

Another question followed.

"I suppose I could claim I was a Baron, were I so inclined. Would that make any difference?"

Duran shook his head. So fast . . . so incredibly fast. And so strong. Was the man human? Then he bit his lip.

As Merhlin of Avalon dismissed the security force, copper-haired woman touched his black-sleeved forearm. The woman's eyes glittered in the light.

This time, instead of dismissing Helene, Merhlin surveyed her coolly, then offered his arm.

Duran gulped the last from the goblet in his hand, choking it down, and ignoring the burning in his

roat. He clutched the empty goblet as if he wanted to
ush it into powder.

Instead, the unbreakable crystal squirted from his
ngertips and struck the ornate floor tiles, bouncing
way from him.

Clink! Clink. Clink.

He could see his sister Aermee look up in surprise,
nd then avert her eyes as she recognized that he had
een the culprit. The couple next to him drew back and
ooked away.

The sound of the bouncing crystal echoed in Duran's
ind as he turned away, but he was not quick enough
o avoid the smirk on Helene's lips as she swept up
e ramp with the man called Merhlin.

Duran swallowed and slowly retracted his steps
cross the hall. Even people he did not know drew away
distaste as he headed for the exit not taken by
Merhlin and Helene, the exit that began the long walk
ack to the family suite, and, in all probability, toward
quiet talk with his mother, the Baroness. Either
hortly, or the next morning, when Aermee would have
eported her extreme embarrassment at his behavior.

Duran sighed, loudly enough to cause another set of
verted faces.

LX

HE COPPER-HAIRED woman shook her head, tossing the
listening curls back over her bare shoulders, conscious
f the effect as she again exposed her breasts. She
traightened her back as she reached for the crystal
vineglass.

Leaning back against the pillows, she brought th
crystal to her lips, first to scent, then to sip.

Gerswin refrained from shaking his head. The hai
line of her jaw and the ever-occurring cruel glint in h
eyes were so at odds with her slenderness and th
softness of her skin.

He whistled three notes, double-toned, more as a te
than anything else.

Helene shivered at the sounds, but said nothing an
took another sip that became a gulp.

Gerswin paused before beginning another song, for
ing himself to keep his face almost impersonal as h
watched her reactions.

She raised her eyebrows, arching her back again.

Gerswin began another song, not a love song, fo
Helene had proved strangely indifferent to the gent
songs, the wistful ones, and had been aroused by h
adaptations of the military themes, the ones where h
had played hope against force, honesty against betraya

"That's right," the woman whispered hoarsely as sh
set the wineglass aside. "That's right."

Her lips parted, her tongue running over her lowe
lip, wetting it and retreating. Her breathing deepene
as his double-toned notes built toward what he woul
have called hope and its betrayal.

Her shoulders shifted, her hips beginning to mov
with the conflict of the song, as she began to lea
toward him.

Gerswin could see her darkened nipples stiffenin
further as whatever fantasy played out behind he
too-bright green eyes intensified with the last notes c
the song.

Even before the tones died away, her fingers wer
digging into first his forearms, then his back as he i
turn drove into her, directly, brutally, and withou
finesse or foreplay, knowing that such power was wha
she wanted, what she expected.

"AaaaaaAAAAHHHHH!"

Her cries filled the not inconsiderable expanse of th

bedroom as her legs locked around him in a series of thrusts, and as her body arched into him and upward, toward.

Waiting until she subsided, he did not leave her, but turned his head to start another song, with a more muted conflict theme, drawing her into another series of releases, more gentle than the first, and letting himself go as well, trying to shut out other faces, other places, with a final thrust more brutal than he had intended.

"Ooohhh!"

Helene lay against him only momentarily before easing back onto the bed, propped against silken pillows, a faint smile on her face.

"You are a magician."

The coolness of her tone brought him back to his purpose.

"Never said one way or the other." He managed a cool mocking tone, which masked the contempt he felt, both for himself and for her.

"Where did you come from? I've never met anyone so strong."

"Anyone you couldn't wear out, you mean?"

Without the spell of his music, she might easily have outlasted him, and then some, but that wasn't the question. He needed certain revelations from the copper-haired harpy.

"I would scarcely confess that, even if it were true."

"What would you confess? You know, I know nothing about you, except your name and status. You could be some Baron's young wife, for all I know, but he'd be a fool to let you run this free, and twice the fool not to."

"Oh?"

Gerswin matched her smile with one a shade more mocking. "But then, you'd never let yourself be bound, would you?"

"That answer takes no magic."

"But you do admit I possess some small magic?"

"I'll admit that, at least in some areas." She sat up

and took the wineglass, downing the remainder of tl
wine in a single gulp.

"Will you admit that you're sought after?"

"Surely. But for what? Body? Or money?"

"Both. For your wealth by the older, and your bo
by the younger. Like that angular-faced young fellc
who couldn't keep his eyes off you at the arena.
puppy dog."

"Him. He's nothing."

"Some Baron's offspring, I presume, ready to pr
pose a contract in an instant."

"He already has."

"But you're here," laughed Gerswin, "instead of
young what's-his-name's arms. Not that you couldr
be and still have accepted."

"Duran wouldn't know what to do. No strength. M
magic."

"Seemed capable enough for a youngster."

"Youngster is precisely right. He'll never grow u
He'd never be more than just a tool, even if I did acce
his contract."

"That indicates you have not. You're a hard lad
willing to use anyone . . . or your own magic
Gerswin forced a leer, let it be seen that it was force

"Why not?"

"You feel no guilt," asked Gerswin with a quirk
his lips, "about holding your body out to this Duran
get him to do whatever you want?"

"Of course not. Why should I? If you can use yo
magic to get my body—not that I mind—wl
shouldn't I use my body to get what I want?"

Gerswin laughed, a hard bark, knowing that tl
hidden scanners had more than enough on tape.

"Poor Duran . . . poor anyone. Whoever gets yc
won't know how to handle you."

"Duran won't get me. He's too weak. Besides, I
probably find a way to avoid the contract even if he d
everything I asked."

"Everything?"

Helene stretched, tossing her copper curls off her
are breasts.

"Sing me another one, a stronger one." Her eyes
rightened as she slowly dropped her head, letting her
air fall back across her breasts, before tossing it over
er shoulders, squaring her shoulders, emphasizing her
anslucent skin, her nipples again taut with anticipa-
on.

Her tongue moistened her lips once more as Gerswin
egan the progression of double-toned notes, this time
eaving the theme of betrayal versus betrayal.

LXI

DURAN'S LONG STEPS took him toward the portal of his
ather's screen center. He barely nodded at the security
onsole as he passed through the endurasteel pillars,
ut his carriage stiffened and he slowed as he recog-
ized the figure in black sitting in the chair across from
is father.

His second surprise was the stillness, for all the
creens had been blanked, save one, which displayed
nly the name "Helene" upon it.

The man in black stood, as did Jorge Fugazey.

"I believe you have at least seen Merhlin, Duran,"
ffered the Baron to his son.

"Twice." Duran's tone was as angular as his strained
ace.

"Merhlin has brought me some rather impeccable
eferences, which I have checked thoroughly, as well as
ome rather interesting information."

"I see."

"The question was whether I let you see it befor
making my decision and whether I asked your opinior
or whether I did what I thought best and merel
informed you."

Duran inclined his head. "It must be rather earth
shaking for you to have consulted with and gone to th
difficulty of investigating a total stranger."

Both his father and the stranger ignored th
unconcealed bitterness in his tone.

"Before we continue, Duran, I suggest you view th
segment of the tape on the console. I can verify, an
have done so, that the speaker is indeed Helene, an
that the tape has not been altered. There are no stres
levels in her voice."

The older man's voice contained a sadder note, on
that brought Duran up short as his father continued
for he had never heard it before. "Knowing how yo
feel, please remember that the one thing I have neve
done is lie to you. That is also why I have gone to th
trouble of having all aspects of this thoroughl
checked."

"Why all the sudden concern?"

"Because I would prefer that you leave yoursel
something besides the choice of suicide through a wom
an and suicide through stupidity or stubbornness."

Duran swallowed. For his father even to have admit
ted the stranger, and then to have spoken so directly ir
his presence, meant that the man was either immensel
powerful or in his father's trust, or both.

"There is a sound block around the screen. For you
own peace of mind, I suggest you use it."

Duran glanced from the pale face of his father to th
impassively hawkish visage of the black-haired strang
er, then walked to the console and tapped the soun
block controls. The wall of silence enfolded him.

He touched the stud to start the sequence, sinkin
into the swivel as he watched Helene's unclothed figur
swim into view on a rather imposing bed, tossing he

glittering curls off her naked breasts.

Duran wanted to shut out the words, to turn away from the scene even as his eyes drank in the cruelty and lust in her face and the slender voluptuousness of her body.

He did not turn, forcing himself to hear every last word. Mercifully, the sequence was short, the betrayal shorter.

He reran her damning words twice, then blanked the screen.

After sitting there silently for several minutes, he dropped the sound block and stood, turning to face the other two, his eyes scanning the man identified as Merhlin, wondering how old or how young he was.

Certainly older, but how much?

He was letting his thoughts drift, Duran realized. Concentrating on the moment, he eased himself into the vacant swivel next to his father.

"Do you want my opinion?" he asked. Even to himself, his voice sounded thin.

"Do you want to give it?" asked his father gently. "You don't have to give it, you know."

"It couldn't have been faked," Duran admitted. "Don't tell me how, but I know that." He paused and pulled at his chin. "Does it matter? I don't know. I know I should be able to accept her for all her faults, knowing what I would get and what I wouldn't. Or I should be able to say good riddance."

"What is the price you pay for taking her?" asked Merhlin.

"A man has to die. But all men die."

"Would you stake your life on that?" asked Jorge Fugazey.

Duran looked from his father, the Baron, to Merhlin and back again.

"I'm not sure I understand."

"For all practical purposes," added the Baron, "you may regard both Baron H'Llory and Merhlin as allies and dependents of Commodore Gerswin."

Duran sat immobile. After a time, he spoke.

"Does that mean you are withdrawing your support should I continue my efforts to have Commodor Gerswin removed?"

"No. It means that the Commodore can remove o negate any protection I can offer. That would mean some risk. Considerable risk. That I cannot deny, no could I let you proceed, should I choose to, withou your knowing that. That is why I thought you should see the tape. You are my oldest son, and you will b sacrificing your life for someone who cares nothing fo you. From her, you would have neither respect no love."

Duran looked at the floor. "Do I have to decide now?"

"No. It might be better if you thought it over."

Merhlin rose to his feet. "Fear my actions have caused a great deal of trouble, but I have been as hones as possible, and I think it would be better if I with drew."

"Do you call that honesty?" Duran's hand stabbe toward the console he had so recently sat before.

"Helene is free to make her own choices. So are you You can live or you can die." While Merhlin's ligh baritone penetrated, his tone was gentle, as if instruct ing a child.

"You think I'll die?"

Merhlin took a step backward. "That is what you must choose, Ser Fugazey."

"Are you betraying Helene, then?"

"Scarcely."

As Merhlin's eyes caught Duran, the younger mar felt as though he were pinned in his seat.

Merhlin bowed to Jorge Fugazey, the bow of ar equal, Duran observed, and said, "I will depart . . . as I arrived."

He stepped out through the portal, which closed behind him.

"What did that mean?" snapped Duran.

"Duran . . . your foolishness could have cost us both arly." The Baron Fugazey's voice was harder, in a signed way, than Duran had ever heard it.

"I don't understand—"

"That's right. You don't understand. Console three ta. Run it before you utter another word."

As Duran stumbled toward the indicated console, e older Fugazey stood. His steps took him in a tight cle, and his eyes darted to the console where his son adied a series of scenes.

When Duran had completed his assignment and anked the screen, he turned and eased himself toward ere the Baron stood.

"I sound like a locked loop, but I can't say I under- nd. Could you explain . . . please?"

"Duran, those last scenes. Who was there?"

"Me, Mother, Aermee, you, Donal, Frynn."

"And the vantage point?"

Duran glanced down. Never had his father asked so any questions he couldn't answer. Accounting and v—there he could hold his own. The same for rketing, tariffs. But this?

The Baron swung his head from side to side slowly.

"Do you know who Merhlin is?"

"No. Does it matter?"

"Yes. While I do not know exactly who he is, I know at he is. Besides being supported by Fernand Llory, who by the way fears him rather thoroughly, d besides being, shall we say, an agent of Gerswin, 's a professional assassin of assassins, who, if he's o I think he is, was the one who broke the Guild, the e whom the Eye Corps refused, it's rumored, to ack."

Duran looked absently puzzled, knitted his forehead a quizzical gesture, and looked up to see the contin- d disapproval in his father's face.

"It's obvious that your life has been too sheltered, ıran." The Baron wiped his forehead with the back his left hand. "I'll put it in simple sentences. That

sequence showed clearly that Merhlin could have ass
sinated every one of us in less than a three-hour peri
and done so without triggering a single security prec
tion within the villa.

"That sequence with Helene showed that Gersv
would rather not do so, and was directed at me, not
you."

"At you?"

"At me. Gerswin simply delivered a clear, tv
pronged message. First, that Helene isn't worth
conflict over, and second, that if I disagree he und
stands he would have to destroy the entire family,
just you, and that he is fully capable of doing so."

Duran could feel the color draining out of his fac

"Now . . . I see you are beginning to understand.
you also understand that Merhlin saw you did
understand and left so that you could not act before
could discuss the matter?"

"But why?"

"I don't know. Gerswin is not adverse to violen
necessarily, though he tries to avoid it." Jorge Fuga
looked at the blank screens arrayed to his right. "T
second sequence had a preface, but it blanked after
first scan. He said he hoped I would understand
remember his words clearly. He and Merhlin speak
the same tones. He said, 'Once I had a son . . .'"

The elder Fugazey shook his head. "Too sentiment
but it makes no difference. He's offered us a way o
one that doesn't ruin us, and a way to save face."

"He's insulted you!"

"If showing me that your intended is both a bit
and a tramp, as well as not up to keeping her word,
refraining from destroying me and everything I've bu
because of your stubbornness and inadequate resear
and if doing it with enough tact to keep it quiet—if
this is an insult, then by all means think so. But I w
with great regret, inform Gerswin that your quar
with him is strictly personal and does not involve Fug
House. While I love you, Duran, hard as that is for y

comprehend, I also love Margritte and Aermee and
nal and Frynn. And if you want Helene after all this
d after all she has already put you through, what you
lly want is suicide."

"What will people think?"

"Nothing. They won't know, unless you tell them."

"But . . . Helene?"

"You confirm to her that you have totally withdrawn
ur offer for contract, with great regret, and you leave
r free to follow her heart, as you cannot meet her
nditions. What can she say? If she tells anyone the
ason is because you refused to murder someone you
not know, then you come out looking like you have
tter judgment than you so far have shown. The only
estion in people's minds is why it took you so long to
through her."

"You leave me no other choice."

The Baron Fugazey sighed. "No. I do not. Someday,
rhaps, you will understand with your heart as well as
th your head."

Duran matched his father's sigh.

"I understand now. But don't expect me to like
. . . not now."

The two regarded each other across the open space
tween them.

"May I go now?"

"You may go, Duran."

"I will send confirmation of my withdrawal as you
ggested. Then, I think, I will leave for New Avalon."

Jorge Fugazey nodded, but said nothing as his son
t. An even deeper sigh escaped him as the portal
sed behind the young man.

He had not told Duran that he had sent a copy of the
quence showing Helene to the Baron Daeris, with his
vn notation that any further action against one Com-
odore Gerswin would be most unwise, particularly
om the viewpoint of the Commodore, Fugar House,
d Baron H'Llory.

Daeris would understand, even if Duran did not.

LXII

"Now . . . IS THERE any other business?"

Eye sat in his customary position at the end of t[h]
Intelligence conference table, sat in his shadow[ed]
splendor, flanked by his two shadowed regents, a[nd]
surveyed the room.

Silence prevailed as the uniformed Service office[rs]
looked back and forth at each other, finally fixing the[ir]
gazes on a single and white-haired Rear Admiral.

"It would seem that your contemporaries feel y[ou]
have something to say, Admiral Thurson."

The round-cheeked Admiral smiled ruefully. "Und[er]
the circumstances, I guess I have little choice." [He]
cleared his throat with an apologetic gesture befo[re]
continuing. "We received a rather disturbing repo[rt]
from New Avalon, which we managed to track back t[o a]
confirmation from a source in Fugar House. Of cours[e,]
we reported the information to Eye Corps. I w[as]
wondering what the current status or classification [of]
the follow-up might be."

Eye nodded so imperceptibly within his hood th[at]
the movement was unremarked by anyone else, parti[c-]
ularly since all eyes were on Admiral Thurson.

"I presume that you are referring to the appare[nt]
reappearance of a man calling himself Merhlin [of]
Avalon?"

"That is the report we received."

"As you know, there is no system or locale know[n]
strictly as 'Avalon' within the Empire or other know[n]

human systems, which indicated that the man using the name was doubtless an imposter. Neither the man nor that identity has surfaced since the incident you uncovered. Consequently, Eye Corps has not been able to trace anything further on the individual in question, since we were unable to obtain any sort of firm biological identification, and since the few holos we were able to obtain revealed gross physical parameters applicable to at least ten percent of the male Imperial population."

"Ten percent?" That whisper came from someone behind Thurson.

Thurson nodded. He cleared his throat again. "A literature search revealed that the only Avalons in history existed on Old Earth. I presume that Eye Corps efforts to identify this Merhlin, also a mythical figure from Old Earth, attempted to tie Merhlin to those with Old Earth ties."

"That was attempted, but no degree of certainty was possible, and in view of the Imperial position on Old Earth, without certainty, no action would have been possible."

Thurson nodded. "Mythical figures can be rather difficult to lay to rest."

"What are they talking about?"

"Thurson's on to something."

While the whispers should have been inaudible to Eye, they were not. Nothing within the conference room escaped his eyes or ears, enhanced as they were by his personal equipment.

"Should we be able to determine the identity of any true malefactor, of course, and should the Emperor concur, we would take the necessary steps to resolve the problem."

Again Admiral Thurson nodded, not bothering to wipe the dampness off his forehead.

"Are there any other questions? Any other matters to be brought before the Council?" Eye paused. "If not, the formal meeting is adjourned. I might also add that

since Admiral Thurson's retirement will become effec
tive before the next meeting, we all wish him well." Eye
stood.

Thurson managed to keep his jaw from falling open
in the quiet hissing of whispers that circled the confer
ence room.

"Just promoted to Vice Admiral . . ."

". . . never announced it . . ."

". . . really hot, whatever it was . . . poor bastard
. . . likely to be found dead of heart failure within
weeks . . ."

". . . why you never ask questions . . ."

Eye strode out, flanked by his regents, and the
Service officers clustered around Thurson, who had
taken out a large white cloth and was wiping his
forehead, despite the chill that remained in the room.

LXIII

HIS FACE WAS as always, the same blond, curly hair,
hawk-yellow eyes, although the image was frozen on the
screen.

The Senior Port Captain of Ydris glanced at the
image, then at the contract on the console, then at her
own work sheet on the third screen.

"Aboveboard and foul in the dirtiest way possible,
Corso! You devil!"

She smiled in both wry admiration and humor.

The ex-Imperial officer she called Corso had her
caught squarely by her own ideals, and those of Ydris.

If she failed to recommend his offer, then the com

munications system he had developed would become
the tool of the commercial interests and eventually
would sell out to the highest bidder, no matter how
noble the initial purpose. That such a bidder would use
the system against Ydris was also inevitable.

If she endorsed his proposal, then Ydris would
inevitably become an information and commercial hub
second only to New Augusta. Even there, Corso had
calculated cleverly. The distance was great enough that
New Augusta would gain more than it would lose—at
least for decades.

His motivation—that was what bothered her. Why
would anyone go to the tremendous effort and expense
of acquiring the equipment, developing detailed operating plans, and obtaining the necessary permissions for
the key systems . . . and then turn it over to someone
else?

He'd offered a clear explanation, right on the
databloc.

"Isbel. You're going to ask why. Answer is simple. I
need an interstellar communications system I can
trust, one independent of the Empire, and one that will
maintain confidentiality.

"I can afford to build it. What I can't afford is the
time and dedicated people to run it. And I need
someone whose ideals will prevent them from corrupt-
ing it. That's you and Ydris."

Should she trust him? Could she afford not to?

She smiled wryly and touched the stud that would
forward the proposition to the Council. Her recommendation to accept was attached.

The Council would accept it. Like her, Ydris could
not afford to decline, could not afford to pass up the
chance to control her own destiny.

Still . . . she wondered why the mysterious man
known only as Corso was willing to fund such an
altruistic enterprise, only for a minute return on his
investment and years before any repayment of the
principal was due.

LXIV

"BUT I CAN'T be!" protested the woman. "I can't be."

"It is not a matter of debate, milady," answered the physician as he looked back at the console. "Contraceptive implant failure is rare, to be sure, but not unheard of."

"Have you reported this to my father?"

"Of course. You are the only Daeris of this generation. How could I not? He said he already knew."

"He knew? But how? I'm not one of his brood mares!"

"That, milady, is between you and your father." The doctor's eyes were calm and level, as gray as his dark gray hair.

She glanced from one side of the office to the other, idly wondering if she could reach the balcony that overlooked the grounds. Then she shook her head.

Not that way. If worse came to worst, her father could have the heir. At least once it was over he could have no objection to her living her own life, and outside the restricted sphere of a Baron's controlled environment.

She unthinkingly tossed her glittering copper curls back off the cream of her tunic and over her shoulder. Was it already tighter than she remembered?

Despite the controls and the guards, she'd managed to get herself in trouble, and he hadn't said a word. Not a word, almost as if he'd hoped for it. But he'd known, known before she and the doctor had! How?

She bit her lip.

Her father had known.

What else did he know?

She looked again at the balcony railing, then back at the thin older doctor.

"What about decanting?"

"Your father—"

"Damn his fundamentalist beliefs! Damn him . . . yes, I know. . . . Of course, I know . . . how else could it possibly be?"

She glanced again at the balcony.

"Milady . . . ?"

"Yes, Hierot?"

"Is there anything else? Before you go?"

Helene shook her head with a quick motion, a violent, short snap. There was nothing else. Not now. Not ever.

She looked toward the balcony.

LXV

WHEN THE COMMANDER'S—strange how she could never keep from calling him a Commander, although he never used the title and had retired from the Service as Commodore—face filled the screen, as soon as the image cleared and went real time, the question was out of her mouth.

"You bought another biologics complex? For what? Do we need another full-scale research facility?"

He closed his mouth, as if he had been about to say something else and had decided against it. He waited.

"Why did you buy it?" she repeated her question.

"I did not buy it. Made the first payment, and obligated you to complete the contract."

Lyr's mouth dropped open. "You . . . obligated the Foundation. How much?"

"Fifty million?"

"Fifty million? From the Forward Fund?"

"That's what it's for." He frowned. "An acquisition grant, not for research. Production."

"What does production have to do with promoting biologic research?"

"Read section three, clause five of the Foundation goals."

Lyr worried at her lip, brushed a graying hair off her forehead. When he cited sections of the bylaws, he was invariably right.

"I don't suppose you would like to tell me why you have involved OERF with production now?"

"Lyr. Someone has to translate research into reality. Done what I can personally. But took the commercial fields, and plowed money back into research, back into the Foundation."

"I know."

"Hope that some more spin-offs from what the Foundation had stimulated would be appearing. They're not. Not one. Yet I'm making creds. It's almost as if—" He laughed once. "Never mind."

He looked below the screen, then back at her before continuing. "Need certain technologies developed now. No other way to do it. But don't worry. It's profitable."

He grinned. "That's another problem, I know, but that's one you can solve."

"You have such illusions about my abilities."

"No bitterness, please." His tone was gentle.

"All right." Lyr bit back the intemperate comment she had almost launched and frowned at the screen, waiting to see what else he said.

"Is your dream beyond a dream still the same?"

"My what?"

"Once we talked about dreams beyond dreams. ours was a chalet on Vers D'Mont. Do you remem- r?"

"That was in another life, Commander."

"Another life? Perhaps, but is the dream still your eam?"

"There are days, Commander, when it is even more tractive than it ever was. Why do you ask? Do you ally care? Or is it just to humor me?"

His expression tightened, as if her words had been en more barbed than she had meant.

"I thought you could tell when I was humoring you. id you ask that . . ." He shook his head. "Never ind."

"You know I have never tried to undermine you—no atter how outrageously you behaved." This time ere was anger in her words. "You never let anyone now how you feel. You make me guess what you really ant, and once in a while I even get a pat on the head." he paused, but not enough to let him speak. "More kely, you tell me to give myself a pat on the head."

Surprisingly, he only nodded. "You're right, Lyr. Not o much I can say that will rebut that."

"Don't you ever get angry? Don't you ever get hurt?"

"Yes. I do get angry, and I have been hurt, and I will e again, no doubt." The gentleness in his voice isarmed her own lingering anger.

"When?" There was more curiosity than steel in her ne.

He sighed. "Rather not go into details. Let's just say at I've buried two sons, three lovers. Not technically orrect, but all five are dead. Some were killed to strike t me, and some were killed when my back was urned."

"And you can take it that calmly?"

She could see his face harden.

"Quietly. Not calmly. I have thrown my share thunderbolts, and the guilty and I have both paid. Pa in full. Still paying."

Lyr shivered as the coldness seemed to rush from t screen and enfold her. She wondered, again, wheth his anger was the cold of deep space, the devastati destruction of absolute zero.

"You still make them pay?"

"No. They paid. I still pay. Will with every mile le in life."

He smiled his grim smile and laughed softly. "B enough of me . . . I asked about you."

"I'm not sure we're finished. . . ."

He sighed once more, and the grim smile was r placed with a still sadness, the guarded look of a ma willing to take an assault without attacking in return raising a defense. Lyr did not recall ever having see that expression, the weariness in his eyes, or the sudde vulnerability.

"What else would you like to know?"

"I don't know. Except that after all these years, I sti feel like I don't know you. Like you feel all things mor intensely than any man should, and yet you show s little. As if what you do is consuming what you are."

His shoulders gave a small shrug. "You're probabl right about the last. But I warned you about that in th beginning. Told you that I was a fanatic."

"That doesn't excuse it."

"Not trying to excuse it, Lyr. I know what I am."

"Do you? I wonder."

He smiled, and the expression was momentaril boyish. "All right. I know at least some of what I am.

"And what about the rest?"

"Guess I'll find out."

This time she was the one to shake her head. "Heav en help us all when you do."

"Not that bad." He grinned. "Enough of this sombe stuff. Let's get back to what I asked."

"What did you ask?"

"If you still had a dream beyond a dream."

"Some days. Why do you keep asking?"

"Every once in a while I care about people's dreams, little more often than they think."

"I stand reproved. I think."

"Not reproved. You're right, but can we leave it at that for now?"

"Why?"

"Because the timing is getting critical. A number of things are coming together, and you'll probably need more staff, and I'm not sure I can afford much more introspection. Not now."

"What do you mean?"

"More large purchases, some more acquisitions, that sort of thing."

"I'm not sure I understand, but you do much more than you're doing, and I'll need more staff."

"Go ahead and add what you need."

Lyr took a deep breath, feeling as though she had somehow missed more than the quickest glimpse into the Commander's soul.

"What about you?" she asked, trying to steer the conversation back onto a more personal level.

"Probably more traveling. Trying to coordinate. Headed for El Lido next, the way it looks. Not sure past that on the specifics."

"But what about you?" she asked again.

"I'll survive. Somehow. Always do. Probably always will. Not much else that I can do."

"Try to keep in touch, Commander." She paused, and her voice softened as she finished. "And take care."

"I will, as I can. Keep doing your best, Lyr. You're the only one who can keep this end together."

The screen blanked as her mouth dropped open. She had never expected either the admission of her efforts or the abruptness of his closing, not after the disclosures she had forced from him.

She rubbed her chin. On the other hand, perhaps he

had to break the connection quickly. Perhaps he could
not afford to become too personal . . . perhaps.

Shaking her head, she cleared the screen.

With his attitude and more purchases like the last,
her efforts might not be enough to keep the Empire
from digging deep into the Foundation, and while the
Foundation might endure, she wondered about the
implications for its Trustee—and for its administrator.

LXVI

THE SHADOWED MAN studied the arrangement.

The single guard sat in a shielded riot box set in the
wall, swivel set high enough that he could survey the
sloping lawn in front of the wall without his eyes being
more than a slight angle from the screen that switched
from snoop to snoop.

The chair itself was an indicator. Gerswin had
watched as the present guard had replaced his predecessor, watched as the seat had lifted slightly when the
guard's weight was removed.

From the shadows he dropped his glasses.

While he would rather have handled it personally, on
a face-to-face basis, that was certainly what Carlina was
expecting. She had obviously studied his past interac-
tions and was counting on his reputed sense of fair play
and direct action with principals.

He shook his head and slipped soundlessly back
along the relatively unmonitored pathway he had
tracked through the surrounding grounds, back to the
flitter.

He took a deep breath as his quick and light steps cleared the unmarked boundary of the estate and as he entered the undeveloped tract where his flitter waited in the small clearing.

After a short flight to a more distant location, he changed craft, from a small black one to a larger black one. Once inside his ship, and seated before the control console, Gerswin touched the communications studs. The picture remained a swirl of color.

He recognized the swirl as a scramble from the receiver, a protective pattern that blocked even his own command access codes. His lips quirked as he waited to see how soon and if the pattern would clear.

Fully two minutes passed before the abstract color patterns resolved themselves into the picture of a silver-haired woman, with a straight, firm nose and violet eyes. Gerswin knew both eye color and nose had been purchased from a high-priced cosmetic surgeon.

Before she had risen to become Administrator of CE, Limited, on El Lido, Carlina D'Aquinio had displayed muddy brown hair and eyes, and a much larger and wider nose.

"Shaik Corso! I had not expected you. I thought someone was testing our security system." Her smile showed the warmth that only years of accomplished insincerity could project.

"I regret the inconvenience, Carlina, but your recent reports have displayed a rather depressing lack of profitability, and I thought I might be of some service in assisting a rather rapid recovery." Gerswin doubted that his smile was nearly as warm as Carlina's.

"Oh, dear Shaik, you shouldn't have bothered. I'm afraid there's little you can do to change that. You know, our overhead has increased so much. You remember all those fancy hidden entrances and gas systems that Delwar had installed—I assume it was Delwar—that led to his replacement? Well, I thought they were really too much of an invitation, and I thought about replacing them. But then I found a few others that even Delwar hadn't known about, and decided I would never know whether I had ever found them all. So I moved the headquarters, and I turned the old buildings into the administrative center for our latest ventures, and they're guarded by DomSec."

"That showed a great deal of initiative, Carlina, especially since you were relying on my good faith."

"Now that you're back, Shaik, you could call a meeting, but, you recall, under El Lido law the meeting would have to be held in headquarters unless you could get a two-thirds vote, and to do that you and I would have to agree."

"That is true, and I might consider that." Gerswin smiled. "How is Ferinay?"

"Poor Ferinay. He suffered a second and rather unfortunate stroke last month, and the doctors say he will never be quite the same again."

"You have your own successor?"

"I don't plan on leaving in the near future, particularly since we have just landed the armor contracts for the Ministry of Domestic Security. They helped me with the design of our new headquarters. Did you know that?"

"I can't say I'm particularly surprised. How did you get around the rule prohibiting contracts with police and armed forces?"

"What provision was that?"

"I think I understand," Gerswin responded. "And, of course, they believe that the Shaik Corso who founded CE, Limited, might be a fiction, or should remain a silent partner."

"You do indeed understand. Perhaps a slight improvement in the reported profits might encourage that?"

"Might that have something to do with the fact that you are having difficulty tracing the origin of my call?"

"Dear Shaik, you are so suspicious."

"Is there anyone else with you, Carlina?"

"Why do you ask?"

"I was hoping for a witness."

"To what?"

"Just a witness, but it would probably be immaterial. ood day, Carlina. Remember that an honest thief ays bought."

"Is that a threat, Shaik?"

"No. I make no threats. Good day."

Gerswin broke the connection, then tapped out an- ther combination and waited as the relay finished the rcuit.

"Rodire and Fergamo." The dark-haired receptionist as plain, but real, and a welcome sight after Carlina. Gerswin smiled at her image. "Shaik Corso for amline Rodire."

"Will he know you?"

"Hope so. I'm his landlord, so to speak."

"You're *that* Shaik Corso? I'm so sorry, but I xpected . . ."

Gerswin laughed, a single bark. "I know, you ex- ected a dark and mysterious stranger who mangled ords and sentences."

"No . . . no . . . ," she protested, apparently unsure hether he was joking or serious.

He smiled. "Don't worry."

"I'll get him."

Hamline Rodire, Senior Partner, appeared on the creen. In spite of his mental picture of Rodire's aging nce he had helped the then-younger attorney found n independent practice, he found it hard not to stare t the eagle-beaked and silver-haired advocate.

"Hamline . . . it's been longer than I thought."

"With you, Shaik, I suspect it always is." The older- ooking man grinned, and Gerswin was reassured by he twinkle in the green eyes and the warmth in the oice. "You never age."

"Are things going well for you?"

"Personally, quite well, although we only get the

required minimum from CE, Limited, since Carlin
consolidated her hold there. Most of that
boilerplate."

"Yes."

"Are you calling about Carlina?"

"May be time for—let's say I need to transfer son
of my holdings—time to place some more local co
trols. A few strings, however."

"Such as?"

"You'll have to vote my proxies when you call th
shareholders' meeting."

"The annual meeting was just two months ago."

"There will be another shortly."

"Carlina has made both her estate and headquarte
into personal fortresses."

"I understand, but you need not worry. After
complete my business, I do not intend to return to
Lido, not for some time, and I need to leave control i
local hands I can trust. I trust your honesty, and yo
will see why."

"You make things sound so mysterious."

"Nothing mysterious at all. Since Carlina insists th
might makes right, I merely intend to point out to he
why that can be a dangerous philosophy." Gerswi
shook his head abruptly. "You still have that estate c
yours?"

"Why . . . yes . . ."

"Still like it as much as when you first purchased it?

"Probably more," laughed the advocate. "You aren
. . . that is . . . I didn't exactly purchase it, you know.

This time, Gerswin shook his head evenly and slow
ly. "Hamline, has Carlina managed to instill distrust a
over this planet?"

"No . . . not exactly . . ."

"Excessive caution, I can see. Is she as well con
nected to the Ministry of Domestic Security as sh
implies?"

"Unfortunately . . . yes."

Gerswin wondered if he ought to write off El Lid

completely, since CE, Limited, had been designed as a
profit venture and since he did not need anything
beyond the proof that the plants did work in wide scale
production. But Hamline and a few others deserved a
chance, if they would take it. He wondered if they
understood the price, really.

"Remember the wonderful time you had with the
windboards? And the place where you met a stranger
who decided El Lido needed an independent advocate?"

"Yes."

"Have lunch there tomorrow. Bring some transfer
orders for CE, Limited, common and preferred stock."

"What—"

Gerswin broke the connection. While his end could
not be traced, he wasn't about to underestimate
Carlina, or Domestic Security. Even so, they would
have had a hard time, since he had tapped into the
system from a reflector satellite he had deployed before
leaving orbit. He doubted that the local technology
existed to tap his beam without some knowledge of the
Caroljoy's location.

He stood up and stretched. Then he sighed before
heading toward the sealed and shielded locker. Dirty
work required dirty weapons.

The man who had been a Commodore bit his lip, but
did not hesitate. Simple graft was bad enough, but to
sell out to a central government with enough control to
publicly name the secret police the Ministry of Domestic Security was beyond redemption.

Removing the two cannisters from their long resting
place in the hold took a few minutes. Setting up the
gear he needed and checking them through the equipment in the hold took nearly an hour. Gerswin left both
objects clamped in place and climbed out of the
ramped three-by-three-meter space that was uninhabi-
table except when the scout was planetside.

He settled back in front of the console.

"Interrogative screen tap status."

"Negative. No energies detected."

"Interrogative satellite scan."

"Negative. No energies detected."

"Code Jam Trap Two. Code Jam Trap Two."

His fingers touched the studs of the keyboard. A though the communications trap program was di played, the trap code kept the AI from understandin the contents of the program.

"Interrogative open channel access. How many di ferent commnet systems can you access simultan ously?"

"Private systems or public nets?"

"Some of each. Try an eight private to two publi ratio."

"Under operating parameters, ten per standard se ond for a maximum of three minutes."

"Stet."

Gerswin set up the modifications he needed, the accessed the official and unofficial maps of Lidora. A he expected, the headquarters of the Ministry of Do mestic Security was clearly marked.

He smiled to himself as he ran the two locato programs for the two cannisters that waited below to b fitted on the launchers of the armed flitter that waite outside in the other side of the hangar bunker tha temporarily housed the *Caroljoy.*

That done, he pocketed the course discs and returne to the sweltering space beneath what had once been th crew room to remove the two long cannisters and t reseal the lockers and the equipment.

After closing the hatch plate, he left the *Caroljoy* an stepped into the cool air of the bunker, air that retaine a trace of the mustiness of a space seldom used. Th lands adjoining Rodire's estate were left unmanaged and Rodire was responsible for insuring that the ta payments were made, that the land was posted, an that would-be settlers and squatters were quietl evicted on a periodic basis.

Wherever possible, Gerswin liked to set up sucl

emote retreats. Usually after five or ten years even the
people who had constructed them had forgotten where
they were. After less than a year, most people had
forgotten their existence, particularly since Gerswin
used them so little and tried to arrive at night and as
quietly as possible.

Two flitters waited on the far side. Gerswin directed
his steps toward the armed and shielded one, not that
there was any obvious external difference between the
two. But with Carlina's allies, he would forsake some
speed for arms and shielding.

He rolled one cannister under the port stub, nearly
under the intake cover, and returned for the second,
which he edged under the starboard stub. Then he
retrieved the tools from the adjoining bay.

His skills were rusty, and all in all it took him nearly
three hours to convert the two missiles and to mount
them to his satisfaction.

He completed the job, returned the tools, resealing
them in their protected containers, and returned the
empty cannisters to the *Caroljoy*. After that, he
climbed into the ship to stretch out and, he hoped, to
sleep until morning.

Sleep there was, and dreams as well, dreams of dark
ships dealing death, and of corvettes with orange
screens failing, and of iceboats disintegrating, and of
landspouts hurling flitters into purpled plains clay.

He shook himself awake once, trying to escape from
the tumbled images of the past, but when he slipped
back into slumber and restlessness, the images reappeared.

Caroljoy, young in the darkness, aging into a white-
haired and fragile duchess as he watched, useless words
caught in his throat. Kiedra, reaching for him and
throwing herself into Lerwin's arms, then aging into
madness with their daughter's death. Young Corwin,
their son, turning gray and disappearing into a cloud of
ashes. And the other devilkids, Lostwin, Glynnis, each
walking down a long dark tunnel away from him,

marching proudly toward certain death as he urged them on.

A man in black smiling as he watched a hellfire flash across an airless moon to flatten a pleasure dome, smiling a smile of contentment, his lips quirking like a dark devil's.

"NO!!!!!!"

He sat up with the sound of his own scream in his ears.

Both his thin undersuit and the sheets on his bunk were soaked.

Slowly the one-time Commodore eased himself of the dampness where he had suffered, and, without a word, stripped off his own damp sleeping clothes, then ripped the sheets from the bunk. He wadded all of the damp articles together in short and savage motions, then took them across the small cabin to the clothes fresher where he unceremoniously stuffed them inside.

Then he stuffed himself into the personal fresher.

After emerging, he donned a uniform brown tunic and trousers, his normal boots and belt. Then he added a few items to the disguised equipment belt.

To settle his thoughts, he fixed a small cup of liftea and alternated sips with a ration cube, trying to refine his approach to Hamline.

He'd picked the Windrop Inn because he knew it was one of the few places where Hamline and whoever shadowed him would have to walk. Neither flitters nor groundcars were permitted in the shoreside blocks of the Bayou Rio.

He sipped the last of the tea and replaced the cup, cleaning up the small mess he had made before returning to the control cabin.

After five minutes spent on completing the exit programming for the *Caroljoy*, he was easing the unarmed flitter from the hangar bunker. He wanted to be early. Quite early, in order to be in place before the opposition.

LXVII

HE MAN WITH salt-and-pepper hair studied the sheet of
ntique paper again, rereading the brief message.

Momentarily, he set it aside and carefully wiped his
orehead, not wanting anything that could trace it back
• him to touch the sheets. He wiped his gloved hands
n a clean towel before picking the sheet back up and
•tting his eyes study the brief message again.

Sire:

Anonymity is not necessarily the refuge of the
coward, but necessary if one must continue serving his Emperor. The rebirth of old myths can
only spell the end of the Empire, yet Eye and the
Eye Corps ignore those myths. They claim it is
done in Your name. Why was Merhlin not traced?
Why could the Eye Corps not discover who stole
Service hellburners? Why does Eye systematically
remove Service officers loyal to the Emperor?
Why have flag officers with early retirements been
killed by so many "accidents" so soon after
retirement, particularly if they opposed Eye and
supported the Emperor? Check on the background of Vice Admiral Thurson, if you can, as
one example.

Folding the single sheet into an equally ancient
nvelope, he stood and slipped the envelope inside his
unic.

With the hour of open Court approaching, he coul place the missive in the Emperor's hand with no on the wiser, and should the new Emperor turn it to Eye even that functionary would have difficulty tracing th envelope from more than half a thousand of the Em pire's peers who would have had such an opportunity

In any case, the risk was no worse than alread existed, not with Eye already trying to isolate the youn; Emperor.

The junior peer who had once been a senior office shrugged. Unless His Majesty Ryrce the Quiet silentl removed Eye, his days and the Emperor's were proba bly numbered.

Cling.

He stood and released the hold on the portal.

An older man, slender and dark-haired for all that h was a decade or two older than the man he visited stepped into the small antechamber.

"Ready to visit His Majesty, Selern?"

"As ready as I'll ever be, Calendra." He debate telling the other about his letter, then decided agains it. One could never be too careful, especially since Ey had to be one of the peers normally in New Augusta.

"Let us hope he is more outgoing than on the las open Court."

"Extroversion does not necessarily make an Em peror."

"What else does he have?" asked Calendra wryly.

Selern shrugged. "Too soon to tell."

"You may be right."

Selern followed Calendra through the portal, and th two walked side by side toward the Grand Thron Room.

LXVIII

HAMLINE RODIRE WIPED his forehead again.

"You all right, squire?" asked the pilot.

"For some reason, I'm warm today, Jorio. Just warm."

"You are sure you are well?"

"I am fine, just fine," lied Hamline. More than ten years ago, it had seemed so easy to take on the whole planet. Now Corso was back, looking as young as ever, those hawk-yellow eyes demanding allegiance and—harder to deny—justice, and it wasn't quite so easy.

"Anyone trailing us?" The fact that he could ask the question without raising Jorio's suspicions about the reason would have embarrassed him a decade earlier.

"Not close, if they are."

Rodire leaned back in the wide rear seat, tried to ignore the whisper of the wind past the canopy as the litter sped toward Bayou Rio, tried to push away the glimpse of sadness he had glimpsed behind Corso's eyes, the sadness that made Rodire feel decades younger than the wealthy Shaik.

Where Corso had come from, Rodire wasn't sure, though he had strong Imperial connections of some sort. Nor was the source of his wealth known, only that he had set up CE, Limited, with a unique biological process, one that allowed production of a cheap nonpolluting organic thread substitute for standard synthetic hydrocarbons and silicons.

From that, CE, Limited, had branched into a number of other products, including most recently battle and stun vests for the planetary police, since Carlina had discovered that the thread produced by the CE proprietary hothouse "plants" could be interwoven with synsteel threads to produce a cheaper, lightweight, and effective body armor.

In return, the Ministry of Domestic Security had employed some of its agents to track down employees who had taken cuttings of the plants to insure that the company remained the sole supplier of the special organic thread.

Rodire frowned as he recalled the developments. He had not remembered Corso ever worrying about employees who tried to grow their own plants. Rodire had mentioned it once, and Corso had laughed it off by pointing out that even a garden full of the plants would only support a family and that most people didn't want to work that hard merely to get thread.

"We're nearly there, squire."

"Fine, Jorio. Fine. Just wait for me, please."

The pilot set the flitter down and eased it toward the left edge of the paved square on the gentlest of ground cushions.

The rear door popped open, and Rodire let his stiff frame carry him down the steps. He glanced around to get his bearings. It had been years, but from what he recalled, the inn should be off to his left.

He turned, taking a firmer grip on the case with the documents within.

"I beg your pardon, ser."

Hamline's head shot up at the intrusion, ready to snap until he saw the brown uniform of Domestic Security.

"Yes, officer?"

"I suggest you return to your flitter, ser. This area has been cordoned off . . . Hamline . . . And please try not to react too strongly, old friend."

Rodire choked down a response, and shot a glance at

e officer, recognizing, with a chill, the same hawk-
llow eyes, realizing that the uniform was not quite
andard.

"Yes, Officer Corso, I'll do . . . as you say." He
anaged to drag the words out.

Rodire turned back toward the flitter, which, he
ted absently, Jorio had not shut down. The "securi-
" man followed.

"What is the matter, squire?" Jorio peered from the
ckpit.

"Nothing, except the officer has indicated that this
ea has been closed. We'll have to . . ." Rodire looked
ck at Corso.

"Why don't you return to your estate?"

". . . go on out to the country place. . . ."

"But, squire . . ."

Rodire reentered the cabin, and, while surprised that
orso followed, was more surprised when the Shaik
ted a stunner.

Thrumm!

Clank!

Corso yanked the unconscious pilot from his seat,
cking aside the dart pistol that had not been fired by
rio, and set the body on the cabin floor before settling
mself behind the controls.

"Let's see . . ."

Rodire watched, half-numb, as Corso's hands played
ver the controls, as the steps retracted, as the cabin
oor closed, and as the pilot's canopy snapped into
ace.

Click. Snap.

"There's probably another homer planted some-
here, Hamline, but we'll have to see. They can't
bject if you merely go home. Besides, they don't
nction well at low levels. Carlina's friends are out in
rce, although they didn't close off the pad. That was a
berty that I took. Funny . . . no one even protested,
nd that's not a good sign."

The attorney sank into his padded seat, not looking

at his own pilot, who he had never dreamed would ha
been armed.

"I'm not sure I understand."

"You do. Or you will. You will. Got those form
Fine. Make out the transfer orders to transfer thir
percent of the common stock from me to you."

"Thirty percent? Thirty percent?"

"Right. Gives you working control and no excuse
You still have twenty-one percent, I assume. How mud
does Carlina control?"

Rodire nodded to Corso's first question.

"Yes or no? How much? I can't look at the moment

"Yes," rasped Rodire. "She controls around for
percent. Don't know what she owns. Worked under th
rules that off-planet proxies are controlled by th
administrator."

"That will end. Fill out the forms. Leave the ce
numbers blank. We can fill those in later, when I gi
you the actual share certs."

Rodire opened the case, grasped it to keep fro
spilling the contents as the flitter banked.

"Just another few minutes . . ."

"Until what?" asked Rodire. His voice sounde
hoarse.

"Until we're where we need to be."

The advocate listened to the higher roar of the win
and sharper pitch of the turbines. A glance outside tol
him that Corso had the flitter racing scarcely above th
trees.

"Isn't this dangerous?"

"Not so dangerous as getting shot down, or trackir
. . . some of the wilder storms I've been through."

Rodire forced himself to try to relax, but found h
arms gripping the armrest on the right and the sea
cushion on the left.

The whine began to drop. The wind's whist
dropped. The advocate felt his stomach rise into h
throat before dropping back into place. He squinted a
the summer light was replaced with dimness. Th
turbines quit.

"You can fly this, can't you?"

Rodire looked up to see Corso standing over him.

"Yes . . . of course . . . still do sometimes."

"Good. When I'm done, you'll have to fly yourself to your estate. Not that it's far. I assume you know where we are."

"I can guess."

"Let's go."

Rodire stumbled out onto the bare tarmac. His eyes caught sight of an armed flitter across the bay, and another larger and blacker shape on which his eyes had trouble focusing. Rather than force his eyes to make out the black ship, since Corso was leading him there in any case, he turned to take another look at the flitter.

His eyes widened as he saw the two missiles mounted under the wing stubs.

"Corso . . . where . . . those are missiles . . . that . . . ?"

"Oh, yes . . . those. We should get to that shortly."

Rodire scratched his shoulder absently and followed the Shaik up the ramp into the shadowy ship. The space inside was smaller than he had anticipated, with only a small control room, and a crew room not much larger, where Corso sat him in a small collapsible chair.

"Will these take care of it from my point of view?" Corso thrust a file at him.

Rodire took the file. Inside were sets of the original share certs, all authenticated by the Imperial Bank and signed over. Only the transferee space was blank.

"How did you get that? They're not supposed to do that."

"It's legitimate, believe."

"I believe you." Rodire shook his head. "That's more than enough. But what do you want me to do?"

"They're yours. Thirty percent of the common stock, as the proxies for my remaining small interest."

The advocate wiped his forehead, once, twice. "For . . . ?"

"Who else?" Corso caught his lower lip with his teeth, then let go. "Once Carlina ceases to be a factor, you need to be Chief Operating Officer, at least long enough to get someone honest to run CE. That's what I want, and what El Lido needs. Get away from dealing with the government unless it's impossible not to. And destroy the company, plants and all, if you have to take orders from Domestic Security."

"But the Ministry of Security . . ."

"I'll make them leave you alone."

Corso turned away toward the wall of blanked screens and indicators.

"Commence Jam Trap Two. Commence Jam Trap Two."

"Commencing Jam Trap Two."

The coldly feminine voice that answered chilled Rodire to the bone. He wondered again who Corso really was, wondered how he had gotten involved. Rodire looked down at the fortune in his hands, then up at the slender man facing the controls.

Corso swung back to Rodire.

"Hamline. You have everything. Time for you to get to your estate. Sit tight. Sit tight for at least twenty-four hours. Don't leave your estate. Your town house is on the north side of Lidora, is it not?"

The attorney nodded.

"Call your children—you didn't remarry, I assume —and have them flit out within the next two hours. Call it a personal crisis, but get them here.

"Don't ask me why. Just do it. Hope all goes well, but the future is more important than a few people, even those I like, and that also includes you and me."

Corso barked a single, hard, laughing sound that expressed neither humor nor relief.

"Now . . . go. I'll open the bay port from here. Take the folder and your case."

Rodire mechanically took the folder and put it in his case, the case he had not even realized that Corso had brought from his flitter. He stood, and his steps carried him from the crew room and through the lock, down the ramp, and back to his own flitter.

LXIX

Gerswin shook his head sadly as Rodire's flitter wobbled out through the open hangar bay.

"Hope he makes it."

Half the hope was for Rodire. The other half was for CE, Limited, and the people of El Lido. One way or nother, one Shaik Corso would be a quiet persona non rata for a number of years, assuming his plans worked ut.

He redirected his attention to the AI.

"Interrogative status of trap jam."

"Code Trap Jam sustained for four minutes forty econds. Initial links verified at 2,645."

"With a standard repeat factor, how long before the lanetary commnet freezes?"

"Probe thrusts indicate system approaching eighty ercent of capacity. Estimate capacity in twelve mintes."

Gerswin nodded.

The trap program was designed to link every possible eceiver and fax outlet and to keep the connection open nd unbroken. As a self-replicating program, the longer he system remained operational, the farther the programs spread. The end result would be the total paralyis of all public communications systems. The odds vere that the unclassified military and security systems vould also be paralyzed because some of the terminals nd screens in government offices would be employed or both systems. The open transmit links would also

create an enormous power drain on the planeta
system, enough to grind some segments of the planet
a total halt.

The last feature of the trap program was that, if a
terminal was not purged of the program, the san
chain could start all over again once power was r
stored, although without the massive input used l
Gerswin, the commercial systems and the governmer
could eventually confine the damage and regain co
trol.

The program worked. The remaining questions we
how completely and for how long.

Gerswin touched the *Caroljoy*'s controls, made son
adjustments, and stood, surveying the cabin. Still wea
ing the pseudo-DomSec uniform, he left the shi
walking down the ramp without watching the loc
close behind him as he hurried toward the arme
flitter.

The concealed bay doors opened as he went throug
the checklist, and, within minutes, he was airborne. H
kept the flitter just above treetop height, and shifted h
communications monitors to the military frequencie
since the civilian frequencies were already dead.

"Gnasher two . . . vector to homestash . . ."

"Negative, Gnasher two. Operating emergenc
power. Beyond trace range . . ."

"OPNET Emergency. OPNET Emergency! Clear thi
frequency! Clear this frequency."

Gerswin watched, scanned the board, and waited a
the flitter skimmed the trees on its way toward Lidor;
roughly fifty kilometers westward. No other transmi:
sions sounded except for a series of high-pitche
squeaks, and he shifted frequencies again when h
realized that the one he had monitored was now bein
used for data transmission.

"Far Cry, negative your last . . . negative you
last . . ."

"Thunder one, arrived DomSec. Thunder two, pro
vide cover."

Gerswin nodded. So far so good. The DomSec boys
ren't used to being under siege. He checked the
ward farscreens, but outside of the background
ergy levels, could detect nothing specific.

"EMERGENCY!"

"SSSSKKKKRRRR . . . !EMERGENCY . . . Due
failure of the communications network and wide-
read power difficulties, the Premier and the Ministry
Domestic Security have declared a planetary emer-
ncy. Repeat, a planetary emergency. All unautho-
ed flitters and other aircraft have fifteen standard
nutes to land. All civilian craft are immediately
ohibited in the Lidora capitol area. Any aircraft in
: capitol area will be forced down or destroyed. I say
ain . . ."

Gerswin edged the thrusters back from full power.
'd reach Lidora, or the point he needed to reach
tside Lidora, within minutes, and there was no need
waste the power yet.

In some respects, he wished he could have done the
 from the *Caroljoy*, but had she been modified to
rry weapons, even he would have been unable to
tain certification, and he needed that certification to
;it New Augusta and the more developed systems
at actually inspected and guarded incoming ships.

In any case, to have made sure of the targets he
ould have had to drop below orbital defenses, which
:ated the same problem he faced now—namely, how
 keep clear of the mess he was about to create. The
her advantage of using the flitter was that both the El
do government and the Impies would have to investi-
te local sources.

Gerswin checked the course line against the targets.
Taking his right hand off the thrusters momentarily,
 wiped his forehead with the back of his sleeve. The
omSec uniform was hotter than he would have pre-
red.

Cling!

The farscreen alarm sounded, and the pilot checked

both the screen and the horizon at two o'clock. A bla
dot of increasing size was aimed toward him.

His scan showed that the forest beneath was thinn
and the terrain becoming hillier as it gradually r
toward the eroded plateau on which the center
Lidora was built. Gerswin had chosen his course
bound over the Great Parkland, hoping to minim
the chance of groundfire. At a time when the planet:
communications and power networks seemed une
attack, he doubted that the Ministry of Domes
Security would be deploying large numbers to cover t
parks.

"Flitter over the Parkland! Flitter over the Parklai
Reverse heading. Reverse heading."

Gerswin debated whether to answer, finally touchi
the comm stud.

"Gnasher four, returning DomSec. I say aga
Gnasher four, returning DomSec."

"That's negative, four. That is negative. Divert
return homestash. Divert or return homestash."

"Understand and will comply. Diverting. Dive
ing."

Before he moved the stick, Gerswin touched t
release button for the first missile. Next, he trigger
the combat harness, simultaneously rolling in towa
the oncoming patrol and pushing the thrusters arou
the forward detent into full combat thrust.

The dark dot swelled into a lightly armed poli
flitter.

"Gnasher four . . . change course . . . FIRE C
THE SUMBITCH!!!"

Gerswin dropped the nose, then eased the stick le
then back into his lap, coming up over the police flitt
At the last instant he cut power, dropped his own no
and triggered the heavy stunner at point blank ran
into the police flitter's canopy.

Thrrrimmmmm!

He did not watch the DomSec flitter spin downwai
pilots and electronics hopelessly dead.

"Unidentified combat flitter, bearing two seven zero. reflit two, he's yours. Fireflit two, I repeat. Fireflit /o, range and destroy. Range and destroy."

Gerswin smiled grimly. The Ministry of Domestic curity certainly wasn't prepared for any real resist- ace. Not that he had expected it would be. Unfortu- tely for the people.

Scanning the farscreens quickly, he recentered the tter for the last few moments to provide the steady unch platform he needed. Then he touched the sec- d release stud.

With the faint lurch of the departing missile, he nked hard left and jammed the thrusters to full wer as he turned tail eastward back across the Great arkland, the whine of the thrusters screaming full tch.

He checked the distance readout and the time. oughly another two minutes before the first missile ached target. By then his separation would be more an thirty kays. Not wonderful, but enough that the tter would be beyond the worst of the shock wave.

He dropped the flitter until it skimmed scarcely eters above the trees, then scanned the clock again.

Less than a minute.

"Two incoming released . . . interrogative defenses. TERROGATIVE DEFENSES!"

"Lasers not up. DomSec Control . . . be roughly ten ore . . ."

"That's not—"

Ssssssssssssssssssssss!

The screaming hiss blocked all transmissions.

Gerswin flinched in spite of his training and experi- nce as a second sun flared behind him. He did not are look back, trying to coax more power from the hrusters as he waited for the second blast, the one argeted for the CE, Limited, headquarters.

Ssssssssssssssssssssss!

Before the first blast had faded, the second flared, hough it had been the first launched.

Gerswin kept his eyes on the controls, mechanical
checking the indicators as the armed flitter screeche
toward his base, listening to what scattered transmi
sions he could pick up.

"Gnasher two . . . tachead . . . repeat tachead .
DomSec HQ . . . other capitol target . . ."

"CLEAR THIS FREQUENCY! CLEAR THIS FR
QUENCY FOR EMERGENCY USE!"

". . . terrorist attack on Lidora . . . nuclear wea
ons . . ."

"Lucifer . . . fallen . . ."

The flitter bucked as the attenuated shock wav
struck.

Gerswin eased the nose back up as the flitter almo
dipped into the trees, let the craft climb a few mete
higher to keep from hitting the trees with the ne
wave.

"Can you read . . . Gnasher one? Can you read . .

"CLEAR THIS FREQUENCY! CLEAR THIS FRE
QUENCY!!"

". . . casualties . . . thousands . . . small nuclear d
vice . . . air launched . . . near surface impact . . ."

". . . the evil . . . upon is . . . upon our souls. .
repent . . . repent . . ."

Crmppppp!

The nose flipped up thirty degrees with the secon
shock wave. Gerswin let the flitter ride and eased
down, checking the heading, and beginning a gent
bank toward the north.

". . . read this . . . homestash . . ."

". . . repent you of your sins . . . Lucifer . . ."

"CLEAR THIS FREQUENCY!! CLEAR THI
FREQUENCY!!!"

Gerswin adjusted his course as he brought the flitte
level, tapping out the access codes on the transponde
to open the hangar bunker.

"Another flitter from the east approaching." Th
cool tones of the AI chimed in on the private overrid

"Interrogative ETA."

"Three plus after your arrival."

"Stet."

Instead of powering down for a conventional approach, Gerswin left full power on.

At two kays out, he dropped the thrusters to nearly idle, raised the nose, and bled the speed back to thirty kays. Just before the flitter started to fall like a headsman's ax, he added full power, nose up, and dropped though a left-hand turn, mushing to a complete stop in the hidden bay.

He snapped off power, opened the canopy, and unstrapped himself in a single motion. As soon as the canopy was retracted enough, he vaulted clear and sprinted toward the *Caroljoy*.

He made it inside, instants to spare, as Hamline Rodire's now battered flitter wobbled inside and nushed into the armed flitter.

"Screens!"

"Screens on."

"Begin departure power up."

"Beginning departure power up."

Gerswin watched the silver-haired attorney struggle out of the safety webbing that had triggered on his anding/impact. Rodire fought his way free and stumbled toward the *Caroljoy*. In his right hand was a pistol-shaped object.

Gerswin pulled a long-barreled stunner from beside the console.

"Drop screens."

"Dropping screens."

Gerswin dashed for the lock and the ramp.

"You were looking for me, Hamline?"

"I . . . am . . . looking . . . for . . . you . . . you . . . iller . . . Corso . . . ," panted the advocate, starting to ring up the weapon.

Thrummm!

The stunner bolt sizzled past the older looking man's houlder.

"Drop it, Hamline. Now!"

". . . never listen . . ."

Thrummm!

Clank!

Rodire clutched his numb right arm with his left, then let go and knelt to scoop up the fallen laser with his left hand.

Thrumm!

Gerswin watched him drop before he moved toward the half-conscious man.

An image crossed his mind, of another man, retching out his guts at the results of a hellburner blast. Of a man going into single combat to avoid unnecessary casualties to a potential enemy.

Gerswin swallowed, once, twice, as he pushed the mental images away and moved toward the fallen attorney.

LXX

RODIRE BLINKED, SQUINTING, although the light around him was dim.

"You awake?"

The voice was familiar. Then he remembered. Corso! The demon he had thought was merely a man! The man who had launched nuclear weapons into the capitol! When Lisa had been downtown . . . He tried to lurch toward Corso but could not lift himself off the bunk.

"I see you are."

"You are a killer, Shaik. Nothing but a killer."

"Admit to being a killer. But not just a killer. Never said this would be easy." Corso laughed once, the same annoying bark that was not a laugh. "You're as much to blame as I am."

"Me! I didn't unleash Lucifer. I didn't kill ten thousand innocents! You did! Not me! You!"

Corso sighed, and his shoulders dropped. "You really don't understand, do you?"

Rodire wanted to scream. Instead, he frowned. What was there to understand?

"Farscreen shows energy concentrations," interrupted the cool voice that had chilled Rodire before. "Standard heavy search pattern."

"Interrogative time before reaching detection range."

"Estimate fifteen standard minutes, plus or minus five."

"Stet. Commence checklist. Hold at prelift. Hold at prelift for voice command for lift-off."

"Understand checklist to prelift. Commencing immediately."

"Commence checklist at full-power status."

"Full-power status. Commencing checklist."

"Stet."

Rodire felt as though the Shaik were living in a different universe, and squinted, trying to let the younger man's words penetrate, trying to understand why Corso would say that he, Rodire, didn't understand.

"Hamline. Not enough time to explain. I'll dump what I can. Fast. Hope you can understand. Then I'm throwing you out."

As he talked, Corso had approached the bunk and touched something Rodire could not see. The harness released and retracted away from the attorney.

"Don't move. You're going to be dizzy if you move your head quickly, and you can't afford to pass out. Now. Where to start? All right." Corso's words were quick, more clipped than usual, and burst out in short groups. "You live on a repressive planet. Law controlled by a few firms. Food by a few family enterprises. Bureaucracy by a few others. People don't have much freedom to change. Personal freedom adequate, until Carlina started linking with DomSec. Declining now. Probably get worse, possible police state.

"Not enough education for most people to resist. Change has to come from the top, to begin with. People like you.

"Thought you might help. Thought a new business, built on new lines might start people thinking. It did, except Carlina, her type, decided CE was another route into the standard oligarchy. You let her do it, when you could have stopped her. Could have sent a message to me.

"Could have set up another administrator strong enough to stop her. Maybe I expected too much of you. You're a product of your culture. Unable to see beyond the patterns."

"But . . . my family . . . ," protested Rodire. Didn't the man understand? Carlina had no children, no heirs, no hostages to fortune.

"The future of your family was lost the moment you put their immediate comfort above your ideals, Hamline. So were you. I didn't know. Should have. My fault. Precedent here is terrible."

"Precedent? Is that all you think about?"

"Precedent is everything in your culture. Carlina' precedent means that everything new, everything that offers hope, can be turned into another instrument of repression. How could anyone ignore that? But you did. We'll both pay."

"ETA ten minutes, plus or minus four," added the cool voice from the control room.

"Get up. Slowly," commanded the hawk-eyed man. "You have to survive. For your remaining children. Not for them, for the people you betrayed once already."

"Betrayed? Who betrayed whom?"

"Hamline, would you please use your brains?" Corso's hard voice seemed tired. "You betrayed them when you refused to stand up to Carlina. You betrayed hem again when you failed to notify me. You betrayed them a third time when you let her join forces with the secret police. You put your immediate family and comfort above the needs and rights of all the people. Don't talk about betrayal to me.

"So what did I do? I destroyed—crudely, but time was short—both the top of DomSec and CE, Limited. Shows that the system can be brought down. That might makes right doesn't always triumph, or at least, that there is a greater might to fear. Gives you an opening. That's all. The rest is up to you. Now get moving."

"Where?" Rodire slid to his shaky feet.

"Home. As soon as you get out of the scout, head for the far bay. Remember? Tunnel there. Comes out about a hundred meters from your estate. Take it and move. DomSec will blast anything in the air and around here, you included. Turn this into rubble."

Rodire stumbled as he entered the lock. "But what do I do?"

"What you should have done in the first place. You run the damned company. You treat the people like people. Not serfs. If you don't, you and your descendants will suffer. I mean *suffer*! Now get down the ramp. I'm lifting. If you're around when I power out, you'll be fried. Wasted too much time talking."

Rodire fell on the hard pavement as the ramp retracted. He staggered to his feet as he heard the lock door clank shut, and lurched toward the far bay and the tunnel.

Wheeeeeeee.

The whine spurred his lurch into a shambling trot.

When he finally reached the oval portal, he rested against it momentarily before hauling himself upright to survey the mechanism.

No access plates. No levers, and only a small wheel. He tried it. It spun easily clockwise, and the portal began to open. He peered inside, where the lighting was dim, but adequate.

Whhheeeeeeeeeeee!

Staggering inside, he took a step before turning back and spinning the other wheel, the one on the tunnel wall. The portal closed smoothly, cutting off the sound.

As he remembered what Corso had said about the security forces, he trotted raggedly down the tunnel, gasping with each step.

After fifty meters he slowed to a walk, his legs cramping with the aftereffects of the stun jolts his body had taken, but he kept putting one foot in front of the other, one in front of the other. Underfoot, the flooring began to vibrate, first lightly, then enough to make his steps feel unsteady.

As quickly as it had come, the vibration halted.

Rodire kept walking, but looked back over his shoulder. He could no longer see the tunnel port where he had started. In front of him, the smooth-walled tunnel began to slope upward, and a dark splotch appeared ahead in the faint ring of light that the walls reflected into the distance before him.

Even though he was walking slowly, he was still panting.

Crump. Crump.

The muffled concussion shook the tunnel, hard enough to make him stagger, but he continued to move forward toward the exit portal.

Crump.

Reaching out with his right hand and touching the smooth plasteel of the wall, he steadied himself, then plodded upward.

Whhhirrrr. Crump!

The tunnel no longer seemed to stretch forever, but only a few yards toward a round black doorway of some sort.

He stopped and took two deep breaths.

Crump!

The floor beneath vibrated, and he lurched forward.

Finally his right hand touched cold metal, and he halted, trying to catch his breath, hoping that the wrenching cramps in his calves would ease.

He waited, wondering if the explosions would continue.

Crump!

He began to spin the wheel, watching carefully through the ever-widening slit, and listening.

Stepping into a moldy cellar, he frowned as he looked up to discover that just the foundation remained of whatever structure had once stood above him. Then he glanced back at the still open portal, which was beginning to close itself, to see how the vines had been planted to conceal the relative newness of the tunnel exit. There was no exterior wheel to open the portal, and the exposed portal looked no different from the rest of the weathered foundation.

Rodire dragged himself toward the overgrown ramp that led to the ground level of the forest.

Wheeeeeee.

At the sound of the eastbound flitter, he ducked, then straightened. No one, assuming they could scan under the old and gnarled trees that covered this end of Corso's lands, was going to bother with a tired old man on foot.

Once out of the foundation, Rodire could see enough through the wide-spaced and massive trunks to get his bearings. His own lands lay less than a half a kilo ahead.

He limped forward.

Wheeeeee!

Crump!

Rodire shook his head. The security forces were late. Everyone was always late. He'd been late. Corso had been late, and now the remainder of the DomSecs were late, as if more force could undo what had already been done.

He shrugged as he plodded toward the immaculate white stone wall that marked his estate. He could see Eduard and some of the staff standing higher on the upper lawn peering toward the column of smoke behind him where he knew the flitters were still circling

He supposed he had some work to do. He shrugge
again. Not doing it wouldn't bring back Lisa. If Cors
didn't like the way he ran CE, then Corso could have
any way he wanted. Rodire wouldn't block him
Carlina had, and what was left?

He refused to think about what might happen if th
terrible Shaik were thwarted a second time. "You wi
suffer . . ." That had been clear.

Rodire sighed. No walls and fortresses for him. H
might survive, and he might not, but one experience i
watching Corso had been enough. One trip throug
hidden tunnels had been enough. And one daughte
lost because he had not done what he had promised to
stranger was quite enough. Quite enough.

Corso might be the devil himself, but he kept hi
word. Both ways. And few enough did that.

The trees thinned as he neared the white stone wall

Eduard caught sight of his father and began runnin
down to the wall.

Rodire smiled at the sight of the long-legged teenage
covering the bluish grass more in leaps than in strides

He waved, and his son waved back.

LXXI

As RODIRE STUMBLED down the ramp, Gerswir
launched himself at the control couch, throwing the
harness straps around himself even before he settlec
fully into position.

"Retract power connections."

"Power connections retracted."

"Retract ramp, and seal for lift-off."

"Ramp has been retracted, and locks are sealed. Ship is fully self-contained."

"Interrogative power status."

"Power status is point nine nine plus."

As he spoke to the AI, Gerswin tapped out the Omega code on the comm link to the nerve center of the facility he was about to leave. Shortly, hopefully well after he had lifted clear, the inside of the hangar bunker would self-immolate in a raging inferno, leaving no trace of its history or recent usage. With the DomSecs likely to pinpoint his base of operations . . . he shook his head.

Nothing had gone exactly as planned. Now —another perfectly good retreat, another perfectly good source of revenue, both lost. Lost because . . .

He could dwell on that later, assuming there was a later. His eyes scanned the data and representational screens, checking the reported positions and projected search patterns of the approaching DomSec flitters.

His fingers continued through the lift-off checks as he studied the screens and as he spoke again.

"Get the DomSecs on audio. Local tactical."

"Local tactical on audio," the AI repeated without inflection.

A hissing began as the AI tried to raise the signals to audibility without the direct link to the facility antenna array.

"Fareach two . . . negative on energy flows . . ."

". . . port, three zero. Vector two six zero . . ."

". . . Thunder three. Say again . . . three . . ."

". . . casualties estimated at three zero thousand . . . three zero thousand . . ."

The man in the counterfeit Lidoran DomSec uniform tightened his lips, wiped his damp forehead, and touched the control keys once more, watching the screens to ensure that the departure gates were fully retracted and clear of obstructions.

"Target contact, Beta class flitter, at ten kays, bearing zero eight zero," the AI's cool voice interjected, overriding the Lidoran transmissions momentarily.

"Thanks."

Gerswin's fingers touched the last key on the board prior to the lift-off sequence, and the whining that signified full power-up began to build.

"Going to be a *full* power lift," he remarked to no one in particular.

"Acknowledging full power lift," the AI answered his remark that needed no answering.

The *Caroljoy* edged from the center of the hangar into position before the tunnel.

Whhhhheeeeeeeeeeeeeee!

The scout slipped up the tunnel and burst through the carefully maintained gap in the trees, a black streak screaming like lightning back toward the heavens from which it had struck.

". . . target at two six five. Target at two six five . . . Tentatively identified as deep space craft."

"Gnasher two, cleared to attack. Cleared to attack."

Gerswin had already dismissed the flitters. Most atmospherics didn't carry high acceleration missiles, nor missiles with any range. Even if the DomSec flitters had, unless they had launched those the moment they had acquired the *Caroljoy* on their screens, it would have been impossible for them to have caught any scout on a full power departure.

The real problem would lie with orbit control, and whether there were system patrollers close at hand.

His departure was programmed for atmospheric envelope exit on the opposite side of El Lido from orbit control. While the DomSecs could speculate, they couldn't be absolutely certain until he actually broke orbit.

"Switch to orbit control frequencies."

"Orbit control on audio."

Gerswin continued to scan the screens, checking the ever increasing gap between the *Caroljoy* and the

DomSec patrols, noting how the security flitters began to use their shorter range missiles on the recently vacated retreat.

The *Caroljoy*'s auxiliary screen showed the energy concentrations around the facility as the DomSecs turned their thwarted fury on the concealed hangar-bunker already far behind and below.

"Facility self-destruct has commenced," the AI noted.

Gerswin nodded at the announcement. Shortly, between the destruct thermals and the DomSec bombardment, there would be nothing left but fused and broken metal, stone, and ceramics, over which the DomSecs could pour to their hearts' content.

"Orbit control, this is Thunder three. Interrogative intercept on outbound target. Interrogative intercept."

Instinctively, Gerswin checked his position. The *Caroljoy* was almost clear of the envelope, and, as he had plotted, in position with the planet between him and orbit control.

"Thunder three, outbound target screened from orbit control. Projected course beyond range of either orbit control or patrollers on station."

By now the rear screen showed an El Lido whose image was rapidly becoming a disc that would fill less than the entire rear screen.

Monitoring the scout's power status, Gerswin shook his head. Eighty percent, down twenty percent just for lift-off. No wonder he had gotten clear so quickly. But power was expensive, even on Aswan, if one considered the acquisition costs, and speed was paid in power terms.

Then, everything about El Lido had been expensive, he reflected as he returned his attention to the representational screen, which now displayed the entire system, including El Lido and its orbit control.

Two winking red dots along the general course line to system exit corridor one indicated the two on-station system patrollers.

Gerswin had already sent the *Caroljoy* hurtling along a different course—the one to the less favored exit point. The second corridor, because the system's irregular gas corona extended farther on one side of the system, required more travel time in-system before a ship could reach space clear enough for a jumpshift.

He calculated, hands hovering above the console. Roughly, at his present screamingly uneconomical acceleration, he could have reached the jump point along corridor one in two hours.

Worrying at his lip with his teeth, he checked the screens again.

"Time to jump?"

"Three hours, plus or minus point five."

The farscreens were clear, except for the distant patrollers, not surprisingly, since jumpship travel anywhere was scarce, and to El Lido, isolated as it was, even scarcer.

The red lights of the patrollers, flashing against the darkness of the representational screen, seemed almost accusing.

"Accusing about what?"

"Inquiry imprecise. Please clarify," requested the AI.

"Disregard," snapped the once-upon-a-time Commodore.

What had gone wrong? Or had anything?

The biologics would continue to be produced, and Hamline would doubtless exert some effort to improve social conditions. And thirty thousand casualties represented . . . what? An initial payment?

"Are you still asking too much of people?" he muttered, not letting his eyes leave the screens.

"Question represents a value judgment. Without further data, no answer is possible." The AI's cool feminine tone was like ice down his spine.

Whose values? Whose judgments? He had killed or injured thirty thousand people, some theoretically innocent, because he felt it necessary, because he felt his

wn creation had been perverted to serve an already
oo-repressive government. Did he have that right?

"You took that right the day you decided to restore
Old Earth."

Did that make him right?

He shook his head. Right was a value judgment, as
he AI had said so coldly.

Had he been too hard on Rodire? Had he expected
oo much of the young idealist when he and his
children had grown older? Did the children make that
much difference?

*Corson, what would you have been like, had we shared
a life? Would you have turned me, too? Turned me from
fire and ice?*

He pushed that thought away from the trails down
which it had led him too many times before.

"Time to jump?"

"Three hours, plus or minus point two."

Why did people let themselves be ruled so easily?
Why did they let others enslave them? Why didn't they
fight?

"Why didn't they fight?"

"Question imprecise. Please reformulate."

The businessman who was an idealist with a vision
and who had been a Commodore did not rephrase his
question. Instead he stood up and turned away, pacing
from the cramped control room into the equally small,
but less cluttered, crew room.

Finding the techniques to reclaim his home had
proved difficult enough, and the refining and producing
was even more difficult. Plus, refinement and production required resources and funding, and while obtaining both had been the technically easiest part, it had
been by far the most time-consuming, and had created
the most problems. But without the resources to bank-
roll the development and the field testing and the
production, all the Foundation's research products
would be worthless.

Then, still unknown, was the question of the Empire.

While it would certainly continue to passively oppos any wide-scale adoption of the techniques the Founda tion was developing, how soon would the forces ma shaling against Gerswin be able to turn the Empir against him.

He had Lyr to thank, time and time again, fo turning the inquiries and blunting the attacks, but Ly and her allies could not hold back the tide forever.

He shook his head. One thing in his favor was tha his opponents did not know where they stood. No would they for years to come, though Gerswin coul sense it now. And his own stupidity in using tacheads Thirty thousand innocents because he hated tyrann and personal greed. Thirty thousand innocents becaus he had held others to his standards. He shook his head Better to write off an enterprise, or to wait until no on suspected he could return. Brute force wasn't th answer. Yet, knowing better, he had turned to it.

He shook his head once more.

"You'd better hope it's considered an isolated case You'd better hope."

He walked back toward the controls, thinking abou Rodire, and about the man's family.

Corson, where are you? Beyond? Never? Martin . . .

But Martin he had not known, even briefly, onl known about when there was nothing he could hav done.

He reseated himself at the control couch, tilted now into a standard seat, and tried to refocus his thought: on his next operations.

He couldn't afford another mistake like El Lido. No for himself, or Lyr, or Martin, or the people involved

Not ever.

LXXII

THE GOLD STARBURST in the center of the console flared.

The man known as Eye stared at the golden light, which remained burning brightly. Behind his shadow mask his mouth nearly dropped open.

The Emperor's call—but why?

He frowned, wondering whether he should answer the almost mythical summons, still sitting before the console.

Three red lights blipped into place on the screen readouts, and his eyes widened.

He shook his head. Apparently the old procedures still held. All his defense screens were down.

What was it that Thurson had said years ago? That the myths always triumphed in the end, whether a man believed in them or not?

With a sigh, he stood, not that he had much choice as a squad of Corpus Corps assassins bracketed his private portal.

"The Emperor awaits you, ser."

While all gave him a wide berth, they seemed almost excited as they escorted him along the secret tunnels, tunnels he thought only known to the Eye and the two Eye Regents.

"How did you know this was the way?" he asked the Corps squad leader.

"The Emperor gave us the map, ser, after he dropped your screens, ser."

Eye said nothing further until the tunnel narrowed, a

narrowing that reflected nearness to the Palace.

Opposite the portal that exited in his own gues[ ]
quarters, assigned to him in his person as the Duke o[ ]
Calendra, the Corps squad leader halted and touched [ ]
databloc against the inlaid tile of the Imperial seal tha[ ]
stood man-tall on the right side of the corridor.

The seal swung back to reveal another tunnel, on[ ]
that seemed to lead upward.

With a shrug, Eye let himself be escorted away from
his own quarters and toward whatever destination the
Corpus Corps killers had in mind.

Even with his age, he had no doubt that he coul[ ]
have dispatched at least two of the Corps troops. Bu[ ]
there were eight, and he did not want to give them any
excuse to kill him out of hand.

He had reasoned with the Emperor before and occa[ ]
sionally gotten his point. Reason provided a bette[ ]
hope than attack.

The squad halted at a liftshaft.

"Go on, ser." The squad leader gestured. "This is as
far as we go."

"Alone?" Eye asked with mild sarcasm.

"Alone, ser."

Eye shrugged and stepped into the shaft, letting
himself be carried upward.

The trip was but seconds long before he stepped out
into a small room. A single Imperial Marine stood
before another portal.

"Lord Calendra, the Emperor will see you shortly.
You may sit, if you wish."

Eye shivered. That the guard knew his real name[ ]
even while he wore the privacy cloak and black shadow
of Eye did not look promising.

He studied the guard, debating whether he should
take on the single impressive specimen who stood
between him and the portal or whether he should still
opt for his chances in reasoning with the Emperor.

The almost unseen haze that stood between him and
the Marine decided him. That it was a screen of some

ort was clear, but of what intensity was not. He
decided to wait.

Frowning to himself, Eye tried to determine how he
might have failed the Empire, or displeased the Emperor.

Could it have been the incident on Harkla? Or the
uprising in Parella? The commercial war on El Lido?
That had been messy. But a commercial war?

He shook his head. Could the Ursans have sprung
something new on the Fleet? Or was the Dismorph
resurgence more of a threat than he had reported?

"Lord Calendra, the Emperor awaits."

Eye stood, straightened his black cloak, and stepped
evenly toward the portal as the Imperial Marine moved
aside.

Once through, he found himself in a small study,
scarcely larger than the formal office of a small commercial magnate. Solid wooden shelves lined the sides
of the room, while the Emperor sat behind an apparent
antique writing desk, his back to a full window overlooking the formal Palace gardens.

"Your pleasure, sire," Eye stated evenly as he inclined his head and waited.

"Have a seat, Calendra."

In private, His Imperial Majesty Ryrce N'Gaio
Bartoleme VIII did not appear any more impressive
than in public. His eyes were bulbous, bright green, and
set too close together. His hair resembled plains grass
scattered by the wind, and his fat cheeks gave him the
air of a chipmunk. Only his deep bass voice was
regal—that and the dark sadness behind the bright
eyes.

Eye settled himself into the small chair and waited.

"This is something I would rather not do, you
understand, Calendra, but it has been too long, and
there have been too many Eyes, your predecessor
among them, who seemed to feel that they represented
another force in government besides the Emperor."

"I am not sure I understand, sire."

"I am not sure you do either, Calendra," answered the deep voice, resonating as if separate from the almost comical figure behind the desk. "I am not sure you do either."

The Emperor pointed a surprisingly long finger at the head of the Intelligence Service. "Tell me. What is still the one weapon that the people of the Empire fear most?"

"Nuclear weapons."

"And why? There are greater forces at man's command."

Eye shivered, but forced himself to reply. "I suppose it must be because of what happened on Old Earth."

"Exactly! And during your tenure, twice have those weapons been used. And you have yet to discover how those weapons were removed from Imperial control or by whom."

Eye looked down, then raised his eyes to meet the green glitter of the Emperor's gaze. "Neither has anyone else, sire."

"No. But they are not Eye. Nor are they specifically charged with insuring that such weapons do not enter private hands." The Emperor paused. "Do you have any idea as to who might have obtained them?"

"Ideas, yes. Facts to support them, no." Eye smiled a grim smile. "At this point, would it make much difference?"

"Not really, since we're being candid."

"Then, since he has brought me down, he may as well bring you down as well, sire."

With a calmness he did not believe he possessed, Eye triggered his own internal nerve destruction, trying to look alert even as his thoughts began to blacken, as the toxins poured through his systems.

Let the devilkid's revenge be Eye's as well.

His mouth dropped open in a chuckle that he never completed as the Emperor, His Imperial Majesty Ryrce N'Gaio Bartoleme VIII, shook his head sadly and pressed the console summons for the disposal squad.

THE BEST IN SCIENCE FICTION

FRED SABERHAGEN

☐ 55327-6 BERSERKER BASE $3.95
    55328-4   Canada $4.95

☐ 55322-5 BERSERKER: BLUE DEATH (Trade) $6.95
    55323-3   Canada $8.95

☐ 55318-7 THE BERSERKER THRONE $3.50
    55319-5   Canada $4.50

☐ 55312-8 THE BERSERKER WARS $3.50
    55313-6   Canada $4.50

☐ 48564-6 EARTH DESCENDED $2.95

☐ 55335-7 THE FIRST BOOK OF SWORDS $3.50
    55336-5   Canada $4.50

☐ 55331-4 THE SECOND BOOK OF SWORDS $3.50
    55332-2   Canada $4.50

☐ 55333-0 THE THIRD BOOK OF SWORDS $3.50
    55334-9   Canada $4.50

☐ 55309-8 THE MASK OF THE SUN $2.95
    55310-1   Canada $3.95

☐ 52550-7 AN OLD FRIEND OF THE FAMILY $3.50
    52551-5   Canada $4.50

☐ 55290-3 THE WATER OF THOUGHT $2.95
    55291-1   Canada $3.50